# The
# Last Hanging
# in
# Scots Bend

## Jack Hammond Jr

## Disclaimer

This is a work of fiction. Names, characters, locales, and events are from the author's imagination. Any resemblance to actual persons living or dead, places or events is entirely coincidental.

Published by Lujack Press
Chesterfield, South Carolina

ISBN 978-0-578-16396-3

To the memory of Sharon Ann "Veda" Hammond

1951 - 2014

---

Even in our sleep, pain which cannot forget
falls drop by drop upon the heart, until,
in our own despair, against our will,
comes wisdom through the awful grace of God.

Aeschylus

# Prologue

## Scots Bend - 1912

Two men in a well-tended open runabout pulled by a gray Morgan gelding drew up to the old Keitt plantation cemetery near the church. The driver got down and tied the Morgan to a single hitching post. He walked around the back of the runabout to the passenger and helped him to the ground. The passenger was even thinner than he had been as a dispirited and starving cavalryman coming home from the surrender in Durham forty-seven years before. He ambled through the cemetery leaning heavily on a hickory cane with a worn deer's antler for a handle, pausing at many of the graves. To his friends and family, he whispered the dates that circumscribed each life, greeting them by name as if they were waiting there for him. To his enemies, he softly cursed a taut, bitter epithet that only the two of them understood. Watching from a distance, one might think his actions were a simple man's way of mourning, of remembering all those people now gone, and while that was partly true, the whole truth was the man paused at each stone to gather his strength before moving to the next person.

He approached a section of the cemetery separated from the rest by an ornate cast iron fence, struggled weakly to open the gate, entered and leaned against a tall marble obelisk in the shape of a tree trunk, with the family name, Cason, cut into the base. Around the obelisk, nearly seventy appropriately arrayed markers and stones witnessed both the

Cason family's size and its steady presence in the community over time. The man visited each grave inside the fence, paused at one, his nephew's, John Brooks "Stash" Harris, scratched at the ground with his cane and spat into the dirt covering the grave. Finally, he stopped between two markers and sank to his knees. He could have been praying, but he was not; walking the cemetery exhausted him, and he rested to still his rattling breath.

Even before birth, when the man lay impatiently inside his mother, a tiny cluster of cells quietly formed in the glandular lining of his stomach, waiting until a bacterium out of the beginning of time triggered a mutation that changed them to cancer. For several years, the cancer silently multiplied through the stomach lining, crept up his esophagus, and invaded his lungs. From there the cancer spread to his brain, and to his other organs. The man's body was shutting down. Leland Cason was dying.

He kneeled between the graves of his only son, James Leland "Little Lee" Cason, Jr., and his wife, Margaret Lowery "Mae" Cason. Close beside them were three more graves marked with large white river rocks he had retrieved from Steerpen Creek to mark two stillborn children, and a pretty daughter who lived three days before she left them. His name, James Leland "Big Lee" Cason, Sr., born September 12, 1842," already marked his place beside Mae. Big Lee took a carpenter's pencil from his pocket and wrote in the date for his death; he wrote tomorrow's date, September 12, 1912.

He struggled to his feet and looked back to the runabout. The driver, a mulatto named Tally Bishop, came quickly to meet him, opened the gate, entered the Cason plot, and offered his arm for support. They walked at Big Lee's pace to the runabout. Tally helped Big Lee into the carriage and went around to the other side, climbed in, and taking up the reins, started the gray on the road home. They traveled south along Scotch Road, and when they came to Greer's Mill and the intersection with Big Spring Road, Tally reined the gray to a stop. Scotch Road divided the millpond, twenty acres or so on the west side and five acres on the east next to the spillway and the mill.

Across the pond to the west, a group of boys gathered on a white sand-clay bluff that rose thirty feet above the water, and one by one, most jumped in. Two boys bolder than the rest mocked those who simply jumped, and after a minute, one arced off the bluff in an elegant swan dive turning a quarter turn to his right as he fell. The last boy strutted back and forth across the top like a bold bantam rooster, crowing and clucking, mocking the other boys, and then with a longer running start, leaped out, flipped twice, and waved both hands with the middle fingers extended derisively at his friends in the water. The two men watched the boys for a while, Big Lee thinking of other days when he, and then his own son and nephew did the same. The men turned to the east observing the activity around the gristmill, pointing out one thing and then another, marking the comings and goings, having a quietly intent conversation.

When they finished, Tally turned west onto Big Spring Road and after a mile further, drove into the Cason Farm. They passed the remains of a house marked by a lonely blackened chimney covered in honeysuckle and wisteria, and drove on to the yard of a small tenant farm house. Tally dismounted, hitched the gray to an iron ring attached to the door of the stable, helped Big Lee to the ground, and again offering his arm for support, the men climbed the steps and entered the house.

Tally walked with Big Lee down a hall into a bedroom and lowered him to sit on a cedar trunk at the foot of the bed. Tally rolled up a runner beside the bed, placed one knee on the floor, leaned down and pulled up a section of the floor that revealed a rectangular reliquary hidden underneath. He retrieved an Enfield rifle wrapped in oiled cloth, laid it across Big Lee's lap and helped him remove the cloth and wipe the rifle down.

While Big Lee caressed the rifle and lifted it to his shoulder once, Tally removed the other items and spread them on the bed beside Big Lee: a medal with the inscriptions front and back, "Southern Cross of Honor," and "Deo Vindice," a small satin pillow filled with Mae's hatpins, a box of cartridges, .58 caliber bullets with the powder charges wrapped in paper, a handful of percussion caps, two razor sharp cane knives, a coil of hemp rope with a hangman's noose on one end, and a dog-eared family Bible. Big Lee picked up the satin pillow and held it close to his cheek, breathing in as deep as his rattling breath allowed and then he softly touched the pillow to his cheek, laid the pillow on the bed beside him, placed the percussion caps, the cartridges, and the rifle on the bureau and asked Tally to place the other items back in the reliquary.

Big Lee lay back on the bed to rest while Tally went outside to put the Morgan in the stable and the runabout in the barn. In the dream-like moments just before sleep, the memories triggered by the items wove into a synchronous montage of dark and light, of good and evil. Big Lee saw the way his wife dutifully recorded important family events in the Bible, how she proudly displayed her hat pins on the bureau. Then he saw images of men in blue falling in front of the Enfield, and images of other men falling in front of it after the War. Then he saw the hanging, so real he could have been standing on the gallows again.

What he saw disturbed him, but finally, he slept soundly. When he woke an hour later, he listened to the activity outside. Big Lee heard Tally enter the house, and he struggled to raise himself from the bed. He put the cartridges and the percussion caps in his shirt pocket, lifted the Enfield to his shoulder again and looked down the barrel through the sights. His vision blurred and he blinked several times trying to clear it. The Enfield was heavy for him now, and his stamina waned quickly, the end of the barrel drifting unsteadily. He wondered if he could hold the rifle steady enough for the shot when he needed it.

Tally knocked softly on the door and entered without waiting for a reply. Big Lee asked him to carry the Enfield, and took a walking stick with a fork at the top from behind the door for support as he walked and to steady the Enfield when he needed it. Forty thin notches stretched down the shaft of the walking stick, each one representing a man slain by the Enfield. The two men looked at each other and smiled, remembering scores settled and times past. Tally offered his arm again, and the men walked out of the house and into the yard. The late afternoon sun lay big and orange just above the horizon. While they sat in the willow oak shade beside the stable, a nearly imperceptible breeze stirred the leaves, and cooled them. They talked about trifling things to pass the remaining daylight and watched a cumulonimbus cloud building up to suggest an impending storm.

As the sun was setting, the men watched quick flashes of lightning inside the cloud lighting up its gray outer shell. The storm continued to build and marched out of the west until it towered ominously above them. The wind picked up leaves and bits of debris from other plants, blowing west to east, and then suddenly reversed its flow, the storm pulling the hot evening air into it from every direction, building energy minute by minute. A wall of rain marched through the woods and when the men saw it break from the woods and race across the field, they moved into the stable to watch the storm's assault from the stable's protection. The big Morgan was restless and Big Lee sat near the stall door where he could calm the horse with his voice, and the horse nuzzled him for comfort.

The storm spent its opening fury in less than a half hour, and settled into an easy rain that would last until dawn. Big Lee retrieved an oiled leather shoulder bag from the tack box and placed the cartridges with the percussion caps in it to keep them dry, and wrapped the Enfield with a light saddle blanket. Tally carried the Enfield for him, and the men set out walking in the rain. Big Lee's frailty stopped them even before they exited the yard, and that established the pattern for the entire night, fifty or sixty feet, and then a pause, then fifty or sixty more, then rest. He leaned heavily on Tally, and several times Tally thought he might just pick Big Lee up and carry him home, but he knew it would break whatever determination Big Lee had left, and out of his respect and a shared need to tie up loose ends, he did not. It would take most of the night for them to walk through the woods to the bluff overlooking the millpond; then they could finally rest, and wait.

# Scots Bend, 1898

## Stash Harris

The sun peeks in the window of my cell as soon as it rises above the horizon. Out of habit, I am always awake when it comes, and after the solitude of the long, empty night, I like to watch the sun and listen as the day begins to move. When the sun's first rays peek in, a thin sliver of light appears high on the back wall and walks its way down, widening as it goes, warming the cell bit by bit. I hear the town waking up, the activity building with the daylight. Reversing the way it winds down at night until all you may hear is a mother calling to a child staying out too late, or a dog barking at something unfamiliar, Scots Bend wakes up, the activity ramping up with the optimism of another day.

Since I've been up here in the jail, I've learned when the Calders close their house at night and when they open it in the morning. Their house sits on the northeast corner of the town square where Scotch Road and Main Street intersect. The jail sits on the southwest corner, close enough for me to hear murmuring conversations on the Calder's front porch, but not close enough to make out much of what they are saying. The only thing I can ever make out clearly is when Hugh Calder drinks his toddy at night, and sings old campfire songs to his wife too loudly, usually something like this:

"Lovely maid I would say good-bye,
I'm a young volunteer, and my heart is true,
to our flag that woos the wind;
then three cheers for that flag and our country too,
and the girls we leave behind."

Then I hear his wife laughing, saying "I hear you Hugh, it sounds like idle boasting, to me, just plain idle boasting. Those younger days are all behind us now," and Hugh responding, "Come on inside little lady. You can see young for yourself. I'm won't be leaving you behind anymore," and her, "Ok! Ok! I don't mind. You'll be asleep in two minutes anyway."

The courthouse is on the northwest corner across Main Street from the jail. I might as well complete the picture of the square for you by saying that there is a general store on the last corner, the southeast one, and inside is the post office. Sitting here in the jail, I hear all the activity around the square; most of the time, I could set a clock by how regular people are in what they do up here. Thomas Barentine walks from his house down East Main and opens the store at 7:00 every morning. I know this because he and Mr. Calder always exchange the same greetings. It's always Mr. Calder, "Hey Tom," and some judgment about the weather like "It's going to feel like winter today, Tom," and Tom calling back, "Yes, Mr. Hugh, or No, Mr. Hugh, the almanac says warm today," and some other little comment or two.

I think people in town move only by the clock, nothing else. We are different on the farm. We move by the light, by the weather, by what the land needs, and the stock, and the seasons, and a thousand other little things that I can't even name. A good farmer just knows what the farm needs, not just by some schedule that is supposed to tell when to start and finish a task, but also by what's in his blood. Something moves along the bone and muscle inside him, some little breeze at dawn stirs and tells him, "Do this," and he does. It's that simple. When people lose their connection to the land, to all the living things around them, their lives becomes different, and not in a good way.

I am John Brooks "Stash" Harris. My Daddy was Jacob Harris and my mother was Margaret Cason: everybody called her Maggie. She was Leland Cason's sister, and over time, that's how my Daddy and the Sheriff, Big Lee, became friends, well that and they had a lot of things in common. Daddy was born up in Robeson County, North Carolina, a place called Saddletree. He was born in 1839, a few years after the Indians up there had the right to vote and bear arms taken from them. Daddy didn't know any different; he was born to it, but it was hard on my granddaddy and the others who knew how it was before the Scots came in trying to take over and disenfranchise the people who lived there since time began. I guess I should say that Daddy was one of those people, the Indians I mean, and so am I, but we don't talk much about it down here. We're white down here.

When the War came, the Indians didn't want to join because they thought the Union winning might be a good thing for them, but the truth is that at first, they couldn't have joined to fight if they wanted to. The Confederates kidnapped a lot of them and put them into slave labor building the fortifications down at Fort Fisher. Later on, after the killing got started, the Confederates took about anyone who would go fight. For the Scots up in Robeson County, the Indians were a worse problem than the Negroes and had been for a long time. When it came to the Negroes, those Scots could keep them as slaves, sell them, or kill them without much problem, but with the Indians, they didn't know quite what to do.

They tried to turn the Indians into Negroes by saying that's what they were on the census and on any other legal document they could find to say it on like whatever they said was God's truth. They tried to steal their land any way they could. They tried to bind them over to somebody over a trumped up debt if they were young enough and worth having, and if they weren't, they tried take everything they had anyway. Later, they tried to kill as many of them as they could. Those Scots tried everything except taking them for who they were and living beside them like neighbors ought to. Here's a plain, well known fact. Unless you are one of them, those Scots up there don't make good neighbors.

Daddy eventually had to go down to Bennettsville where more people with color lived to join up and fight. He did it because Grandpa convinced him that fighting for the Confederates might gain him some favor after the War. It didn't exactly work out that way, but that's another story by itself; when he went home things were pretty much the same, maybe even a little worse in those lawless times, so he ended up walking over here into South Carolina to be a white man. He met Mama, and she got some of the Cason land so they made a life down here for themselves and us.

There were three of us children, but out of all of them, I am the last one. Mama and Daddy are gone too, like I said earlier. Now you may wonder why I admit, if you want to call it that, about Daddy being one of those Indians and walking down here to become a white man. It's pretty simple. I want my children to know who they are. I might not be here later to tell them myself. Now you should understand that being Indian isn't something we talk much about, but still, I want them to know who they are. Daddy walked over into white, for a reason. It's not hard to figure out why.

My wife Ella, her sister, and brothers moved up here from Montrose in the spring of 1888. This is how it happened. Daniel Calder stood up in church one Sunday and told about how six Quick children down there lost their mama and daddy in a fire. Some people knew Moses Quick, the daddy. Their baby brother died in the fire too, but the six older children got out. We had all heard about it. He said it was a Christian thing to do to take them in. If the church people divided them among the members at least they could be close to each other. He said he had prayed about it, thought we ought to take them in and that if we didn't, who would, and God only knew where they would end up.

There was some murmuring, reasons why first one and then another couldn't take them in, and questions like why didn't the people down there take care of them like it was more their responsibility than it was ours.. About then, Aaron and Aline Therrell stood up and said they would take them all in, and that settled it. The Therrells always had bad luck with children and buried three little ones before they got one boy to stay. Then, that one boy grew up and hopped a train west thinking to get rich somewhere somehow and send for them. They still haven't heard from him.

Now some people can find something bad to say about everything, and it was some of those same people making excuses about why they couldn't take those children in who said Aaron Therrell only wanted those children to work on the farm. What they said may be partly true; he needed help just like everybody else, but the next Sunday, you wouldn't have thought that was the reason when the Therrells and their brand new family walked in. Everyone in the church had their eye on them. Aline Therrell was in front with the two youngest, a boy and a girl on each hand. Then two more boys walked in trying hard to be little men. Next in line was a girl. She was the prettiest thing I ever saw. The last of the children was a boy of about fifteen, and then Aaron Therrell, herding them all in like a brand new papa, grinning from ear to ear.

That prettiest thing turned out to be my Ella, and when I watched her walking in, it seemed like the church and all the people in it faded away until she was only one there with me, standing wide-eyed, watching her. Right then a feeling I never knew before took me over. I was about to turn eighteen and I found out a few days later she was sixteen. I don't know if the first real flush of love happens in a split second for others; all I can say is it happened to me.

I could see Ella was nervous, like anyone would be in that situation. Everything was all new for her, and I saw she still had a long shadow of grief on her face and the remnants of mourning lingering in her eyes. The shock of what happened to her family was still too close. I felt her sadness, but I sensed the fragments of her shattered hope too, and in that moment she became all I ever wanted.

I wanted to be the one to put the shattered pieces of her hope back together again, to put my arm around her, to hold her, to make her feel alive again. A few weeks later, I found a reason to kiss her, and a future opened up for me in a way I didn't know existed. That kiss was hope for me and although we didn't know it then, it was hope for us too, and for Brooks and Janie too. It was that simple. Now I've mo-mocked up all that we had together, and there isn't any way to avoid what's coming.

# Big Lee

I am up to watch the sunrise every morning. Heavy rain clouds lumber out of the southwest, covering the sky, leaving a thin slice of blue sky along the eastern horizon allowing the sun's first rays to weave into the cloud bottoms. A light, steady rain is falling, a rain that promises more. Seven evening grosbeaks cross the yard in front of me, lighting in the willow oak, chittering their antediluvian song to the rain. They wait for the scattering of oats, rye, and sorghum I sow into the yard every morning, and when I reach into the grain barrel, they flash and whirl above the yard excitedly.

I have a love for the mornings that all men who survive wars have, a love that comes from still being alive, from waking up after the unsettling night into what is as normal a day and a life as a day and a life can be after doing and seeing what soldiers do and see. Even after all that I've seen and lived through, even after all the men I've killed during the War and after, even now that I've lost my wife, Mae, my boy, Little Lee, and a lot of others, I am still glad to be alive, to feel the breeze on my face, to see the sun rise and set, to see the stars at night, and to hear the world alive around me. Even with all the living that has faded into memory, all that is lost forever to me, even with the loneliness and the sadness, some days are good, some are not, but both are different sides of one coin, and no one knows what side of the coin turns up on any day. It's all simply being alive in the world, and I am glad in it.

I live with a need to set some wrong things back to right out of the turmoil and change over the past thirty years.

That is why I wanted to be the sheriff. I believe I've earned it with the things I've done and who I've become here. People believe a sheriff upholds the law in every circumstance and what they believe insulates me; what people believe creates a protective shell around me. There is real power in what they believe, and in what they don't. I use both to my advantage when I need to make a thing right that I could never make right strictly by the law. This is a rambling way of saying that I can do some things that regular people can't, and I do when I have to.

Some things I can't make right no matter how much I might want to, and it frustrates me. Isn't that the way it is? I have the power to affect so many things, but when it comes down to the power to change what I really wish I could change, I am helpless. I wish Mae was still here. I miss her. A day never passes that I don't think about Little Lee and the man he could have become. I am powerless to bring either one of them back no matter how much I wish I could, or how much I pray, or how much I spend one long night after another reliving it all to see what I could have done differently. The clock won't turn back, and now, another hard task is all consuming, and I already see that I won't be able to make it disappear or change the course of it. At the same time, I know I have to try.

I am standing under the stoop in front of my stable, out from the house, avoiding its emptiness the way I do most days. In my hands, a cup of warm coffee releases fragrant steam; I breathe it, then sip the coffee that warms and wakes me. Behind me, inside the stable, my good saddle horse, Ben, is impatient, neighing to let me know he is ready for the morning regimen, the combing, the brushing, the feeding, and he hopes, the ride into town. Ben is the grandson of my cavalry mare, Maddie, who carried me through the War and back home, and lived to be twenty-nine, and twenty-nine more years would not be enough with her. Ben's grandsire is

Butler, Gen. Wade Hampton's war stallion that he rode up here with the Red Shirts back in 1876, and while we worked the crowd at his election campaign speech over at the courthouse, Tally took the opportunity to breed Butler and Maddie, and it worked out.

I'm riding Ben into town, but I like to make him wait. I enjoy his antics when I take longer than he thinks I should. He is Maddie come back to life in his demands, and he reminds me of the times when the War weighed heavy on me, when I doubted that I would live to see home again, and Maddie seemed to know it, and nuzzling me, she grounded me, reminding me of home, of the simple doing of little things that makes a life beyond the interminable War believable.

Now Ben does the same, wanting the daily regimen, demanding the constancy of activity that pulls us along into the future, the doing of one little thing and then another and another that becomes living one day and then another day and another. Even though there are other people around, inside I am alone, and I need the constancy of one task that leads to the next and the next, building each day, and Ben helps with that. I keep my work horses, my Morgan geldings, in the stable at the jail, and, I have a mule, Sockeye, that I am keeping for my nephew, Stash Harris, while he is in my jail. I say my jail because for the past twenty-two years, I have been the Sheriff here, and in that many years a man starts to think a job and a place are his own.

I ride Ben except when I need to move prisoners or other people around in the carriage. I have a man uptown, Tally Bishop, who is a good hand, especially with horses. I picked him up on my way home from the War, and he's been with me since. He is a good man, a colored man, a mulatto actually, His daddy was white; in fact his daddy owned Tally's mama before the War. Tally is as solid as a man can possibly be. Occasionally people complain a little bit about a colored man being trusted to help run the jail, but he is loyal to me, and I trust him in any spot no matter what, and if they get too tired of it, they can elect someone else and I will come home to stay.

This farm is my home and always has been. I was born here. Thad Cason came up to this part of the country around 1750. A man could get a hundred acres of land for himself, a hundred acres for his wife, and fifty acres for each one of his children. He and his first wife had seven children when they came, and had another before she died having the ninth. He took a second wife from right here to help him take care of the children, a Cheraw Indian some say, my grandmother, and they had six children between them. That comes to fifteen children and nine hundred and fifty acres. While that amount of land doesn't compare to some of the big farms over in Marlboro County or the Cash land down on the Pee Dee, it's still not a little amount, and that's how we started here.

Ben is not waiting quietly, so I go into the stable to lead him out and take him through the morning regimen, changing his water, cleaning the floor of his stall, feeding him some oats mixed with molasses, and putting fresh hay in. I put a lead on him, tie him off, and start working him by combing him out and brushing him. I saddle him, and when I take the bridle from its hook, Ben starts snorting and neighing, knowing that the bridle means it's time to go, and he puts his head down, nuzzling me, impatiently trying to gather in the bridle. I lead Ben out, the rain still lightly falling, with the clouds now covering the eastern horizon, but in the west, the clouds show signs of breaking.

I rise into the saddle and Ben is steady for me to settle in, and then he is off on his own pace, knowing the way, and I lean a bit forward and let him stretch out a little, spending his impatience and energy in the effort, and then I rein him in and we settle into a rhythm, comfortable, both knowing the other, finding agreement in the pace. We come off the hill, and down at the intersection with the main road, I look across the millpond to Greer's Mill, making a mental note of the activity there, Julia and Tadlock, on the steps, directing a group of five men to some task, and when Julia looks up at me, I rein Ben to a stop and we watch each other across the water, neither acknowledging the other.

Even across the distance, the tension is palpable; I feel the anger building, rising up my spine, the back of my neck tingling, and the five men turn to look at me. Julia snaps a quick command, and the men turn quickly away. "The shrew doesn't want me to see their faces," I say quietly to Ben. The millpond releases its heat into the cool morning air, a mist rising and thickening until it forms an impenetrable wall that for a moment blocks the view. The mist swirls in the thermal current, the wall breaking down, and I can see that Julia is alone across the water, still watching, with the men and Tadlock disappeared. We face off for a good five minutes, and Ben sensing the tension, stands rock steady as if waiting for me to shoot. A fish rolls at the surface. The concentric ripples widen across the pond and dissipate. A great blue heron flies between us, its raucous call interrupting the face off. The heron lands in the shallows, intently stabbing into the water, spearing fish and swallowing them live. Julia ends the face off by turning her back, and with a dismissive wave, walks into the mill.

I pet Ben along the neck, praising him for being steady and start him, tapping him lightly with my heels. I pass the church, the stones in the cemetery standing over the dead, and say out loud to Little Lee, "I'll be back in a bit," thinking about my weekly conversation with him and Mae. While I am lost in that mix of memory and emotion, Ben covers the distance uptown to the jail, and I dismount. Tally comes out and takes him to the stable, and I go into the jail, to Stash, and the hard task I'm facing.

# Julia

M e and Tadlock was standing out on the steps in front of the mill this morning giving work directions to this new crowd of turpentiners we got in here when I saw Leland Cason coming down the hill from his place on that stallion of his. I despise that bastard now, but I've got to admit he makes a good picture of a man and a horse. He's one meddlesome son of a bitch though, and besides him and his crowd owning a big piece of land that we been trying to get ahold of for a long time, he's the sheriff, and he's always snooping around here and anywhere else that anybody's trying to do things to make a little money. He don't like people making money

He's got too much power, and damn him, he uses it to suit himself and his crowd and damn anybody else and what they might think. He's in the way of everything we try to do, but I been hammering away at his ass for a long time, and believe you me, I got him in a tight spot now. Leland has been a tough one for me to get at, and his daddy was for my daddy before us. I got to admit that most people we've been after would've folded up and gone away a long time ago or we woulda found some way to get them, but not the Casons. If Leland manages to hang on, if he keeps on like he's going, he'll be a tough one for Tadlock when I'm gone because he just don't seem to age at all. He looks about the same that he did right after he came home from the war, and he acts about the same too.

I was still a pretty young girl back then, only seventeen when all the boys from here come home, and Leland was one good-looking piece of man, and I would've took him in a minute. That Mae of his would've never stood a chance against me, what with me knowing what I already knew about the ways around a man, but daddy farmed me and my sister Margaret out to a crowd of them bummers when Sherman came through in March of that year, trying to save the place here, and by the time our own boys came straggling home all during that summer and fall, we was both carrying babies.

When we was little, me and Leland kind of liked each other. He was a good looking boy back then, and all the girls liked him. We took a real shine to each other and we might have had something later on when we got older, but at first Daddy wouldn't hear of it, and after the War, me being pregnant when Leland came home, and then having Tadlock got in the way. I thought back then Daddy didn't like it was just because he was one of the Casons, but I guess there was more to it. It seemed to me like Daddy would've been all for me getting with Leland to get a hook into that land of theirs, but he told me not to have nothing to do with Leland, so I moved on to another one.

Anyway, by the time our men came home from the War, me and Margaret both was carrying babies. Mine was Tadlock, and hers was Leonard. Everybody calls him Drip. By the time my baby came along, Mae already had her hooks in Leland and I didn't stand a chance, what with here still being pure as far as anybody knew. Who really knows? My sister Margaret's gone up north now, but that damn boy of hers is still here spitting and sputtering, trying to talk, and trying to drag people around to show them things that ain't none of their concern. People see he's a simpleton and it works out for me if they keep thinking that, but that line-bred bastard is smarter than people think; you can believe that or not. I know.

Leland stopped across the water there, and we locked

eyes on each other for a minute, just a staring match like we have all the time, and those stupid turpentiners turned around to look too, and I barked at them real quick and turned them away. Leland ought to know that a little staring match ain't gonna intimidate me. I'm way past that, and I guess he is too. Those men we got work out real good for some things. They're pretty handy with some things, but at the same time, they are stupid about other things, like letting Leland see what they look like. I don't want nobody around here knowing anything about them, like who they are and what they look like in case I need them to do some after-hours work; some might call it dirty work. It don't take but a little piece of change to get them to do most anything, and when they have run out their string here, it's easy to send them on down the line somewhere else if they got a little bit of money. Most people will do anything for a little jangle in their pocket.

That kind of men works a lot like them girls that spread good cheer over at our brothel. Back in daddy's time, he always used some of his pretty young slave girls for work out at the brothel. He'd try them girls out and when he got tired of them, he'd use them out at the brothel until they got pregnant or got some ailment that didn't need spreading around. Men don't have any pause about sticking their tally-whacker into whatever is around that will let them, so it won't any problem at all for them girls to be slaves or colored either. That was true for Daddy and everybody else too. I will say that most of this crowd around here liked them girls to be light, about the color of caramel icing, but if there won't any like that around, them horny bastards would go on ahead and take a girl black as ink. That's just how men can be.

Now that we don't have slave girls to use for free, we have to pay them girls out there, but men get tired of paying for the same old thing over and over. I reckon that's why they come to the brothel in the first place, so we got connections with a lot of other brothels. There's more out there than you think. We use our girls for a while and send them on down to another brothel and they send us a new bunch of theirs. Some girls really know what they're doing. Every once in a while, I'll see one come in here and turn on their charm so hard that some fool from right here falls in love with them. Them foolish men give them anything they want and some even leave their wives to follow them around like a fawning little puppy. When you get ahold of a man like that, you can really make some money

A long time ago I realized a man is just a piece of clay when it comes to a woman that knows how to use his tally-whacker against him. It's a sight. I like it when I'm sitting up in church on Sunday morning with some of them same men that I make money from out at the tavern and the brothel during the week. I don't give them away though. That would be bad for business. I just say something like, "Why good morning Deacon Taylor! How are you this morning," and then just nod and speak real nice to the wives too like "Why Mrs. Taylor, you and the Deacon got to come down to the mill sometime to fish. The robin and the shellcrackers are up now." Ain't no telling what them poor women's men are dragging home to them, but then maybe it ain't no problem at all. Maybe that's why men come out there. Those women of theirs might of already put the lid on the honey pot a long time ago. I know it happens, and you do to. Whatever the reasons, they pay me good.

To get back to those worker men, we use those turpentiners for all kinds of little tasks. That way when a person turns up dead or missing, or a fire or something else happens, it won't come back on me and Tadlock. Everyone knows how that rambling work crowd can be, the kinds of things they do, so it's not a hard thing for people to believe that what they do, they do on their own without any direction from us. A lot of protection comes in what people are stupid enough to believe, and even more in what they think they're too smart to believe.

I mentioned sitting up in church with men that come out to the brothel and it don't hurt a bit that we go to church. It's a natural thing how people look around the church and think everyone sitting there is too good of a person to do some of the things that seem to happen around here. Going to church works out for us, gives us some extra protection. Jesus ain't never rode me too hard like he does some people, so it ain't a problem for me to go there and be one of them holy ones for a little while. I mean, I know Jesus and all. The preacher baptized me a long time ago. Him or Jesus either just ain't ever rode me real hard like he does some people.

It's always been nothing but trouble between us and those Casons. It goes way back before my time. Them Casons try to be too good to suit us. What's between us has been really rough for the past few years; there's been a lot of hard talk back and forth. Leland's boy drowned in the tailrace of the millpond when the mill wheel caught him and whacked him in the head a few years ago. The one that drowned and the other one, Stash, Jacob's boy, that's up there in the jail now for killing those men was a plain out torment to us for a long time. During the hot weather, there won't no way to keep them off that mill wheel and out of the pool under the dam. I admit it was hot, and anybody wants to cool off, but they didn't have no business down here all the time, and we run them off more times than I can count. I told both of them little bastards that something bad was coming, and see what happened. Little Lee, that son of a prim and proper bitch, that fine woman, Mae, had that drowning coming and so does that other one deserve what he's about to get. You harvest whatever it is that you sow.

After the drowning, Mae come down here every day and

stared at the water and kept asking me and Tadlock what we seen over and over and over. She went crazy, and before she died, me and Leland had hard words over it. That woman quit eating and starved herself to death I think. She was a sight before she died, skinny, like some of them men that come home from prison after the war and just as rough looking, with her hair all run out like she ain't touched it and bare-footed even after it turned cold that year. That pitiful bitch wore her funeral dress every day till it won't nothing but filthy rags. She might have been a good looking, nice woman to Leland's fine man, but she slid down hill real fast after the drowning. Having Leland wasn't near enough to keep her up. He should have had somebody a lot tougher than her to match up to him.

Every time Mae come down the hill, Drip slipped out and got around her trying to show her and tell her things she didn't need to know. It didn't do no good though because he can't do nothing but spit and sputter when he tries to talk. I don't know why. Something just messed up when he was born. When Mae would be down here and Drip was out there with her, me or Tadlock one had to beat him with a stick to get him away from her. After she died, Drip switched over to Leland and tags along at the cemetery with him every Sunday. Like I said, Drip is not the simpleton people think he is, but I need people to think what they want to and what I want them to think.

These people around here are just too stupid to see past what a person acts like and says. They ain't got enough sense to know that nice and friendly ain't always good. In fact, most of the times nice and friendly don't have anything to do with the person that's getting the nice treatment. No, that person is usually the victim you might as well say. Nice and friendly is usually just some slick way one person is trying to get on top of another person. A lot of times that nice and friendly person is kind of like a snake being real slow and patient once it gets on something, or like a cat that's having a good time toying with a mouse before it gets tired and kills it. Nice and friendly ain't hardly ever good.

# Stash

I rode to church this morning with Big Lee, Leland Cason. He has as pretty a team of steel-grey Morgan geldings as you'll ever see. I've always been partial to that color. His team is a shade or two darker than Traveller, but all over the South, the color grey is what people will pay top dollar for since the War. Heads turn when we pass, and it's hard not to feel a little bit proud to be riding with him, even under these circumstances. He is a good horseman. He tends his rig and his team with a caring hand that shows his skill. Well, to be fair, it's not all him; he does have some help from his right hand man, Tally Bishop. There's not a flaw beyond good, honest wear on or about his horses or his rig. I need to say here that he's more than just a good horse man; he's just a good man. He is my uncle, but like most people, I call him Big Lee.

He doesn't control his team with simple force, but he is firm; he makes them do exactly what he wants. Some men have the knack, carrying themselves in such a way to compel people and animals to naturally do what they want. Big Lee is like that. He mastered his horsemanship riding with the 4th during the War. He was just a boy when he rode off with the men from here to fight what they thought would be a short war. Four years later after bearing the colors during the surrender up in North Carolina, he came home a man who had seen too much.

For now, I'm staying up here full time in the Scots Bend jail until my sentencing. I have to stay in my cell some, but most of the time, I go where I please. I can even sit outside if I want to; he says I just can't leave the grounds, and I don't. The jail is a red brick building, matching the Robert Mills courthouse across the street. Around the back is a high plank fence to keep meddlesome people out, and lawbreakers like me in, although if a prisoner wanted to get out, he could. The county's stable with two stalls on either side of a small tack and feed room sits behind the jail and opens into Berry Street running parallel to Main Street. The stable is a pleasant place to be, better than the inside of the jail, especially for a farm boy like me, and I like to sit out there, breathing in the fresh air, playing with the mouser, and helping Tally tend the horses when they are up here like they are now.

I'm not much used to being cooped up inside, and I appreciate the freedom Big Lee gives me, not to make me sit in my cell all day. I wouldn't do anything against him for that and a lot reasons that I'll talk about later. People say I have it easier than I should, and I know it is true. They say Big Lee is as tough a man as there is, makes the prisoners do exactly what they are supposed to do, and that it just isn't right that he isn't the same with me as he is with other prisoners. They complain about it, even though they know they would do the same thing for one of their family. Most would do even more. I've seen how tough Big Lee is more times than I can count, but I've occasionally seen the other side too, like when his eyes filled up with tears while he was carrying my Mama, his own sister, and my Daddy from the church to the cemetery. That is a little part of this story that I might get to if there is enough time.

I intend to tell my own story, as much as I have time for, in my own words since all the talking other people do is bound to change it over time with each telling and the story might become both more and less than it really is. I've always heard people say that if you tell the Widow McBride some little piece of news on Monday morning, especially if you tell her not to say anything about it, the news will run all the way down the county to the Great Pee Dee spreading out like water finding the lowest ground, then turn around and climb back up to Scots Bend as an even bigger story full of absolutely true facts by Monday afternoon. If it is any good and nothing else has come along that is better, those people at church the next Sunday will be buzzing with whatever version settled down there. The Widow McBride is not the only one.

The church I'm talking about going to is my church, or as close to my church as any, and is about six miles south of Scots Bend. It is nothing special, but it's a good enough church, what we could manage to rebuild after the fire burned the one left over from the Keitt Plantation in 1894. Times were hard after the economy went bad in 1893, and even more than that, after nearly thirty years we still hadn't gotten our feet on the ground after the War. We still haven't and I don't think we ever really will, but times are improving a little bit now it seems, or maybe it's just that the younger people are used to the way it is, and the old people that remember how it was before the War are dying out. Maybe that's it; people can get used to almost anything.

Like I said, the church is good enough, has room for about a hundred people, but like a lot of churches it's usually not full except for a couple of weeks leading up to Christmas and a few more Sundays around Easter. A lot of people don't ever feel much of the pull from the church until they start thinking about Jesus up on that cross and him getting up off that sepulcher and those angels rolling that rock away and all. Then they flood in there and act like they have been clamoring at the foot of the Cross all along. It's just the way people are. I might as well admit that most of the time, I am one of those.

The old church was one of only two buildings out south

of town left standing after Sherman passed, and was an impressive place. It was a relic from back in the slave days when the masters let the slaves come to church with them and the balcony was for them. Let probably isn't the right way to say that; those masters made the slaves come if they didn't have any work to do and the last thing that would've happened in those days was that the slaves could go to a church of their own. Those old masters were smart enough to know that all those slaves congregating up together somewhere was just a way for some big trouble to get started. By the time it burned, people mostly forgot what that balcony and all was for, and just thought that it was a big, nice church, and it was.

Now don't get the idea that bastard Sherman had some special respect for a church, letting it stand and all. He did not; he burned plenty of churches, most of them he came to in fact. Kilpatrick even rode his mount right up the front steps and down the center aisle of ours with his horse dropping turds all over the place the whole time, and some of his men did the same, gathering up the hymnals in a pile to fire the church, but they had to ride off in a hurry before they could get it lit when someone sounded the alarm that Wheeler was coming, so it's not like Sherman spared it on purpose or anything like that. Now, I know that some of you reading this might think that the part about Kilpatrick running at the warning of Wheeler coming doesn't ring true, and I can see why you might not believe it.

I've read some of those new histories too, that change things to make out like Sherman's army blazed through here without any resistance at all, but most history writers write to fit whatever fancy there is at the time or to fit their own idea about the way it was trying to make some of their own people look better than they really were. The people around here who lived through Sherman say that even though there was no way to stop that Yankee horde, there was plenty of resistance, like when a bunch of citizens up the county between here and Kershaw, killed eighteen Yankee bummers and lined the bodies up beside the road with a sign on them, "Death to all foragers," and when Gen. Chestnut tracked down seven Yankees who raped a girl and her mother and executed them and sent them to Hell where they belonged. It might have been futile, but there was plenty of resistance. You won't find that in those history books, but it is true.

Anyway, some would say the new church is simpler, plain even, but I guess it is enough for God to do His work in on Sundays, or at least to try. God's work takes sometimes; sometimes it doesn't. To hear the preacher tell it, a man has to step inside the church to get a full dose of God's grace, but I disagree; I think that God is strong enough to do His work any place, like on a man with his ear turned to the rhythmic baying of his dogs striking the trail under the full moon lighting a late fall night, or on a boy with his back against a big longleaf pine listening to the wind singing through the tops, watching the day rise up out of the night, waiting for that first squirrel to bark. I think that, and I'll admit right up front that for a time, a long time, I tried to stay as far away from the church as I could, but the preacher says no, a person has to be in church for God's work to take ahold, and now Big Lee takes me there every Sunday since I'm in his jail and he says what I do and don't do. I think he wants me to be sure about God and Jesus for what might come later, a little thing about going to prison or maybe even hanging.

You wouldn't think it, but people in the church sometimes do more yammering about first one thing and then another than the drunks laying up somewhere getting over a long Saturday night. As soon as they saw me with Big Lee, the whispering started, I guess about that I was getting some special treatment and about all the hoopla around me, and the killing, and the sentencing, because the whisperers were gawking at me while they were doing it. I don't care; people talk.

I got to sit with my wife Ella, and my children. I put my arm around her and my littlest one sat in my lap. My other one got as close to me as he could. My boy, Brooks, is four, and my little girl, Janie, is eighteen months. We all whispered back and forth some, nothing special, just little things like a man and a woman and their children do. I've been full time in the jail since I finished the fall harvest about two weeks ago, and I was up here some of the time, since the jury convicted me at the trial in July. Now don't get the idea that me getting to go do my harvest is some special treatment. It's a fairly common thing here that if a man is settled and not likely to go running off, the law, the Sheriff, will let him go take care of his farm to make sure his wife and children can be safe over the winter. If the man doesn't look after them, who will? Someone has to take care of them.

Ella and my children miss me, and I miss them. It's natural, right? I've never spent one night out from my wife and children until all of this. I'm not like some men around here who take any excuse to be out for a day or two. I like being at home. Ella doesn't cotton to a lot of mess, but it doesn't bother her if I ramble with the dogs at night, make a barrel or two of wine in the barn, or take a little cut of moonshine once in a while. She's one of those women who make it easy for a man to want to stay around. I like it, well, love it is a better way to say it. Even when I run the dogs, I don't usually leave until the little ones are asleep and I try to be the one to wake them up the next morning. Most times I like to get in early enough to wake Ella up first if you know what I mean.

Now I have a question for you. Have you ever been to church and felt like the preacher was talking just to you? Well, that's how it was this Sunday morning. I remember telling Mama once a long time ago that I felt like that, and in that way she had of using every chance she got to control my wild tendencies she said, "That just means you're walking too close to the devil, son," and I said, "Now Mama, I'm not that bad," and she said "You're not that good either." It may be true. I freely admit that I've had my times when I walked as close to the devil as I could without getting pulled in too deep, but I'm pretty sure that this time I've gone too far. Anyway, back to the story. That's the way it was this morning when the preacher started talking about sinning and dying. That rascal looked straight at me like I was the only one there that needed what he was about to say. He had been building up a good head of steam, and when he rolled out "The wages of sin is death," he zeroed right in at me.

That really doesn't give you a good picture of the way it was. The preacher is a tall lanky rascal; he puts you in mind of one of those traveling evangelists, all severe and gaunt, strutting around like a big old tom turkey in April, like he can't quite figure out where to go and what to do, but he's urgent about it anyway. He looks like the Holy Spirit is a parasite that's sucking all the energy out of him, and he's just wasting away, or that's what he reminds me of. If you've ever seen chickens drink water, the preacher looks like that when he's digging into the Word hard, going after one person. A chicken dips his beak down into the water and tilts his head back and you can see his goozle working up and down letting the water down.

The preacher looks just like that. He looks down over his nose into his flock, and when he chooses his victim, he starts up real loud, and then tilts his head back, looks up into the heavens and stretches his hand out in supplication, works his goozle up and down just like a chicken, and strings out "the wages of sin is death" for at least 20 seconds or more. Some of my worst whippings came from me and Little Lee sitting on the back pew getting our tickle box turned over, laughing and mocking that preacher until the pew shook and our faces turned purple.

Now don't get the idea we were just plain heathen. We both knew plenty of scripture, more than most even, and we marched down into those holy baptism waters believing with all of our hearts that we would be so good afterwards, we might become saints. In fact, for a while we both had in mind to be preachers like most boys do when they're in the first flush of salvation and all. We practiced hard at it too. Every chance we got, me and Little Lee took turns standing up on one of those big heart pine stumps in the woods preaching hard to a congregation of one, each other. I saved Little Lee more times than I can count and he saved me too, over and over, but it wasn't long until Satan's hand got the hold back on us.

Me and Little Lee followed a crowd of girls down to the creek one afternoon. We just played the fool and slipped around behind them, and they were so busy talking and tussling with each other, they never saw us. When they got down to the creek, they waded around for a while splashing and pushing each other, and it wasn't long before their clothes were sopping wet. Those girls stripped down to the skin, to dry their clothes I guess, because they hung their clothes up on some bushes and got back in the water. Let me tell you, it was a sight to see. It was the first time me and Little Lee ever saw anything like that and we had a big time watching those girls for a while. When we got bored with that, we slipped up closer to them to steal their clothes, and that's what caused all the trouble.

When those girls saw us, we grabbed their clothes and ran. I know that you already suspect this so I might as well admit that we didn't run too hard. I remember running along leaving those girls behind, and the thought hit me - it might be more fun if they caught me - and in just a few steps, they did. They forced us to take our clothes off too so we would all be even and wouldn't be able to tell our parents, and we all splashed around in the creek for a long time and had a whole lot bigger time with them than we did just watching them. After that first time, we all went back down there and skinny dipped a lot. Me and Little Lee slid real quick back to normal, and in a few weeks, when Daddy noticed we gave up preaching, he said that baptism water must have run off us like rain off a duck's back. He was right about water being the problem, but it wasn't that holy baptism water that got us.

Getting back to the preacher, he usually doesn't let up once he lights in on a person, and he stays on them until they stand up and let go with a "Praise Jesus" or even better, a "Come to me, Lord." I've seen it plenty of times, but today I guess he saw Janie asleep in my lap so he let me go when I made eye contact, just nodded at him and snapped out a quick, "Amen." Or it might be that he thinks it's just too late for me, knowing what all I've done. Everyone in that church knew why he chose me, and I heard what he was saying. I'm not stupid; I heard him. Even with the preacher's caterwauling, Janie didn't wake up, and she didn't even wake up when I handed her back to Ella, and kissed her and I even kissed Brooks goodbye. Brooks, like any boy, took the manly action of wiping my kiss off his cheek and acting like I stuck him with a knife instead. It felt good, and it makes me smile when I think about how mannish he tries to be.

I know people were watching. Some were watching because they feel sorry for Ella or me or the children, and some people even had a few kind words, the normal things, like, "We're praying for you son," or "We're all thinking about you," or "It's going to be all right. The Lord always has a plan," things like that. Some were watching, well, gloating even, because they fall on the other side of this thing. I don't care what either side thinks or says, although I appreciate those good words, because I believe I'm likely to hang over this thing. Big Lee says if the judge sentences me to hang, I'll be one of the last ones hung here, maybe even the last one, since the State is planning to take executions over sometime soon, but either way, I'll be dead, and it doesn't matter to me who does it.

# Ella

I was as nervous as a cat this morning. I've been without
John Brooks for a while, and I knew I'd see him at
church; it was Sunday, and it felt just about like when we
used to be courting, and I'd get real anxious and fidgety
when I knew he was coming. People call him Stash, but to
me, he's John Brooks, and that's all. He's not Stash to me. If
you don't know what I'm talking about, about being nervous
and excited to see the person you love more than you love
yourself, then I can't explain it to you. You just can't imagine
it unless you've felt it, and if you haven't felt it, you can't,
and I feel sorry for you.

Brooks, our boy, was excited too and was hard to handle, but not too bad, just like any four year old boy would be
who hadn't seen his Daddy for a whole week. Janie is too
young to understand, but we being excited stirred her up
too, and she ended up fussy. Things were a lot easier before
everything slid down into the mess we got going on now.
Sunday was always a good day back then; it was a day when
the women would be up early getting some breakfast on and
at the same time starting something to hold over for after
church dinner. The big house was still standing. It hadn't
burned yet and John Brooks' Mama and Daddy were still living, so a lot of kin people were around, and everybody gathered there after church for dinner and then stayed on into
the afternoon most times.

It wasn't but a little ways up to the big house from
where we live. Our little house was the first actual house
built here. Well, the first one was just a little two room shack

built by the first set of Casons that came up here, but it's been gone for a long time. Down in the woods, you can still see some big white flint rocks that held up each corner of the shack, and a pile of rubble with some make-do mortar still clinging to the rocks that made up the hearth. It was a start, and I guess a lot of living went on in that little shack, and then John Brooks' family built this house, and then they grew some more and built the big house along about 1830, and then had to build it again after Sherman came through.

Where we are now is the Cason land, his Mama's people; his Daddy and his people were up in North Carolina around the Lumber River and had been there a long time according to what they say, longer even than the Casons here. They say it was their land before the white men came. When the Scots moved in, they made it hard for other people to stay, but some did, and still do. After the War Papa Jacob got tired of being treated worse than a freed slave, so he just left and came down here to get away from it all and met Miss Maggie. I guess he felt like if fighting in the War alongside everybody else wasn't enough to be left alone to live once it was all over, nothing would ever make it alright to be up there and be left alone. That's what he always said anyway.

John Brooks likes to go down to those white flint rocks in the woods and sit right up in the middle where his ancestors did their living. He's one to think about things. He likes it down there. It's one of his special places and when he took me down there after we'd been courting for a while, it was like he'd let me open the door into his heart. I believe we made Brooks down there not long after we married.

I remember lying back in the leaves after we finished, looking up through those big oaks around the old homestead, listening to the birds, and the wind, hearing John Brooks' rhythmic breathing, feeling like I had everything I wanted, him lying there beside me as content as I would ever see him. Not long after that, I knew I was expecting our first.

Sundays were good days back then. Miss Maggie, John Brooks' Mama, hadn't come down with the cancer yet, or at least we didn't know it, and me and John Brooks wasn't long married. His Daddy, Papa Jacob, was still a strong, bold man like John Brooks is now. It was a good, peaceful time. Now it's gone.

When me and my brothers and sisters first came up this way to live with the Therrells, I liked John Brooks right off, and I thought he liked me too. I saw how he watched me every chance he got, the same way I watched him, like every Sunday at church, and the Therells said he sure was finding a lot of reasons to come by their place that hadn't ever been reasons before.

I tried every little trick I knew to get him to talk to me, but he didn't approach me right off. I thought he was shy, but he said later that he was just being patient, moving real slow, giving me room to get comfortable up here, and get over all that happened in the fire. Whatever the reason was, it worked; that patience made him even more appealing to me, and I wanted him to talk to me more and more the longer he waited. People told me for a while that John Brooks liked me, and finally, I got my nerve up and walked up to him and stood nose to nose with him in the church-yard and said, "Boy, if you're ever going to talk to me, you better start now," and he did.

Tadlock Greer was a little bit older, and he didn't waste any time at all trying to get me interested in him. In fact, he was a little bit of a nuisance, always hanging around and trying to bring me little things he thought I might like. There was something about him though, that just didn't sit right with me, but being new and all up here, I wasn't bold enough to push him away right off and I guess he took that to mean that I liked him, so when it all came out that me and John Brooks were a couple and that Mr. Aaron and Mrs.

Aline said it was fine for us to be a couple and be married, Tadlock went off on a sulk like I was something John Brooks stole from him.

I wasn't ever anything to Tadlock Greer and he wasn't ever anything to me. I might have used him to bait for John Brooks just a little bit, trying to get the jealousy stirring, but that was all, and all girls do that, don't they? At the time, I didn't know about all the trouble between the Greers and the Casons or I wouldn't have added anything to it for the world, but I think Tadlock thought something was true about us that weren't and he's like most of the Greers. He thinks he ought to have whatever it is that he wants.

A little while after me and John Brooks were together, I was walking from the big house down to our house one day in the middle of the day when the men were out doing some work. Tadlock rode up on his horse and got down and walked right up in front of me. I told him he better leave; no Greer was ever welcome on the Cason place, especially not him, but he didn't listen and tried to grab me. I guess he intended to haul me off on that horse. I don't really know, but I fought hard and when I pulled away from him, it tore the sleeve of my dress nearly off. Miss Maggie saw it happen from the porch and hollered down to where we were telling Tadlock he better get gone, and he rode of, hollering back that he'd be back to get me "out of this mess you're in . Something just isn't right in his head. Thank God Miss Maggie saw the whole things and hollered out at him.

Later when I told John Brooks what happened, I saw that fire rising up in his eyes, and he rode straight off, down to the mill to settle up with Tadlock. I never asked him what happened. I was scared to, but I heard he walked into the mill, and smacked Tadlock in the mouth. Some people said Tadlock fell out like a bag of rocks and peed in his pants while he was laying there. I don't know what John Brooks said, but that was my last trouble with Tadlock until John

Brooks went to jail. I'm rambling, I know, but I did see John Brooks at church this morning.

We met out in the churchyard when Big Lee brought him from the jail. I gave him the biggest kiss I've ever given him, especially out in public like that, and I didn't care who saw me. The way he kissed me back and held on to me, I don't think he cared either. Brooks and Janie were all over him, worse than I was, and he was smiling and laughing like there wasn't a thing in the world that was a burden to him.

We went in the church and I tried to listen to what the preacher said, I really did, but my mind was on John Brooks. I just soaked it all up, the way he smelled, and being that close to him and all. I just couldn't get to him the way I would've liked to, and now I've said too much, but it's true, and I'm not ashamed one bit to be thinking about things like that in church, not one bit. John Brooks leaned over to me after a while and whispered, "Listen to that son of a bitch talking straight to me." I hope nobody heard him. He was talking about the preacher. That's my John Brooks. He hasn't changed one bit, trouble or not.

# Stash

A lot of things changed in the years just before Ella came into my life. I've had a lot of time to think up here, and when a person takes the time or just has the time forced on them like I have now, that person can probably go back and see when the life that came before some event ends it and a different kind of life starts. Sometimes, things change so much in a minute or a second even, that the life you had before is gone, and you can't ever get back to it. You can't see those times when they're happening because the living, the breathing in and breathing out, the doing one little thing and then another, sweeps you along like a boat that's cut loose in the river.

Looking back from here, from this place where all I've got to do is think, I see it clear; those years leading up to Ella was one of those times, where one kind of life stops and another kind starts. It all started, and ended, when my best friend and first cousin, Leland Cason, Jr., Little Lee, stuck a gig in a big carp and drowned under the wheel at Greer's Mill. He was a little less than a year younger than me. We grew up together, and he was more like a brother to me than a cousin. I could tell you a thousand stories about the two of us, rambling all over the countryside, measuring ourselves against the world like boys do, challenging it in every way we could think of, but that would take longer than I might have. I may get back to it some if I have time.

We did most things together, but on the day Little Lee died, it was so hot that when he came to get me, I was down in the springhouse just laying there trying to cool off. Heat does that to you, just makes you lazy and makes you want to find some relief. Sometimes during the hot weather we snuck around and swam in the pool below the dam at Greer's Mill. If none of those Greers were around to stop us, we liked to jump on the grist wheel and ride it up to the top, then jump off into the deep pool below the dam. We did it over and over and then we ran like demons when Julia or Tadlock Greer came out to chase us off. Tadlock chased us hard; trying to show his mama how tough he was, until we both turned around on him one day and beat the shit out of him. He ran a lot slower after that.

Anyway, Little Lee drowned just after the Fourth of July. It had been over a hundred degrees for about four or five days straight. Naturally, the cool water draws boys in when it's hot like that, and that's what it did to Little Lee. He told his daddy that he was going to find me, and we would go down to the mill to swim and cool down for a while, and it was such a natural thing that Big Lee didn't think a thing about it. Like I said before, he didn't find me, and ended up down there at the mill by himself. I guess another natural thing is that when a boy sees a big fish, he's going to try to catch it some way. I would've done exactly the same thing, and it could've been me that drowned that day.

Tadlock Greer always kept a couple of gigs and an awl pike leaning up against the mill house in case a big fish came upstream trying to get over the spillway. Nobody knows for sure, nobody saw it happen, except maybe Drip Greer and he can't talk, but we just sort of figure that when Little Lee saw that big sow carp, he grabbed one of those gigs and stuck her. We've both done it a hundred times. When Little Lee didn't show up for supper, Big Lee came by our place looking for him and then he went down to the mill, and the first thing he saw was that big carp circling in the pool below the dam with the gig stuck in her back and about three feet of the bamboo handle out above the water. Tadlock told that Big Lee said right off that his boy was dead. Drip Greer, Tadlock's simpleton cousin jumped up and down grabbing Big Lee by the arm, trying to drag him into the water until Tadlock whacked him over the head with a stick and ran him off.

The word spread quick and drew quite a crowd, and me and Daddy and a lot of others gathering around tried to ease Big Lee's worry saying things like, "You can't think the worst yet; you can't think that he's dead; that boy could swim like a fish," but Big Lee just replied over and over again, "He's dead somewhere in that water. That carp would be laying up here on the bank if he wasn't drowned." I can't say I didn't agree with him. I had a feeling in the pit of my stomach, like I was in some big trouble, or I had forgotten something real important. Some of us went into the pool and swam around feeling on the bottom and in the rocks at the base of the dam, but Big Lee just kept looking at the water, and when the wheel spit his boy out a little bit later, he went in and got him. The carp weighed forty-one pounds. Big Lee wanted to know.

We all crowded around, trying to get a look at Little Lee. Some of the men wanted to look him over real close to try to figure out why a young, bold, boy like Little Lee let a forty-one pound carp pull him in under that grist wheel, but Big Lee wouldn't let anybody close to him. It was a natural reaction I guess, for a father to want to protect his dead boy, that was too far past protecting, and that's all he could think of to do, so that's what he did, protected him from everybody around, and kept all of us away.

So, we didn't get to look at Little Lee close; no one had the nerve it would've taken to stand up to Big Lee, to stand up to the Sheriff, to check Little Lee to see what happened. The mill was about a mile from Big Lee and Aunt Mae's house. He walked, carrying Little Lee in his arms the whole way home and wouldn't let anybody else touch him. It was the longest walk I ever took, with me, Daddy, and a couple of others following along about ten steps behind trying to respect what Big Lee wanted.

By then, all the excitement, the panic, and the wanting to know how it happened had died out, and the shock of Little Lee being dead set in on me and everyone else. Walking along, I stared numbly at the ground, just avoiding the sight of Little Lee's legs dangling off his daddy's arm. His head lay in the crook of his daddy's left arm and his legs flopped back and forth with every step. It was just too hard to see the life gone out of him like that. Then, I noticed a little drop of blood every few steps, not a lot, but about ten drops off and on in the dirt while we walked.

I nudged Daddy, pointed the first few drops out to him and he shook his head, no, and gave me the sign to be quiet, so I let it alone and didn't say anything more. Later on that night, when we were at home, I asked him about the blood I saw, and he said the mill wheel or some rock under the water probably hit Little Lee on the head, and it was too late for it to matter anyway. People offered to take the burden off Big Lee and Aunt Mae to clean Little Lee up and get him ready to bury, but Big Lee wouldn't hear of it. In fact, he wouldn't let anyone, even my Daddy or Mama, stay with them to help.

I said earlier that it was over a hundred degrees during that time, and Big Lee didn't pour his grief out in tears, but in buckets of sweat digging Little Lee's grave the next day and then again, filling it back in after the funeral. Daddy sat with him while he worked, watching him, just to let him know he was there, but neither one of them said a word. The hotter the day became the faster Big Lee dug and the deeper he went.

He went past six feet about four in the afternoon and kept digging. Daddy said he tried to stop him a few times, but Big Lee just kept digging harder and faster, and deeper and deeper, trying to spend his pain. He stopped when the sun set and the daylight began to fade, scrambled up the wall of the grave he dug, and without saying a word, walked home and spent the night building a box for Little Lee to lie in. Daddy was always a curious man, so he measured the grave to see how deep it was. It was seven and a half feet.

Just over a month passed before Big Lee talked to anybody except Aunt Mae, speaking softly to her, coaxing her, trying to get her to eat. Later, it was me and Daddy and God he first talked to. We had the sled hooked up to Sockeye, our steadiest mule, working between two rows of sweet cane sorghum. I drove the sled while Big Lee walked along one side of the sled with Daddy on other side, each working a row of sorghum. Work is always easier with help, so Daddy and Big Lee always helped each other when they could. Me and Little Lee usually helped too, but it was just the three of us now.

They used razor-sharp cane knives, cutting the stalks close to the ground with one stroke, topping the grain heads with another, tossing the grain off to the side to pick up later, and the stalks of cane on the sled for me to straighten. We worked along at a steady pace that matched Sockeye's gait up the row. Suddenly, it seemed as if Big Lee remembered some battle from long ago, and he violently slashed and slashed, working harder and faster, the way Daddy said he dug that grave, mowing down the cane like it was some ancient enemy, cursing violently, "Why God dammit, Why God dammit, Why God Dammit," with every stroke.

At the end of the row, he stood up with his hands in supplication to the sky, wielded that cane knife like his old cavalry sword, and exploded with one final crescendo of "Why God dammit! Why?" that rolled across the field and echoed down the field, stilling everything for a moment with shock at the vehemence of his outburst. In that stillness, no answers came down from God, and we didn't have any either. I heard a door slam behind me. I looked back to see Aunt Mae standing on the porch, still in her tattered funeral dress, looking down the field to where we were. Big Lee saw her too. I watched his eyes fill with tears. Then he looked down at the ground like he was ashamed of something. When he looked up, Aunt Mae was gone, and we went back to work.

When we finished cutting a full load, I drove the sled full of cane stalks up past the barn and under the syrup shed. Big Lee and Daddy walked along quietly behind the sled and we soon fell into the familiar rhythm of the work in the syrup shed, cutting the cane into easy lengths, feeding it into the press, all of us taking turns turning the crank until we finished juicing the stalks. While I laid the paddles around the kettle and started a slow fire under it, Daddy and Big Lee sat in the shade of a black walnut just outside and took a few sips from a new jar of pine top, moonshine with a chunk of pine resin in it for flavor, letting the hard edges of the day round off, shaking the jar watching the bubbles rise, winding down with the day, cooling off with the sun setting in the west, and a big, round, full moon already up in the east.

Big Lee took a slug of the moonshine, and then stared at Daddy with sadness and a question in his eyes. He just shook his head, looked down at the ground and said, "I just don't get it," and then in a minute, sadly, "Jesus Christ." When he looked back up and Daddy said, "What is it Lee," he said so softly and sadly it was almost a whisper, "Jesus Christ Almighty. I just don't understand why?" That was it. So far as I know, he never said another word about Little Lee dying to anyone, but he never went to the church without going out to the cemetery and standing at his boy's grave for a few minutes talking to him. Now, I'm not a judge of whether that shows the tough side of Big Lee or the other side, but it shows something. Maybe like most things do, it shows a little bit of both.

Things changed a lot after Little Lee drowned. Aunt Mae lost her own will to live after Little Lee died. She was a sweet woman, too sweet maybe, and she never got past losing Little Lee. She walked around mourning and simmering at the same time. Little Lee dying broke something in her that couldn't be fixed. You could feel her pain and her seething anger too. She kept walking down to the mill, looking at the water, and she kept asking Tadlock Greer, "What did you see?" over and over again. When he said "Nothing," she just looked at him until he walked away, and then she looked back to the water.

Occasionally I accompanied her, just to keep an eye on her for Big Lee, and Drip Greer came out sometimes and watched the water with her. She later told Big Lee that every day Drip came out, he put his hand on her arm and then pointed to the water and in a private language that only he and God understood, tried to tell her something, and every day Tadlock or his mama, Julia, came out with a stick and beat him until he ran off down the creek hollering and hitting at trees and things. Aunt Mae watched that water for hours, day by day by day, and every time she went there, she asked what Tadlock Greer saw, and every day he told her the same thing, "Nothing."

After a few weeks, Julia, Tadlock's mother, went to Big Lee and said, "Leland, you need to keep that wife of yours away from the mill. She's gone crazy, and everybody's scared of her. It's not good for my business."

Big Lee told her, "Tell Tadlock to say what he saw. Maybe it'll satisfy her. He had to see something. Maybe you saw something too. You and Tadlock ran Little Lee and Stash off from there a thousand times. You were both there; you had to see something."

Julia said, "My boy told you and her and everybody over and over again, he didn't see anything, and I didn't either."

Big Lee said, "Then I guess she'll get tired one day. Until

then, nothing is going to stop her. When he died he took her heart with him."

Julia said, "He didn't just take her heart. He took her mind too. I've seen crazy before and she's crazy. She's just plain crazy."

Big Lee looked at her and said, "Listen to this real close; don't say a word to her. Let her be."

Julia said, "If you can't handle your woman, I know I can, and I will if I have too."

Big Lee told her, "Julia, I've known you my whole life, and we've avoided big trouble so far, and I'm not looking to have it out with you right now, but if you or any of your people touch Mae, I'll put a bullet right there," and he tapped her in the middle of her forehead. "I said let her be, and I mean let her be."

Julia replied, "You won't do shit; you ain't never done shit," and walked away.

Aunt Mae refused to eat enough to keep a bird alive. Little Lee was fifteen when he drowned and he showed all the good traits of his daddy, his courage, his level-head, and at times his fearlessness. I don't know whether we learn those things or if they are born inside, but Little Lee had them all. Some people called him foolhardy for how much he seemed to challenge the world. Maybe that was born in him too. I really don't know, maybe so. Until now, I've never thought about it that deep. It seems that way now with the way things ended, but Little Lee also seemed to have another side, the best from his Mama.

She was a kind, sweet person. I've known her to nurse orphaned calves with the same care she would have given her own child, and one time she wrestled the last two pigs from a big, angry sow intent on eating them like she ate the other eight from the litter. Aunt Mae nursed those baby pigs the same way she did those calves, and when we butchered them, she wouldn't have a thing to do with it until they we cut them up to where she didn't know them anymore. Little Lee had that part of her too. I saw it more times than I could count. Anyway, losing him was hard on everybody, but especially hard on his mama.

It wasn't long before Aunt Mae completely gave up. She got weaker and weaker, and when the winter came, she took a rattling cough that turned into pneumonia, went to bed, refused to eat or drink, and died. So Big Lee lost his boy and his wife within six months of each other, and I lost my Aunt, and my lifelong best friend. Like deaths close to a person do, they left a big empty space that never filled up until Ella stepped into it. Thank God for her. They say that the Lord gives and the Lord takes away, and maybe that's true since as soon as the living seemed to shudder to a stop for a while with Little Lee and Aunt Mae dying, and it seemed to move again when Ella came. I don't know how Big Lee filled up that space or if he ever has. I don't know how he even breathes. I just don't know.

# Tadlock

I'm a Greer and that ought to be enough for anybody. See, that name means something around here. Julia Greer, I call her Mamaju, is my mama. I don't really know who my daddy is; he was dead before I can remember. That's what Pop Henry and Mamaju told me; they said Kilpatrick's men executed him when he got caught spying. He died a hero they said. That's what they say anyway, but you know all about what they say. We had a nigger one time that hung around here waiting for the little work we gave him every once in a while, and one day he got the blackass over some little something and told me that Pop Henry was my real daddy, that the man Mamaju claimed was my daddy wasn't nothing but a common no-count thief, a bummer that got caught stealing some silver dinnerware that Kilpatrick was hauling home to his wife and got hisself shot in front of a firing squad.

Pop Henry is Mamaju's daddy, my own granddaddy, so you can figure what that means, but back then, I wasn't but a little thing and didn't understand what it all meant and I thought it was a good thing that Mamaju was my mama and Pop Henry was my daddy. They were the two people that meant the most to me on the whole earth. I told Mamaju what the nigger said, and she went straight out with a big walking cane she kept around and beat him down into the ground. He laid there for a long time until some others slipped up and hauled him off, some of his family I guess.

While Mamaju was beating that nigger, I tried to run off with my idiot cousin Drip, but Pop Henry made me watch with him, and he just laughed and laughed watching Mamaju beat that poor man down, but I felt sorry for him. I kind of liked him, the nigger I mean. He was kind of like a pet to me, and did about anything I wanted him to do like pulling me around in the cart, or cleaning my fish, or going with me to feed the stock, just little things like that. We didn't ever see him back around after the beating, and I missed him for a while, but I got over it. People like him disappeared all the time in those days.

I grew up tough. Pop and Mamaju made sure of it. They always told me that any Greer, even the least Greer, like Drip, was head and shoulders above anybody else, especially all these so-called good people around here. It was the Casons and others like them they were talking about and eventually I grew up hating them without really knowing why, but it really didn't matter why. I hated them with a passion. I just did like most people do growing up and took on what my own people thought. Later on, a lot of things came along that gave me some reason to hate them, but you probably know about some of those already. If Pop or Mamaju ever caught me backing down from any of those people or even just trying to be friends and get along with any of them, one or both of them just beat the shit out of me. Hating those people and trying to find ways to get at them was what they expected of me, and then later it got to be fun, kind of like a big game.

I remember way back when I was in charge of keeping people out of the swimming hole below the grist mill, it was Stash and Little Lee that was the most aggravating to keep out. They always came down here from up on the ridge like they didn't have a place they could swim otherwise. There's plenty of other places. Sometimes it seemed like a game to them too, just to see if they could get away with it. When I was younger, I thought they were fine; when I was a whole lot younger, I thought they we could all be buddies even

though I was older. Both of them were bold and rambunc-
tious like I was, and it was hard not to like them, but Pop
and Mamaju wouldn't allow any part of us being friends. I
got beat over and over, anytime I let my guard down with
those two, and I ended up hating them, just for the trouble
they caused me.

Looking back it seems like I was always in some kind of
contest with those two: to see who had the best horse, to see
who could kill the most squirrels, to see who could catch the
biggest fish, and then later with Stash, a little while after Little Lee drowned down here at the mill, to see who could win
the girl. Ella Quick is who I mean. By the time that competition came along, when Ella came up this way to live with the
Therrells, I already had a couple of fine little mulatto boys
off two pretty Negresses that Mamaju made me be with
from out at the brothel. She picked them out for me, to
make me a man she said, and I didn't fight it too much, but
when Ella came along, it was her I wanted to be with me,
and make a family in my own house, respectable like if you
know what I mean.

I thought a man of my means ought to have a respectable house and a wife and a family, and I had already tried to
make a respectable house with Nell and we had a boy too,
but that whore ran off to be with George Cason, but bad
things come with bad women. Eventually, he reaped a bitter
harvest with her, god damn his soul, and so did she. I think
the only reason Ella went with Stash was because she felt
sorry for him about Little Lee. Nothing else could've been
the reason, not with all the things this Greer had to offer.

I was around the mill when Little Lee drowned. It wasn't
like him to come down here by himself. It was usually him
and Stash together, but for some reason, he came by himself
that day. The fish had quit the spring run, but the pool below the dam was full of all kinds of fish like robin, shellcrackers, catfish, suckers, and a few huge carp. I'd seen some

roiling the surface, trying to find their way over the dam. I always kept two or three gigs, and an awl pike leaning up against the millhouse just for those suckers and carp because it was a lot easier to gig them than to catch them with dough-balls on a hook. The way you did it was to gig them and pull them up close to the bank, and then if they were too big to pull out alive, you used the awl pike to stick into their brains to stun them. Then you could pull them out easy.

That day, I went out back and saw Little Lee struggling with something big stuck on the end of the gig, and when I ran over there, I saw he had a big old sow carp, one of the big ones that I'd been watching, trying to haul it up over the rocks onto the bank. I hollered at him, "You little bastard, this ain't yours. There ain't any right of yours to be in here. Give me that gig," but he was a stubborn little son of a bitch and wouldn't turn loose.

He said, "This creek isn't yours, and this fish is mine. Come on, help me pull her in!"

I said, "It's my mill and my gig! Let go of it you poaching little bastard," but he wouldn't let go so I grabbed my awl pike to stick the fish on my own, and get a hand in on claiming it, but Little Lee dragged it away from me, and wouldn't let me get to it, so I went inside to get Mamaju to help me, and when I came back out, that carp was swimming in circles around the pool and Little Lee was gone. I figured that he must've gotten scared or smart, one or the other, and run on off, and I thought it was a good thing he did. It wasn't until later when Leland came down here looking for him that we all found out that he drowned. The stupid, aggravating, little bastard must have fell on the rocks fighting that fish and drowned. That's what happened.

I was surprised that Leland didn't ask more questions right after he brought Little Lee out of that water, but he just carried him up the ridge towards home and buried him a couple of days later. It was really pitiful the way Mae, Little Lee's mama, came down here and looked at the water every day like the water was gonna give up some answer to her. People started coming down here watching Mae in that black funeral dress of hers standing there by the water, crying and begging and wailing, asking god for answers. She did that till she took to the bed and died, and Mamaju and Leland had words over it, her coming down here and drawing a crowd. Ever since then, Leland makes me nervous the way he looks at me and the way it always seems like he's watching every little thing we do, like it's any of his affair.

Mamaju says he's obsessed with us, that he'll do anything he can to get us, like he's got any reason to, and he's taken a special liking to Drip. Drip was out there watching Little Lee fight that fish, but that idiot bastard can't say a word and wouldn't know the sun from the moon anyway. He can't tell shit about what he saw, so I don't know why Leland is so damn interested in him. There's nothing to tell anyway but that Little Lee wrestled with a big fish, bit off more than he could chew, drowned and now he's gone. That's all.

# Big Lee

S ometimes it seems to me that all I went through before
Little Lee and Mae died was just a way to get me ready
for their deaths. You can live for a little while thinking the
way things are is the way things will always be. It's just a
child's way of thinking, children having no experience yet to
think otherwise, but those times eventually end for all of us
don't you think? For me, by the time I went off to the War, I
knew a little bit about death, but like most people when
death first strikes close them, I just followed the custom,
copying what the older people did, and then pushed death
out of my mind as quick as I could so I could get on with
living my life. Everyone does that. Still, just like the sun
coming up in the morning and setting in the afternoon, people around me kept dying like they always have and always
will.

By the time I went off to the War, I had even seen one
person killed. One Sunday after church the family, the aunts,
uncles, and cousins, gathered up at the big house like we did
on Sundays. I was around twelve; I forget exactly, but I do
recall that it was a hot, thick day near the end of dog days.
After we ate dinner, the men and boys went outside so the
men could smoke and slip inside the barn for a drink, and
the boys could argue and tussle about with one another. Like
it always happens when men and boys get together without
women around, the smoking, drinking and boistering talk
boiled down to one idea. Every single person there thought
they had the best horse, and every single person there
thought they were the best horseman. Most of us did have

good horses; it was just an issue of pride and necessity be-fore the War, and every man and boy there claimed they were the best rider or the best trainer, or both.

One of the cousins traded in horses, and had a tough one that he couldn't completely break. It was a fine horse once he settled down, but he wasn't worth much money to a horse trader since he always bucked and reared a couple of times before he settled down for riding. It didn't matter how many times a person rode him; he always did the same thing. Even if a rider got off him during a ride, the stubborn horse did the same bucking and rearing when they mounted him again. He'd sold the horse three times and had to take him back every time.

Now there was another cousin, Lane Pittman, who fan-cied himself to be the best trainer around and said he could break that horse, bragged that he had a foolproof method that had never failed him before. We knew what he would do; we'd all seen him do it a few times. We never thought it was dangerous, because he was damn agile around those green horses. Lane got up on the horse and let him buck and rear one time. Then, on the second time when the horse reared, Lane pulled back hard on the reins and leaned back at the same time. When the horse got off balance and started falling back, Lane was supposed to jump off the same way he had so many times before. It was the horse falling and hitting the ground that would break it from rearing, but this time Lane made one little mistake; the one little mistake that turned out to be the only one in a his life that really counted.

Lane had on some new Sunday shoes. We'd been trifling with him about them, kicking dust on them, spitting close to them, just little stupid mess like that. We didn't know it and he didn't either, but the soles of those shoes were a little bit wider than his regular working shoes and his left foot snagged in the stirrup. I think he realized while he was fall-ing back with that big horse on top of him that he was in big trouble. He hollered "No!!" real loud and tried to pull his left leg free of the stirrup, but he didn't make it off in time. The horse fell straight back on him, and drove him down into the dirt. The horse kicked and squirmed, rolled off him. The pommel dug into the middle of Lane's chest.

We all rushed in to him, but that quick, he was too far gone to know we were there. He stared up through us, into the sky and his eyes glassed over. He wheezed for about a minute, not really breathing, just a reflex attempt to get air, blowing pink foam out of his mouth and nose when he exhaled, and then he just stopped. It was my first time seeing somebody killed, and it was a hard shock. It just plain scared me for a man to be laughing, talking, and bragging about how good he was doing something, and then have the same thing kill him a few minutes later. One tiny mistake is all it took, and I carried the hard memory of Lane dying around with me not knowing that seeing him die was just the beginning of all the dying I would see in my life.

A few years later, I bought into all the secessionist fervor going into the War like most of the young boys around here. I took it all in, hook, line, and sinker. Henry Greer was one of the ring leaders around here, and I remember him and the rest of the war-mongers made it sound like Sumner and Stevens and the rest of the abolitionists were the spawns of Satan sent to earth to trifle with just us, and that it wouldn't take two weeks to teach them their lesson and shut them up. You know it didn't work out the way they said, and to make it even worse, there were quite of few of those like Henry Greer who didn't want any part of the War once it came. Some of them paid someone to go in their stead. Henry Greer was one. I can't remember the poor fellow's name that went for Greer, probably one of those drifters he liked to hire, but I do remember hearing that the man got killed the first time he ran up on some Yankees.

Anyway, I went on off to the War when I was sixteen. I

thought I was a man. I had been doing some things that men do, and thought that's all it took to be one. I graduated to moonshine when I could find it. I guess every boy around here starts slipping out to the wine barrels early, and I've known some boys to be pure drunks as young as ten or eleven, but moonshine is a whole other thing that comes later, and I started stepping up to drink the man's drink. Not too long after I started with the moonshine, I discovered that Julia Greer liked to take her clothes off as much as I liked for her to take them off. I know it's a lot now to think that me and Julia ever had anything like that between us, and it does seem like another life and another person even, but it's true. When that started happening with Julia, I really thought I was the cock of the walk. I thought every little girl around here was just waiting for me to come strutting by and show a little favor their way, but when I tried that same tack with Mae, she set me straight real quick. That might have something to do with why I married her a little while after the War ended.

My unit stayed in South Carolina for a while down around Beaufort and Charleston, sometimes venturing over into Georgia to a little bit south of Savannah. There was a lot of activity, but nothing like what we would see later. Except for the Yankees using their navy to harass our ships and to occasionally put soldiers on the ground to run little raids and such, most days we just tried to stay as far inland as we could to avoid the malaria and other low country illnesses. We got a big alarm one day about some Yankee boats moving up the Combahee River, raiding the plantations down there for supplies they needed, and freeing as many of the slaves as they could while they were there.

While the Yankees were storming about the countryside setting houses and barns on fire, an old escaped slave named Harriet Tubman they brought with them to talk to the slaves, was busy convincing as many as she could that the

Yankees weren't anything like what their masters had told them. If it wasn't for her, most of the slaves would have stayed put. Before she convinced them otherwise, most of them ran from the Yankees like they were the hounds from hell. After she talked, some went along, believing that freedom was a good thing, and I guess it felt good to them. I read later that all told, about a thousand slaves took off with the Yankees, but even before we left down there, quite a few had come back home, and they straggled back down to their old homes, the only homes they ever knew, for years.

While I was down there, I saw some dead scattered about, and I thought what I saw steeled me to seeing dead men lying about. One that sticks in my mind was a dead slave boy with the back of his head split wide open. When we rode up to one of the plantation landings on the Combahee, the Yankee gunboat was already gone downriver. There was a big crowd around that dead boy and they were all moaning and wailing over him. He was one of their people. When we rolled him over, a chunk of his brain fell out on the ground. A damn cat darted in there and snatched it up before we could stop him. I can still see that stupid cat running off with a chunk of brain dangling from his mouth. I hate cats. I always have.

That poor slave boy was probably was about my age. His people told us he was going to leave with the Yankees and got scared right at the last minute. He tried to get away from the boat, and one of those Yankee soldiers whacked his head open with a sword to keep him from telling where they were. Sometimes there just isn't any winning in a War, and I kind of felt sorry for him.

It was when we went north to fight with General Hampton that I found out that what I'd seen so far was just a little taste of the dead and dying. Death and dying were our constant companions, and it drove a lot of men insane. I don't know if I was one of them or not, but I do know this. A thing broke inside me that has never healed, an idea about what living means. If it sounds hard, it is hard, and that is part of what broke inside me, the idea that living is easy. Sometimes living is harder than dying or watching someone die.

When we went up north to fight, our Enfield rifles had better range than what the Yankees used and we were pure hell for a while until the Yankees caught up with us. Most that rode in the 4th were good shots before the War, but shooting every day made us pure out and out deadly. I have to admit that nothing is quite like picking an enemy off from further away than he can even think about hurting you. It's powerful, but at the same time, every time you see a real, living and breathing person drop in front of you, something inside you changes in a way that you just can't ever get back. So all along, people dying around me made my heart and my soul hard enough to endure Little Lee dying, and Mae dying too, and it hardened my heart enough to allow me to do what I've needed to do over the years. God help me.

I'm not in the business of true confessions or anything close to it, but when we came home, a lot of things had to change. We had to correct them, and I will say that I helped change things back to a way of life we could tolerate; damn those arrogant sons of bitches that came down here thinking they would rule us, when even Lincoln himself said that we were all Americans. Damn them all and all those opportunistic bastards they sent down here trying to suck more life out of our home. Some said wait, be patient, but to hell with that. I waited on God or fate or whatever during the War too many times to think it was going to be any different after the War. Sometimes a man just has to do a thing that needs doing. Every son of a bitch that fell in front of my Enfield earned those notches in my walking stick and that's all I'm going to say about that for now.

# Stash

You know how it is. People talk about the innocence of youth all the time, and there is such a thing. I know just like you do, a person lives for a while believing everything their parents say and everything they hear in church and it's a shock the first time they realize things aren't exactly the way they've been taught. It's a disappointing thing, but the sooner you accept a different way of thinking about the world, the better off. I lived the innocent life for a little while. I never saw the truth about all the constant conflict between the Casons and the Greers. Conflict isn't even the right word to use. It turned out that it was an outright feud like it is now, but for a long time me and Little Lee didn't see it. The grown-ups sheltered us as long as they could I guess, the way I tried to shelter Ella, and Brooks, and Janie.

Everything was just fun for us when we were young, even when the Greers came storming out of the mill to run us off from riding the wheel to jump off into the pool under the dam. We just thought it was a game. Now that I think back on it, I see it wasn't ever a game and I don't think the Greers sheltered Tadlock at all. It seems he knew from the start we were the enemy, judging by all the things he did to us growing up. It was either that, or his pure meanness is just an inbred thing. The first time I really knew all that "Love thy neighbor" stuff was just wishful thinking was the first time Papaw Cason took me and Little Lee to see the Mothers. It became my favorite place of all the favorite places we knew about, and I think it was Little Lee's too, but we never talked about it being a special place the way I am talking to you; it was just one of those places that drew us back over and over.

We were just boys, not pondering God, or a just world, or good and evil, or how things are, or are not. Not that we didn't talk and ramble about in ideas and smart talking like we were smart men. We did a lot, especially when we were both thinking to be preachers, but we were just boys, and none of it amounted to much. That kind of talk for boys is akin to the foolish and daring physical things they do measuring themselves against the world out there, like riding that mill wheel up to the top and jumping off into the pool, or gigging a big sow carp alone, or racing through wiregrass during the middle of July thinking they are moving too fast for a rattlesnake to bite them. Once boys get a little bit of knowledge about almost anything they have to rush out and find somebody to contend with about it and measure their mind and their words against the other to see who knows the most, which is smarter. It's the same as any bunch of animals getting the pecking order straight, just with words and ideas, well, not just with those, sometimes with tussling, and wrestling, and fists, when the words aren't enough, and we did our share of that too.

Anyway, stretching out along the ridge on our side of South Prong Creek, the fat litard stumps of ancient longleaf pines stretch out like the stones in an old cemetery marking nameless graves. I call it the witness ridge because like the stones marking the dead, the stumps scattered through the new growth pines and wiregrass along that ridge bear witness to what was here long before we came, and beyond that, to the greed of the men who sucked the life out of them, and cut them down.

The first time Papaw showed them to me was one day in early October, the day cooling fast, the golden-hued fall light shimmering, me, Little Lee, and Papaw Cason, walked along the creek bank and when we got to a place where the ridge rolled down to end on a bluff about twenty feet high above the creek, we turned north, climbing the ridge and walked into a new growth pine forest mixed with blackjack oak, wiregrass, wild lupine, prickly pear, and occasional tufts of broomsedge. The three of us could reach around the pines with just our hands when we put them together. Papaw said they were about forty years old, "We planted these."

I couldn't have been more than eight years old and like I've said before, Little Lee was a year younger. We moved slowly with Papaw, quietly too, a hard thing for two boys on a ramble with their Papaw, but we watched him closely, copying him as he moved with stealth and grace, the way he said you needed to move in the woods, until a covey rose, the quail exploding from the cover of a broken-topped blackjack, startling our hearts into a racing rhythm, matching their staccato wing beats, me and Little Lee quick to the chase for a moment, and Papaw standing in the dappled sunlight, with his hands easy in his coat pockets, smiling, calling to us, "Come on back boys. We didn't come for those birds, this time."

We turned west and followed the crest of the ridge, the silver grey stumps of cut longleaf pine becoming more frequent and larger. "What happened to these trees, Papaw?" Little Lee asked, and me too pestering him for an answer, but he was quiet, not answering. After a quarter of a mile or so, we came into a grove of larger, living longleaf; a man could still reach around them, but he had to be a grown man, it took Little Lee and me together to reach around most of them. The stumps of even larger, older pines stood, sentries between them.

I asked again, "What happened to these trees, Papaw?" me and Little Lee standing on one of the stumps, scuffling around, pushing and tugging at each other, trying to push each other off.

"People cut them down. People used them up making

turpentine and tar, and then they cut them." Papaw said, walking over to where we stood on the stump. "Take this tree right here. I bet it was five hundred years old when they cut it, and that was probably over a hundred years ago. Most of these stumps are like that."

We didn't really have any idea what four or five hundred years meant, or even ten years, being just boys, but Papaw's mood, serious, even a bit melancholy, got our attention. It was kind of like when we walked into church with him; he was always a little bit different than he was any other time. When he walked over to us, he sat on the edge of the stump, brushing off the top so you could see the rings in it, and told us to count them to see how old the tree was. Try as hard as we could, neither of us could pay attention long enough to count them all, so we decided to be smart and started counting in sections of fifty rings, marking the ones we counted, taking a break to run around the area, jumping up and off of other huge stumps, and coming back to count again. After a while, we counted eight sections and a few more.

After a great discussion between us, and some figuring in the dirt beside the tree, me and Little Lee decided the tree was only about four hundred and thirty years old. "Papaw, it wasn't five hundred years old. See, it only comes up to a little over four hundred," we both said, like four hundred was a little number, just trying hard to get something over on Papaw.

"What about that soft wood on the outside that rotted away? Doesn't it have rings too?" and he had us dead to rights again.

Papaw started counting in from the farthest ring on the outside and said, "If this tree fell yesterday, this is how far back it lived." He counted in, separating a thin slice on the outside of the stump from the rest, and said, "Sixty, this is when I was born." He counted back some more. "One hundred and twenty five, George Washington, Thomas

Jefferson, and Ben Franklin were all alive." He kept count-ing, "One hundred and fifty, the Casons were still in Eng-land, just thinking about coming here," and then he counted nearly into the center, "Four hundred and six years, Colum-bus came here, and remember, this tree was probably cut about a hundred years ago."

"So Papaw, this tree was right here way back before Co-lumbus came?" Now that was something we could get our heads around, and he had our attention.

"Yep, and we don't even know what was here then. There was nothing here but Indians way back then. Come on. I've got something else to show you boys."

We walked along the ridge, going deeper into the grove of larger trees, with him telling us about how tall the trees must have been, about all the species that used to be around that were gone now, like deer, and turkeys, even though you might see a deer or two that got pushed up off the Pee Dee, but never turkeys. To find any of those, you had to go down to the Pee Dee, or up into the edge of North Carolina along Jones Creek, or even further up to the Rocky River. Then he told us about the Carolina Parakeet that traveled in flocks, and when a man shot one, the flock came back over and over and over again, trying to save the one down, until all of them died if the man had enough ammunition and time, and about the Passenger Pigeon, that traveled in still larger flocks, and met the same fate, and even elk, and bison that vanished long, long before white men came.

He stopped, looking around, and said, almost to himself, "It was nothing but greed, our greed that wiped it all out." Then he looked at both of us and smiled, "Well nearly all of it," motioning to us, "come on," and him still talking, "Some people say we thought it would last forever, that us wiping it all out was just a big mistake. Other people said that God put it here for us to use up any way we wanted to, like it was fine if we tore God's creation down and turned it into numbers in a ledger book somewhere, but I think it was simpler than that. I don't think we cared. Most of us still don't. In the end, it was nothing but our greed."

"Our greed, Papaw, some of our people did this?"

"Yep, and some of us still do."

We turned back toward South Prong Creek, and came to the rim of a natural amphitheater on the outer radius of a sharp bend in the creek. The rim curved around a flat area of about two acres tucked in beside the creek. The ridge on the other side of South Prong ended in a drop-off thirty feet high above the creek. The rim where we stood and the drop-off on the other side protected the floor and denied easy access from either side of the creek. Two massive longleaf pines rose from the floor of the amphitheater, and even from where we stood at the top, they towered at least eighty to a hundred feet above us. Papaw said "a hundred and fifty feet, at least," and me and Little Lee had no way to dispute him.

We scurried down the side onto the flat bottom of the amphitheater, where the soil, too damp for the wiregrass, broom straw, prickly pear, and wild lupine on the ridge, lay covered with colic root, spotted wintergreen, fern, and a dense mixture of ground hugging mosses. We ran up to the base of the trees, and stretched our arms out, trying to reach around them. "Come on Papaw, help us," and Papaw came down the wall to where we were and joined hands with us, the three of us reaching around one tree, and then the other, with little room to spare. "These trees are huge, Papaw. How old are these?"

"I don't guess anybody really knows except God, and they've been here so long, he's probably forgotten about them."

"Why didn't they get cut down, Papaw?"

"I don't really know why, boys, but I think it might be because of these high walls on our side, and that drop-off on the other side. Nobody ever figured out how to get them out. I know since the time that I know about, this is Cason land, and we wanted to keep them. We named them the Mother Trees."

"Mother Trees. Mother Trees." We liked the name, and said it a few more times. "Why do you call them that, Papaw?"

"Because a lot of those trees up there on the ridge came from these two trees down here; we dig their seedlings up and move them into the empty spaces up there, and we take the seeds from the cones and plant them. I think more trees come from that."

"Why can't we do that some, Papaw?"

"Well, you can. I'll teach you, and one day it will all be up to you and Little Lee, because I'll be gone by then, but you and the Mothers will still be here."

"Aw, Papaw, you'll still be here. You can watch us."

"I hope I can boys; I hope I can, but me and my Daddy started this planting seeds and moving trees together, and now he's gone, and one day I'll be gone too."

Papaw sat down at the base of one of the Mothers facing the creek, leaning back against the massive trunk, and copying him, we did the same thing, one on each side. He reached out and pulled us close in to him, and we sat for a while, the daylight fading into dusk, the water murmuring in the creek, the wind singing through the pines, the lonely cry of a pileated woodpecker echoing down through the creek bottom inside the coda of other birds' songs, the three of us tucked inside one of those moments that random sounds and smells trigger out of memory from nothingness years later to stop you cold, a time like right now, a time that you can never find the right words to tell about it because it wasn't about anything that the words could say to begin with. Somehow it seems so much more than that. Even now, I can't find the words. Maybe it was the face of God.

Papaw said, "This is a good place, boys. Remember this time. Don't let it get away from you."

"We won't Papaw. We won't," me and Little Lee promised.

Then we heard the sounds of some men coming from across the creek. Papaw took us up to the top of the amphitheater and told us to lie down so the men couldn't see us. "If any trouble breaks out, run back and get your daddies for me. Can you do that?"

"Trouble, Papaw?"

"Don't be scared. Just run get them if anything happens."

"We will, Papaw, we will," and we hunkered down watching over the edge of the amphitheater while Papaw went back down and stood behind one of the Mothers.

We watched four men scramble down the steep drop-off on the other side across from us. Three of the men carried small pails used to collect resin from pine trees. As they got closer, we could see they had bark girdling knives hanging from their belts, and the other accoutrements needed to do the work for turpentining. The fourth man carried a rifle of some description and as he began to direct the other three men to their task, that man turned out to be Julia Greer, and when Papaw stepped out, it was Julia that he called to while the three other men spread out behind her just like when we played war with some of our friends.

"Julia, I told you the last time I caught you here that it wasn't going to be good for you if you came back on our property."

"Well old man," she said, drawling the words out and smirking, "here I am and I don't see a damn thing you can do about it," and she looked back to the three turpentiners with her, and motioned for them to step up.

"Listen, you know you're off your land, and you know these trees aren't yours. We've had this talk before."

"You can't sit with these old trees all the time old man, and what good are they anyway if you can't turn them into money?"

"What good they are is something a greedy old crone like you won't ever be able to understand, and since they are not on your land, it's not your worry. You're just determined to tear down something that's better than you. It's not even the right time of year to pull resin. You just want to kill these old trees for spite."

"You whining old bastard, you think those little words are going to hurt me? I don't give a shit what you say, but here's something plain enough for you. Sooner or later, we gonna suck the life outta these trees, and their sap will be running out in them buckets just like your sap is running out, and then we gonna cut them, just because it suits me, and because you bastards think you're so damn good when you ain't nothing. We'll own this land one day too. You watch." She turned to the three men, and told them, "Tie this old fart up. He can watch us strip the bark off these trees he loves so much."

It was then, for the first time with Papaw, me and Little Lee disobeyed and went running down that bank to him instead of running home like he told us. They all heard us coming, and Papaw ran over to us and gathered us in close, and Julia lit out on a vicious cussing spree with words I never even heard before, trying to get those men to do what she said, and them backing off, saying no, they didn't want any part of tying up little boys. Julia kept cursing, threatening with things like, "You pieces of chicken shit! You're just like every man I've ever knowed, pure shit," and finally she scurried back up the drop-off across the creek and disappeared behind those three turpentiners.

It was the first I ever realized how people really hate other people right down to their bones and the ground they walk on, and when I saw those Greers, especially Julia, in church on Sunday with her billing and cooing like she was a nice, friendly, and good person, it confused me for a while until Papaw said that's how some people acted. He said we didn't have to worry about doing something to people like them, God would take care of it on the other side, and that was good enough to me for a while.

I found out later that it was hard work protecting our land from people like the Greers and those wanderers they hired for their dirty work. Daddy and Big Lee and Papaw, as long as he was able, spent a lot of time in the woods during the turpentine season making sure they never crossed onto our land to rape it the way they did their own.. As the years passed, their land started looking pretty bare from killing off their trees by turpentining too hard and then cutting them for timber after, and it wasn't anything but their greed that caused them to start coveting our land and trying to poach it any time they could get away with it. It's a true fact that our land looked more and more tempting with every year that passed.

Papaw took to his death bed in the late winter of 1894. I sat with him some while he was waiting to die, and we talked about things we used to do just to get his mind off his pain, things like fishing, hunting, rambling in the woods, and a lot of other things, and one day I said to him, "Papaw, remember the first time you took me and Little Lee to see the Mothers," and he smiled and said "I remember. I wish we could walk there one more time. Maybe if things work out, me and Little Lee will come there one day. Maybe we'll see you there. Don't forget to take care of them. Don't let anything happen," and I said, "I won't Papaw, you know I won't, you can depend on me," and a few days later, he was gone, and like a lot of promises a man makes over his lifetime, my promise to him was another idle promise I couldn't keep.

I visited those trees often, and with Daddy and Big Lee,

we chased turpentiners off, moved trees and planted seeds, trying, I guess, to remake a part of the world that was lost, just our little part. It seems so futile now that so many of the people and places that I knew are gone, but if Papaw was here or if he could talk from the other side, I'm sure he would tell me that all the effort is worth it. He would say that a man ought to spend at least a part of his life doing something that will last longer than he does. That's just who he was and the way he thought about the world, and I guess that's why I am the way that I am. Little parts of him and all those other people who are gone now are still alive in me.

It's an odd thing, a thing I never expected, that the world begins to empty out around you. When I think about Papaw and Grandma Cason, and Mama and Daddy, and Little Lee, and a lot of others, I never thought about how it would be for all of them to be gone, about how I would feel to be the one standing here alone, trying to figure this whole thing out, looking for answers that won't come, trying and trying to get just a whisper out of God, not for myself, but just a little whisper from him to let me know that all those people are good on the other side of dying.

The world becomes a sad, empty place, even with all the living still going on all around. I remember the way the world was when I was just an innocent boy, and I remember it rich with the people and the places I loved, full of wonder and magic, like a lush, endless forest. Then I see it withering away, fading into a barren desert. I fight to hold on to the living around me, trying to slow it down, wanting to make it all last, wanting to make it alive again, but I know that even what's left will be gone one day, or I will.

# Ella

John Brooks never talks much about what he's thinking, but I know he tries hard to figure things out about how the world works and all. I think if I tried to figure it all out like he does, it would just make living seem too hard, too much to bear, especially now with all that's going on. It seems like a person just gets tiny little spaces of time where they can breathe deep and enjoy life with all the good around them, and they only get those little spaces when they're lucky. I know about the innocence of children and I know it's true just like you do; we all go through those times, and the lucky ones have more than others. That innocent time ended for me when our house down in Big Springs caught on fire. My Mama and Daddy and my baby brother died in that fire.

Everything that happened to me is a good example of what I'm talking about. We were enjoying living in a real easy time. We were so happy that Mama came through birthing our new brother, Paul, and they were both doing fine. I never told Mama, but while she was carrying Paul, I was scared for her. Our neighbors down at Big Springs, Ellis and Eileen Carson had a big family already, eight children, and when Eileen was carrying their ninth, she just kind of broke down like some women do. Mama said it didn't look like it was going to go good, and it didn't. Eileen had a stillborn in her seventh month and a little bit later, she just up and died too. She never got out of that birthing bed. Ellis told Daddy he thought she just couldn't bear for their littlest one to be on the other side alone, so she just gave up and went over there too. It didn't make much sense to me since she left eight children on this side, but if it gave Ellis some comfort about it all to say it and believe it, I guess it was fine. It didn't hurt a thing.

After Paul came and everything was fine with him and Mama, I decided all the worrying I did about Mama dying like Eileen was for nothing, and it tickled me to have a new baby brother. It was a real good time. Then, right when my guard was down and I relaxed into just loving my life, like it seems to happen too often, the fire came and we lost Mama and Daddy and our new brother, and that little space of good time seemed like one more dream that passed us by way too fast. I don't remember much about the fire and all the funeralizing around it. I think I pushed it way down trying to forget. I say that and mostly it's true, but sometimes memory just lays there waiting for the right thing to come along and wake it all up like the fire that killed John Brooks' Mama and Daddy. Then all of it, even things I never thought about before, come floating up to the top and fill up every thought like they've been there all the time, and I guess somewhere they have.

It's been on my mind a lot since all this trouble with John Brooks got started that it might be me who's brought all this hardship up here. I never thought about that I might be the one bringing all this on John Brooks and his family until the fire that burned the big house and killed his Mama and Daddy. I think about it a lot now. If it is me that brought all this hardship up here, then what is it that I did that makes God keep burning up things around me? For my own Mama and Daddy and little brother to die in a fire and then a few years later for my husband's Mama and Daddy to go the same way seems like more than just a thing that happens without there being a reason behind it. It never occurred to me before that God might be after me, but now I wonder.

Trouble always lay between the Casons and the Greers, but it seemed like the fire that killed Papa Jacob and Miss Maggie started things on a harder path that ended up with those two men lying dead and John Brooks tried and up in the jail for killing them. He never denied it even though I tried to get him to. He said there wasn't a jury in Scots Bend that would convict him for killing two of the Greer men. Everybody around here knows how the Greer men are, so he just said right out he was the one that did it, and never showed any remorse for doing it. I tried to tell him that it wasn't so much that he killed those two men, it was how he killed them and how much some people were saying that he liked it too much, and in the end, he was wrong about that jury; they convicted him and now he's facing a hanging and the only thing that might stop it is a pardon from the Governor. Everybody knows that John Brooks really wanted to kill Julia and Tadlock, but just like it always seems to happen, they came away unscathed.

Now those two hired hands are lying dead in the cold ground. John Brooks is up there in the jail waiting to hang, and I don't understand it any more than John Brooks does. It just seems like the bad wins out too many times. I finally told John Brooks I was scared it was me that was bringing all this down on us, and he wouldn't hear of it. He said the Greers brought the evil in here, and I didn't have a thing to do with it, and I know he was trying to ease me, but it sure seems like the evil follows me, like the fire that killed part of my family followed me up here and killed off Papa Jacob and Maggie.

I don't want to seem too whiny and ungrateful. I know there are good things in my life too. The Therrells took me and my brothers and sister in after we lost Mama and Daddy and Paul. It could've been a lot different for all of us. Now I've got Brooks and Janie, a nice place to live, and John Brooks' family will look after me even if he leaves, so I guess

I should be thankful and on one side I am, but on the other side is a whole different thing. I don't expect everything to be rosy all the time, and it doesn't have to be for me to be satisfied, but the way things have been since the fire down at Big Springs is almost too much to bear. I've heard it said a lot of times that everything has its season. That's from Ecclesiastes, and it's true; everything does, but what I need is a long, easy season in the sun without a bunch of dying and turmoil.

Tadlock Greer still has his eye on me. He told some people down at the mill that he didn't care whether John Brooks was dead or in prison, either way was fine for him. He told them he would be right here real quick to pick things up for me either way. It won't happen. First of all, the Sheriff wouldn't ever let it happen, and the second thing is that I wouldn't let Tadlock Greer anywhere near me or anything of mine. I don't care how hard it gets. Even if John Brooks' family abandoned me, and that won't happen, there's a place uptown in Scots Bend they call Widow Hill. There are about ten small shotgun houses up there where women move when they get widowed. Most of them have children. It's not the best place to be, but it's a place. Tadlock Greer is never going to get his hands on me, and he won't ever get ahold of Brooks and Janie.

When I think about losing John Brooks it takes my breath away. I look at Brooks and Janie and I would do anything to keep them from losing their daddy the way I lost mine. Any mother would. When I lost Mama and Daddy and Paul in the fire, I was scared like I am now. I prayed that God would show us a way to live and it seemed like He took care of us. The Therrells took us in and then for me, John Brooks came along, and I really thought all my prayers came true. It seemed to be so, because even through my mourning, I could see a way in front of me that gave me hope.

I finally let myself believe that God made everything

right again, but when I'm weak, I wonder whether the good was ever Him. I shouldn't question God, but all that's going on shakes my faith. I can't help it. If the good came from Him, then where is He now? Why can't it all stay good? Now, when I pray, I don't ask for much of anything anymore. I just pray for the best, whatever God thinks that is. I pray that God will forgive me for doubting. I quit asking for things when all this trouble came along, because it makes me bitter to keep begging for some relief that won't come, and I don't want to be bitter. I want to live with hope. I want to trust God to do the right thing for all of us even when we don't know what it is, and if a person asks over and over not ever getting what they ask for or even a reason why not, it just takes hope away. Living without hope is a hard way to live. So, I just pray.

A little while ago, I put Brooks and Janie to bed. I came into our little room, mine and John Brooks' and sat in his chair, just trying to find a way to be close to him. It still smells like him just a little bit. Something in the air closes in around me and comforts me, but at the same time, I feel how much he's not here. Missing seems like a little word to say how empty this place feels with him gone. For a few minutes I thought about doing something, some little chore to get my mind off him being gone. Then, I just turned the lamp off and sat in the dark breathing in and out, soaking up what's left of John Brooks in the air. I slid my hands under my nightclothes remembering John Brooks' hands on me, and missed him even more, but I didn't stop. I just kept on, trying to imagine it was John Brooks' hands and everything was fine, and none of this ever happened.

The moon is a few days short of full. I heard one of the children stirring so I walked down the hall to check on them. I saw Janie curled up with her back up against Brooks. He looked so much like his Daddy with his arms up and his hands tucked behind his head. The light coming through the window cut the bed in half. Brooks and Janie lay, half in shadow, half in light. I sat watching them for a long time, the moonlight spilling out to cover them in pale light. When it covered Brooks' face, I saw his eyes open, watching me, as calm as anyone could be. I walked around to his side of the bed, and sat on the edge, reaching out to touch his cheek with the back of my hand. His eyes were dark, like deep, endless pools of liquid. I could see John Brooks in him. He smiled and took my hand. "I want Daddy," he whispered so he wouldn't wake Janie.

"Me too," I said. We sat looking into each other's eyes for a minute.

"I have been praying Mama. It'll be ok," he said.

"Me too," I said, and then I lie beside him and after a little while, fell asleep.

# Stash

I've never seen an actual hanging, just the result of one, and if you had a chance to pick how you would leave here, hanging wouldn't be the thing you would pick. I don't guess any way is a good way, but some have to be better than others. Not having any personal experience yet, it still seems to me that dying ought to be a private thing. It might be nice to have one or two people around to hold your hand or hear what you might say, for you to drift off real easy, but to have a lot of people, strangers mostly, clamoring to watch you die for their entertainment just doesn't seem right. Not all the time, but sometimes it really weighs on my mind that I might hang for this thing I did. I think what I did is good. Well, maybe good is too strong a word, but I know I did what I had to do.

I know what the Bible says about "Thou shall not kill," but it is pretty clear to me that people have figured out a lot of ways for that commandment not to be a hard and fast rule, like during the War, well any war, and at most other times too. I think if you just pay attention to the New Testament, to what Jesus said, the killing thing is pretty clear - you can't do it - but if you double back into the Old Testament like most people do, well then you can find plenty of safe places to back up killing someone, like what Moses and the Jews did to those Midianites, and if you look hard enough, you can find some place to back up almost anything you might want to do.

Those poor Midianites never stood a chance. Moses sent the army in there and told them to kill every single male person they came across, even babies and old men too that couldn't lift a finger against them. Then they killed off all the women except the ones they tested out and found to be virgins. I remember once, the preacher used the story about the Midianites showing off the wrath of God trying to scare me and Little Lee into being preachers again, talking about how He might punish us for walking away.

Just being me, I asked him how was it that you tested out a virgin. I was a curious young fellow. Little Lee just plain out exploded into laughter and that preacher's face turned as red as it did on Sunday morning after he'd been flailing away at the people for a while. He snatched me up and whipped me with a leather strap until I had welts all up and down my legs. Little Lee ran to keep from getting the same. I never did find out how to test those virgins with any sure enough proof, and I still haven't figured that one out. I do know some girls that can turn themselves into virgins all over again anytime they need to.

Anyway, Moses let the men in the army keep the virgins for their own pleasure, whatever own pleasure meant in those days. I have my own ideas about what it means back then, and in this day and time. So, my question is that if God can tell Moses to go in there and slaughter a whole people, steal their land, their livestock, their riches, and then use those virgins any way that suits them, why can't I kill a couple of evil bastards that needed to be killed? Why? I pray about it, and ask God the question, but so far, He hasn't seen fit to answer me, and I'm still stuck up here in the damn jail.

I know there have been hangings where over a thousand people were there to watch, some even more than that, and I can't stand the thought of that many people gawking at me while I'm dying. The last one here drew over five hundred and that was way back in 1855. I hope the last thing I hear isn't a bunch of bloodthirsty idiots hollering things about me dying. A lot of people just go for the show, to see the poor hanging bastard do that jig, that hangman's jig, dancing, kicking, pissing, and shitting all down his pants legs, and some son of a bitch will be there, some greedy bastard selling souvenirs to the crowd trying to make some money off my dying. There always is someone like that. Now that would be a bastard that ought to be hanged, not me; if there is a person there like that, I'd put the rope on him myself before they put it on me and we could go together.

Let me tell you about the time I saw the result of a hanging. I was with Daddy, Big Lee, Little Lee, and Tally Bishop when I saw it. I asked about it a few days ago. I wanted to get the time right, and Big Lee said it was during the wild times before the General, Wade Hampton, won the election and worked the deal with President Hayes to send the federal troops back north along with that bastard Chamberlain. I would have been just under six years old. There was a colored man named Prince Williams. I use the word colored instead of Negro on purpose because Williams' skin was a medium shade, about like light caramel, and if he had been one or two shades lighter he could have walked over into white the way a lot of people did during the upheaval after the War.

He got ahold of a nice piece of the land from the Keitt Plantation when the Freedmen's Bureau split it up and handed it out because the Keitt family abandoned their land up here a couple of days before Sherman and never came back. I heard they're down on the coast near Wilmington on another big piece of land some of the family had down there. They never really fit in here anyway being mostly speculators like a lot of people were before the War. A little while after the War, Williams showed up with papers from the Freedmen's Bureau down in Darlington, and a little piece of money and took about forty acres of land and after a while, a pretty Keitt mulatto named Doll for a wife. I might as well go ahead and explain that Doll and some more like her from the old Keitt plantation had as much real Keitt blood as any of the white Keitts. People don't talk about it much, but it was true about them and a lot of others around here too. I'll leave it to you to figure out what that means; it's not hard to figure. People wondered what Prince Williams' connection was that he could get a good piece of land for a farm, but they mostly let it pass, being so taken up with trying to survive themselves. Then, he started bragging that he had been one of the 1st SC Volunteers, and was part of the reason the Yankees won. It explained a lot. For those of you who don't know, that was the unit made up of runaway slaves that served in the Union army. It was a big deal for the Yankees, and it was a big deal the other way for the people down here.

There were so many veterans from around here who fought hard, and watched other men die hard. When it was all over, most of those men came home plain wore out, and ready for peace. They came home just wanting to pick up their lives or start them over again. At the same time, they didn't come home ready to lie down and let a bunch of Yankees and freed slaves run their business either. They didn't take kindly to the Federal troops left down here, or to all the penance those troops thought the people down here owed. The people around here weren't ready to accept any of it, especially from an uppity Negro who fought for the Yankees, took land from one of the old plantations, and then bragged about it to anyone who would listen. Living was a hard struggle, and with all Federals wanted to ram down peoples' throats, a lot of bitterness hung on.

For a while, the worst that happened to Prince Williams was a whole lot of shunning and some aggravating harassment. Over time, the word about him spread to a crowd of ruffians that usually lay up in an outlaw camp on Little Mountain down in Harden Swamp. They tried to claim the name of Regulators like the ones from a hundred years before and they tried to use that respected name to justify their marauding. A few were just ne'er-do-wells drowning in alcohol, but mostly they were just rough crowd of thieves and ruffians, and a group of them went one night and took Williams out to teach him a lesson, and the lesson was that they hung him. It was a hard lesson.

The next day Doll came uptown and told what happened, that a crowd of men came and took Williams off. Word spread pretty fast and some of the rifle club men went out looking. Daddy and Big Lee thought it might be that crowd from Harden Swamp and headed off that way, and me and Little Lee tagged along. I don't think Daddy or Big Lee had any idea that Williams was going to be hanging there in that tree or they wouldn't have let us go, but we went, and we rode up on Williams hanging from a big white oak about four miles outside Scots Bend just past the Rivers place on the road to Harden Swamp. Now it must have been a nasty crowd of men that lynched Williams because it looked they drug him off behind their horses and beat him and whipped him all over before they hoisted him up on that rope. They built a fire under him and hung him just high enough that his feet were in the top of the fire. The fire burned him all the way up to his waist and embers were lying about where he kicked them out from under him before he died.

God knows that must have been a hard way to leave here. It was a scary thing, especially to a little boy's mind, and when I think about me up there hanging if the judge says so, it's the image of Prince Williams hanging there I see in my head. You know how it is when you're little and something gets in your head, and it just stays there even when you grow up and ought to be able to get rid of it. Big Lee says a hanging, well, a lynching like what Williams went through won't happen to me, he's not going to set a fire under me, or beat me, and I know he won't, but when I think about me hanging, or dream about it, it's the image I see, me hanging there dancing a fancy hangman's jig, a fire burning up my pants legs, me kicking and trying to breathe. It's not a pretty picture to have in your head.

Since I've been up here, I've been thinking about Williams' hanging and those men who did it and this morning When Big Lee came in this morning, I asked him about it. "Big Lee, how come I'm facing a hanging for getting rid of those two bastards when none of that crowd who lynched Prince Williams ever hung?"

He said, "Why are you worrying about it now. I tried to tell you to be smart. Anyway, what would you rather be, dead or stuck in some hell hole of a prison for the rest of your life?"

"Well, Jesus Christ Big Lee, neither one of those choices is very good for me; it's not like I'm going to march up to those pearly gates and say, 'I know you know about me killing those two sons of bitches down there, but now I'm here to walk on those streets of gold.' I'm probably going to be in a hell hole either way."

He laughed at that and said, "I guess that is so, but that is some way to put it."

"You know I sent those bastards straight to Hell, and saved a lot of people the trouble. They deserved to die a lot more than Prince Williams did and none of those men had to hang."

Big Lee said, "Yeah, it might be true, or it might not. You don't know about Prince Williams and the way it was then, and the world was a different place back then. There was so much dying, people were almost used to it, and people still looked at any Yankee soldier as the enemy, and you killed the enemy if you could. Anyway, the world levels things out and the just world itself caught up with most of those men anyway."

I don't understand the just world thing at all, how people get what they deserve; I just can't see it, so I asked him, "What the hell do you mean? That bullshit just doesn't make sense to me. If the world catches up to people even if the law doesn't and makes them pay, doesn't the other side of that have to be if you do something good, the world catches up with you and pays you back for it too?"

Big Lee thought for a minute and said, "It ought to work that way. I see your point, and I just don't know, but I do know this. Most of the Harden Swamp crowd came to hard ends, and maybe that was the world or God or whoever levelling things out. You remember Steve Evans. He passed out too close to the fire on a big drunk. That fire burned his shoes off and got to his feet and legs awful, and when the gangrene set in, Doc Teal amputated them up to his knees trying to save him, but it didn't work, the gangrene had already spread, and Doc trimmed on him twice more, and finally just ran out of room to trim before he died. Now that's the world catching up."

I said, "What about that other side, the side where the world pays you back for some good you've done?"

"I have to say that I don't see that side as clear. It's confusing. Maybe just being alive is good payment enough. I know the whole argument against a just world, Stash. I've had the same things, the same thoughts about how some people die and some people don't, about how some people who do everything wrong seem to have everything and how some people who do everything right just struggle and struggle and struggle, and how it doesn't seem to connect up to anything, but you have to believe something, either that or you could just go crazy."

"I guess so," I said, but the whole time, I was thinking that I don't see myself the same as that Harden Swamp crowd. If Big Lee is right about the world levelling things out and God sees me the same as Steve Evans and some of those others who helped lynch Prince Williams, then the world is going to catch up with me anyway no matter what the judge says. Maybe I'm just done for, but I'm just like you I know; I've seen a thousand times where something bad happened to somebody and you just know they didn't deserve it, and it doesn't help much, to hear that God has a plan, that the world is a just place.

I'm not ready to die. I'm twenty-seven years old. I have a wife and two children and a farm to try to run. I've seen some people ready to let go of living. I've known some people to get so sick or so beat down by living that they were ready to go; I'm not one of them. I wish I was home right now, with my little ones already asleep, and my wife with her warm, smooth skin up against mine. I miss it.

I keep saying over and over I'm not ready for hanging, and who would be, but I can't truthfully say I would have done anything different even if I knew where I would end up. I know how I am, and I feel like I had a good reason, and I've always had a problem telling the truth too much, and when Judge McIver asked me at the trial if I did what they accused me of, I said yes, that's exactly what I did, and the world is a better place without that trash in it. He and Big Lee just looked at each other, and shook their heads. The truth has caused me a lot of grief. Knowing what I know now, I might try to be different and lie if I had it to go over again, but I doubt it, even though it's pretty clear to me, people who can lie do a lot better than people who are stuck telling the truth. Mama said telling the truth is always better, and the preacher says the truth will set you free. Sorry Mama, but both of those things are lies. Remember that.

# Julia

I'm whittling the great Casons down one by one, and now I think I might be about ready to finish those high muckety-muck sons of bitches off. I've got Leland stretched out about as thin as he's ever been. I can be pretty shrewd if I do say so myself and when I try to think about how I'd wiggle out of where he is, I just can't see it. I think I got him in a tight bind. Getting the upper hand on the Casons has been a long time coming, and along with the fact that I just plain hate everything they are, they've been nothing but a constant thorn in our side, in the way of how we want to do business for generations. Even without all of their meddling, there's just something about them that don't sit right with me. I don't know what it is, and I don't care; it's just the way it is, but I do know this.

I'm proud of being the one, the first woman in charge of this Greer thing, and by god, I'm the one that's got the balls that none of our men ever had to get rid of the Casons and the rest of their kind around here for good. I got Stash, that darling son of a bitch of theirs up there in the jail, waiting to be sentenced, hung probably, sweating and wailing about it every day, praying high and low for God, I hear, and when he is hung and dead or in prison, there won't be but one left to get, that glorified war hero everybody thinks so much of, that pompous blow-hard, Leland Cason, who thinks he's so much better than me. It ain't been that long since he lay up beside me like we was something to each other, but finally getting him won't take long now. I'm telling you, I've played all of them like that big fish that killed Little Lee.

I know I sound tough like a man, but I remember what it was like to be a pretty little innocent girl. I really do. That girl is still inside me, and if things had worked out differently, if I was born in a different place, I might have been like these women around here, just a nice little woman for the man like Ella is to Stash, and Mae was to Leland, but that life ended for me about the time I turned twelve. Then was the first time Daddy came into the bed with me. I didn't have no idea what he was about to do, but he did the things a man does to a woman that I didn't know anything about until then, and he told me it was me what made him do them. He said I was just too pretty.

After a few times it got so I just waited on him most nights to come in there and do what he did. It got kind of like I expected it. Mama never had talks with me and Margaret about anything like what he was doing to us. I was just twelve and Margaret was a year younger, and I guess Mama thought nature would just take its course with the boys around here like it does for most girls. Well, it did, but not with the boys until later on. I had Leland for a while before he went off to the War, not just him, but I did have Leland. Whether Mama knew what Daddy was doing to me in that bed at night and what he started doing to Margaret when she showed some buds on her chest about a year later, I can't really say., and I can't really say if she had any idea about me and those other boys later on. I think Mama just kept her head down most of the time, and tried hard not to know.

I know Daddy always had Mama cowed down pretty good. Even if she did know what he was doing to me, she wouldn't have said a thing anyway. She was not like me; she was weak. She just stayed cowed down until she died having another baby during the war. Like I said, Daddy told me I made him do all them things by just being too pretty and for a long time, I was a guilty little girl like he wanted me to be. I ain't guilty any more, not about what me and Daddy did, and not about anything else either.

Daddy was just one of those men that thought he could have or take anything he took a notion to have. I've seen him more times than I can count, nod towards the woods at some pretty Negress nearing the end of a row of cotton or tobacco, and them ease off into the woods for a few minutes for him to do whatever. One summer, I'd noticed Daddy watching a right pretty long-legged girl while she chopped cotton. I saw him ease off into the woods and I followed him a little bit behind. When I came to where he was, that pretty long-legged girl was bent over with one hand down on a big stump holding on, her other hand twirling a stick of hard peppermint candy in her mouth, and her dress up over her back. Daddy's pants were down about his knees and he was sawing away at her, puffing and blowing like he was really doing something. That girl wasn't paying no more attention to him than she would have to a little old green snake, and I saw right into who he was and who he wasn't right there.

When he came in to me that night, I didn't wait for him to get his stinking ass on top of me, I jumped out of the bed, put my night clothes up over my back like that girl in the woods, bent over and asked him where was my stick of candy. He slapped me hard one time, then punched me in the jaw and left me lying on the floor. It was over a week until he came back in. It was the first time that I knew I could take control of any man, any time.

I've heard about some more of that kind of men around here too, more than ought to be. I've seen it tear some girls up, make them crazy, how their daddy or their uncles or their brothers was doing things to them the girls thought was only for their husbands later on. That's what we all heard about growing up, how what we had was a prize to hold back only for our husbands and we had to keep it that way; well, it just ain't true. It ain't like that at all, but what daddy did just made me tough; that's all it did to me.

Like I said before, I've worked it to where Stash Harris is in the jail up in Scots Bend waiting to be sentenced, waiting to be hanged I'm betting if the money and women I've throwed around down in Columbia is any good. It's just too damn sweet that it's gonna be Leland Cason that's doing the hanging of his own kin or giving up his job as the sheriff if he can't or won't. Either way, I can't lose. He'll take the only family left to him off to the prison, kill him at the end of a rope, or I'll raise enough hell with the Governor until he makes Leland resign. He's in a tough spot, and it's nothing but fun to watch that pompous ass squirm around in it. I've made sure he's had a tough way to go, ever since things changed so much between us when we growed up.

Now, my Daddy was as bad as you think he is, but he always made money. We had about anything we wanted. There was a price to pay though. There always is. Daddy traded in whatever made money for him before the War. We had the grist mill, a saw mill, a turpentine still, a moonshine operation out in the woods, and a slave breeding operation. He owned land of course, and claimed to be a planter and to be fair, he did some planting mostly to keep up pretenses, but his main activity attached to the farm was breeding and selling slaves. That's not all. Out in the Sandhills, he kept a tavern with a brothel tucked back into the pines a quarter mile behind it. Me and Tadlock still run all of it we can, but Leland tries his best to shut us down.

Daddy kept pretty active sampling his slaves, and coming in to see me and Margaret at night. I already mentioned it. He claimed sampling them slave girls was to see which ones would attract business to the brothel. I guess it wasn't a long step for him to go from all he was doing with them to offering me and Margaret to those bummers trying to protect his money-making, especially since he was sampling both of us too. There's no telling how many of them young slave girls Daddy bred hisself. I heard him telling some trader one time who came by to look at the slaves what was available that he was the best stud on the place. I hate to think about all the Henry Greer spawn scattered all over this country. They'll be smart all right, but God help us, you better watch them close.

Daddy was big on the secession and took every chance to sermonize about leaving the Union like it was all about states' rights and independence when his interest wasn't anything but him wanting to protect his profit making. None of his bold talk, his secessionist fervor, his states' rights posturing, or his pride, stopped him from kowtowing to those bummers and offering me and Margaret up to them. I will say that it was something of a relief to get Daddy off us for a while when those bummers came.

You woulda thought for all of his rabble-rousing, his firing up every Tom, Dick, and Harry to go off and fight, Daddy woulda been first in line to go off to War, but he never served one minute in the army. There was another boy that I liked other than Leland, and he liked me too, but when Daddy caught me and him together doing what Daddy had been doing to me for years, he got real jealous and offered him a lot of money to go off in his stead to the War. He told him that if he'd go off to the War for him, when he got back, he'd give me to him along with all the money and land he could ever want. On the other side, Daddy threatened to kill him or have him killed if he didn't accept. That was Daddy's way. He'd offer something that looked so good it just seemed like the right thing to do, and then he'd offer something on the other side that was real bad, and most people knew he had a way of making a lot of bad things happen.

My poor little bastard fell like a stalk of ripe wheat before he got the Scots Bend dust out of his nose. I got the news when Daddy came in one night and said, "Well that little pissant you been spreading them legs for is dead and rotting on the field up at Bull's Run. I guess it's just me again," and he crawled in the bed on top of me. I hated Daddy for that, and a whole bunch of other things, and right then something in me broke, something inside my head went wrong and turned me bitter. Still, I kept up with the rest of the boys from around here, hoping they would make it home, especially Leland. Back then, I wouldn't have believed it would all end up like it has, us being bitter enemies and all. Life is like that too many times. We went through the War with the people at home struggling to live, mourning when bad news came home that one of theirs was dead or missing, but at the same time, Daddy just kept on finding ways to make money, finding ways to squeeze money and land out of people beat down with grief.

It seemed to me like all the misery of the War played right into Daddy's hands, and the whole time, even though I hated him, I was watching and learning, and by the time we heard Sherman was coming, I had learned my lessons well. Daddy dressed me and Margaret up real pretty and when them bummers came, he made some kind of deal with four of them, that they could have us if they helped him keep his place. We was still pretty girls, and I think them bummers thought so too. We knew our way around a man since Daddy had been coming in to us at night for years by then, and even before them bummers, we, me and Margaret, both went out on our own and took about what we wanted from the boys, and even a few of the older men around here. Those boys might have one of them perfect little girls too, and them men of ours, a meek little wife at home, but they all took whatever we gave anytime we wanted to give it to them. It was us that was in charge.

Even though them bummers had been raping everything they came to all across the South, they fell in on me and Margaret like they was starving for the least little pleasant touch. There's a difference between sawing away at a girl that don't want it and having a girl that don't mind, one that might even like it, and me and Margaret treated them four bummers like they was courting us the right way. Margaret wasn't like me though. For some reason she really liked them men, one especially, but deep down I hated those sons of bitches as much as I did Daddy, but I had enough sense to know that my best weapon against all of them was between my legs and that's what I used and just bided my time, billing and cooing like a stupid girl, well, billing and cooing like Margaret did.

To say something on their side, they did help us keep our place here and most of our things, except for whatever money changed hands once the real army came through, and then all four of them stayed around for a good while after the War too, and helped Daddy with all his work. Me and Margaret both had babies by them bummers. Well, I reckon it was by them; it could've been them or I guess it could've even been by Daddy. I don't know, and it really don't matter. My boy Tadlock is a good one and Margaret's simple bastard, Drip, ain't so good. He can't even talk but damned if he don't try to tell everything he sees. I hated Daddy and I hated all four of them bummers because I didn't get to pick who I spread my legs for and who I didn't, and who my baby's daddy was. A girl ought to be able to do that much anyway, pick who she wants between her legs, and I hated all them bastards for what they was doing to me.

Somebody hated them more than I did though. Those four Yankees was Daddy's own little army, and I guess some of our own men with enough balls to do something about it decided it was time to weed those bastards out. Those four bummers had been here for a while, long enough for me and Margaret to have our babies and our own men to get home. Them Yankees was riding out to the tavern one afternoon and a sniper shot one right in the forehead. It takes a good shot to do that, to hit a man riding along on a horse right up in the forehead, and when Leland came out, by that time he was working with the sheriff, he said so too, but there was so many of our veterans home with their rifles, he said there wasn't no way to tell who done it. I didn't mind. It was one less dog tagging along wanting a treat.

A while later, the three that stayed was out again doing some of Daddy's errands, and when they stopped to move a tree that was across the road, another one of them bastards fell with a perfectly round hole right in the middle of his forehead. Whoever was doing the shooting was a damn good shot. I've always thought it was the same person. I knew there weren't any reason to send for the sheriff. It would be Leland that tended this area, but Daddy was some more pissed off and raised hell about it with Leland, and Leland just smiled and said to Daddy, "You got no business keeping these Yankee sons of bitches down here. What do you expect." and he was right. Daddy could of got plenty of assholes from right here to do what they was doing. It don't take much to get people to do whatever you want done, especially if it's easy dirty work. I didn't care about that dead Yankee either; it was just one less dog sniffing around, like I said about the other one.

About that time, Margaret and that one bastard that she took a special liking to just up and hauled ass back up north carrying as much money and silver as they could. She left that boy of hers down here for us to deal with, and ain't never come back, not yet anyways. We raised the little bastard, and I guess Daddy felt sorry for him being his own blood and all, maybe even double blood, and kind of let him hang around here like a pet monkey or something. I look for Margaret to come dragging back down here one of these days, but so far, it ain't happened. It'll probably be when she thinks she can get some money or land or something out of what Daddy left.

Along about then, I decided to turn myself into a man. Somehow in my head, I figured it was about all I could do to keep Daddy and that last bummer son of a bitch off me, and I did everything I could to become a man. It wasn't hard; the way I see it, a man ain't nothing but a thin shell of bravado and bullshit. I see a lot of nice boys start turning theirselves into men with filth and whiskers and tobacco oozing down their chin, scratching and hiking their balls around like they're jangling a bag of gold or something. So it wasn't too hard to be a man, except I couldn't grow no whiskers, or a tallywhacker either as far as that goes. I was stupid enough to think being like a man would keep other men off me, but a lot of men is odd. A lot of them liked me as a man, and they kept right on sniffing around me like I was still that pretty little thing I used to be. I got to say it surprised me.

I remember the first time Leland saw me after I turned myself into a man. He just looked at me real funny, and shook his head. He said, "God Almighty Julia, what in the hell do you think you're doing. There's somebody out there better for you than these god damn Yankees."

I said, "Well maybe so, but it ain't your concern. You got sweet little Mae at home, so don't worry about it."

He said, "Damn," and just went on about his business. That was a long time ago.

Daddy and that bummer kept right on with me, and I kept right on hating it and waiting for that sniper to do his work, but I guess that bastard forgot about us or moved away, and in the end I had to get rid of that last bummer myself. I got tired of waiting for that sniper. I couldn't be enough like a man to keep them off me. Me and my last bummer was competing hard to see who could do the most for Daddy. I wasn't about to let the bastard beat me out of my birthright, and I could see he was angling to do just that. I built up a lot of hate for him, and even though I turned myself into a man and a pretty nasty looking one at that, that stupid bastard still wanted to get at what I had between my legs.

We was together one afternoon at the tavern checking up on things there and we started drinking some. I watched that bastard get drunk and he was drooling all over me, fawning over me kind of like a boy does with his first little piece, so I took him out back. I wasn't really planning to kill him then, I swear. It didn't take nothing to get him ready for me. He was like every man about what I was doing to him. I barely touched him, and when he was ready, I pushed him down on his back and dropped my pants and crawled on top of him, riding him like a workhorse.

His eyes was rolled back and he was moaning and groaning having a big old time when something told me to slide my knife up between his ribs into his heart, so that's what I did. The bastard had a funny look on his face like he couldn't believe what was happening, and I felt a power I never knew existed until right then. I got off him and his tallywhacker stood up there like it was something grand but when he sucked in his last breath, it withered away fast, like a fat earthworm does that crawls on a hot brick. I went back in the tavern and told two men that was working for us there "Go out and bury that grinning son of a bitch right where he lays. I saved that damn sniper the trouble." Them drunk bastards at the tavern went wild for me right then and there. I know it sounds just plain crazy, but I swear to god it's true. Some men are just plain odd.

# Stash

As much as I hate it, Greer's Mill is the hub of activity in our area during the week like town is on Saturdays and church is on Sundays. Before the War, every stream that held enough water had a mill on it somewhere. Cassidy's, Polson's, Grant's, Bay Branch, and at least ten others that I could name operated nearby until Sherman's horde burned and dismantled them. To blame everything on Sherman might be too simple although it's easy. Three waves of destruction passed over during the march according to the people who lived through it.

Bummers came first. Hordes of scavengers, thieves, and opportunists attached themselves to Sherman's army and as long as they brought food and supplies back into camp, Sherman allowed them a free hand to take what they wanted. I didn't make the word bummers; that name comes from one of Sherman's own. I read <u>Sherman's March through the South</u> by a fellow that rode with them named Captain David Conyngham, and that is where I learned the word. Daddy and Big Lee bought the book, ordered it from New York, but neither one of them could read it, being veterans and all; it just made them too mad. I read it though. You should too. The people who lived here just called all of them thieving Yankee trash. Like I said, bummers are what their own people called them, but trash is what they were by all accounts, even Capt. Conyngham.

Then came Sherman's own troops and the things they destroyed was almost like what a surgeon does taking things out, but instead of fixing up something, their kind of surgery took the heart out of every community they went through. It was Sherman's own men, under his orders, who wiped out courthouses, churches, houses, grist mills, foundries, blacksmith's forges, stables, anything that people could use to build their lives back. Thousands of deserters, thieves, and freed slaves tagging along like vultures attracted to a puffed up dead cow followed in a final wave of plunder and destruction intent on little more than beating down our people and exacting some perverse revenge by raping young girls and murdering old men. It was an evil gleaning swallowing up everything of any value left, and no matter how much revising all those history people do, they can't wash the memory of all the evil Sherman and his Yankees did out of the minds of the people here.

For reasons that only Henry Greer knows for sure, Greer's Mill stood there untouched. That's where and when the worst of this conflict started. The Greers try to say that Sherman's compassion kicked in right when they got to their place since he was close to leaving South Carolina, but what came later, the fate of other towns and people after he passed here, says no, and if you have a chance to read some of his letters, compassion is not a word you would use to describe him while he was going through here. Some say Henry Greer, Tadlock Greer's granddaddy, made a bargain with Kilpatrick to send him money for as long as Kilpatrick lived. I guess that could be true.

From all I've read, it wouldn't be past Kilpatrick. He did ride that horse into our old church and spread turds all down the aisle of one of God's places of worship where generations had walked down to ask for the grace of God. Gen. Hampton thought Kilpatrick was a weasel of a man without a speck of class, but living my whole life seeing what the Greers do, I doubt Kilpatrick or anyone else could convince a Greer to send a dime of money anywhere without them being under constant threat. What others say is a lot closer to the truth, that it was Henry's daughters that made the deal with some or maybe even all of those four bummers.

The old people tell that when the bummers moved in, four of them rode up on Greer's Mill. They were a ragged lot, like all of them, but like all of them, they rode in on finely bred, but unkempt horses, the very best stock they found on the farms and plantations they robbed. When one horse wore out from hard use and neglect, they simply shot the one and took another. Most had pack mules laden with all sorts of finery, gold, silver, and jewelry, things the army couldn't eat or use some other way. A funny thing happened when they got to Greer's Mill. Those bummers stayed, and when the army came, after a little parlay and an exchange of some silver, the army passed it by, and when the stragglers came, the men protected the place like it was their own. Greer's was the only mill standing after Sherman passed and it gave the Greers a lot of power over everyone when the War was over.

Henry Greer's daughters, Margaret and Julia, were sixteen and seventeen years old, pretty by all accounts, and the old people say those four bummers stayed around because Henry Greer farmed those girls out to them like he would have any of his slaves out at the brothel. It must be so because within a year, both of those girls had baby boys. Tadlock Greer was Julia's boy. Margaret's boy was Drip, a simpleton. Leonard Greer is his given name, but everyone calls him Drip because he drools and sprays when he tries to talk. On the other hand, Tadlock Greer grew up to be the shrewdest, nastiest, most evil spawn that's ever lived, and people say it is that bummer bred in him that just won't wash out. I can't say it's true; I say being a Greer is enough. He is just like one of those little rattlesnakes that you let pass because they keep the vermin out of everything; sooner or later, those bastards grow big, and are going to bite you. There's no bottom to what the Greers have done, or what they are willing to do. You will see that before I am done here.

Sometimes I think a lot of people like the Greers are just in case Christians. They think, "I am going to be Christian just in case, just in case all this about the Bible, and God, and Jesus is true. I don't want to be standing outside in the hereafter, outside those pearly gates watching everybody walking on those streets of gold, so I'll be this Christian just in case." That's how the Greers are. They do some plain evil things and then pile up there in the church like it's all just fine.

You might be curious about what happened to those bummers so I should probably finish that part of the story. What I know about it, I picked up listening to the talk around the gatherings when I was little. I always had an ear for the stories and I was a curious boy. I still have an unnaturally strong curiosity. I want to know things, and I always have. Anyway, those bummers stayed around for a while and became Henry Greer's own personal army. He took full advantage of the turmoil the Reconstruction was down here, and used those bummers penchant for violence to grow his own little empire.

Henry took land - stole it is a better way to say it - when he could. He curried favor with the Yankees running the Freedmen's Bureau down in the Darlington district by sending liquor, women, and money down to them. They made him one of their agents and he went around seizing land and giving it to some of the freed slaves the Yankees shipped in here from all over. It was just something the Yankees did. The Yankees shipped slaves from all over in here, and they shipped slaves from around here to other places. A lot went to Arkansas. Sickles had a hand in all that. He threatened to ship all the Negroes out of some areas, and some people wish he had. Sickles and the rest of the Yankees wanted to break up the loyalty some slaves had for their old owners and the responsibility some of the old owners felt for their slaves.

Henry Greer had enough power and levied taxes on a lot of people he knew couldn't pay, and lo and behold, the Greers ended up with some of that land. Those bummers of his stayed busy for a while too burning some people out, tearing up stills, turpentine and moonshine both, and just in general getting in the way of people starting over and getting their feet back on the ground. A few people ended up siding with Greer just to survive. Most people that didn't grovel to him ended up bankrupt or dead.

Now as far as those bummers, all of them stayed around for a little while, and I've already told a little bit about the dirty work the bummers did for Sherman, so you can see it when I say the people around here hated those men and did everything they could to drive them out. Henry Greer didn't care about what people thought. By then, he gave up any pretense and just went outright and bold after anything he thought he ought to have, and he thought he ought to have everything.

One day, those bummers were riding out from the mill to the tavern and they heard a gunshot. Well, all of them heard it but one. The one who didn't hear the shot fell backwards off his horse, and when the others went to him, he was looking up at the sky with a blank stare, his mouth partially open, and a .58 caliber hole in his forehead. It was probably some old Confederate sniper brushing up on his skills since there wasn't much call for sniping after the War. The investigation was real short; Big Lee was working for the sheriff then and didn't find a bit of evidence that could tie the shooting to anyone. The world was full of good marksmen with enough skill to do a little shooting, with experience a plenty from the War, and plenty of veterans had their Enfield .58 tucked away for special occasions, say, something like bummers staying around.

A while later, the three bummers left were riding out again to do their work and they rode up on a tree that was down across the road. They stopped to move it, and in just a minute, two of those bummers heard another shot and another one of those bummers was looking up into heaven with that same empty look in his eyes and a .58 caliber hole between his eyes. Big Lee couldn't find any evidence that time either, but that shooting encouraged one of the other two that he needed a change of scenery, so he took Margaret Greer and headed north with what was left of his stolen riches to what they hoped would be a little safer place to live.

One bummer stayed down here with Julia and soon became Henry's overseer. He said he intended to hold the spot until his boy, Tadlock, came of age. The last bummer might have been Tadlock's daddy, but no one really knows I don't think, probably not even Julia, and maybe especially not Julia. A lot of people say when Julia decided to turn herself into a man, she fought that bummer over being Henry's overseer; they said she wanted the job for herself, but by then the damn Yankee bummer had Henry's favor.

He did exactly what Henry told him, and he kept the old man's hands clean from the barn burning, still busting, and plain outright killing when that's what it took. I guess it wasn't too long a step from marauding across the South in front of Sherman to doing the same for Henry Greer. When Julia turned herself into a man, she jumped in doing her part too, and it was quite a battle between the two of them to see who could do the most dirty work to impress Henry and curry his favor. It didn't last long though. Somebody out at the tavern murdered that bummer, and Julia stepped on up into what she thought ought to be her job anyway. Some people say it was Julia herself that murdered him. I don't know myself. It was before my time, but people say it.

# Big Lee

When we came home from the War, things were in a mess. Even though we weren't ready to surrender, the War ending when it did turned out to be a good thing. About six weeks passed between when Sherman came through Scots Bend, and when we surrendered up in Durham. By the time we got home, our people were starving. If we hadn't come home when we did, I don't know how many more people would've died. It was a real struggle just to stay alive. Most of the working stock needed for planting that spring and summer was dead, killed by that god damn Yankee horde just for meanness. It didn't matter whether it was a big, rich landowner's stock, or the poorest scratch farmer out there. The Yankees wiped the countryside clean, even down to what the Negroes had.

I know that just doesn't sound right to some people, that the Yankees who were supposed to be fighting and dying to save the Negroes from slavery, burned out everything they had too, and I got to admit, it just doesn't make sense, but a lot of what went on in the War, especially a lot of what went on with Sherman's march just doesn't make sense. Maybe it shortened the War; maybe it didn't. Nobody but God knows the answer to that, but one thing is dead sure. Sherman came through here with the rabble he drug across the South and they stole what they could carry, and burned or destroyed everything else.

They burned slave cabins as quick as they did the finest of houses. They took top-bred horses, hard-working oxen and mules, and believe it or not, they took corn and pigs, and chickens from poor white people that never had a thing to do with slavery, and they took the same things from the slaves too. If a yard dog barked at them, they shot it just for fun. It just doesn't make any sense. They left nothing. I guess it didn't matter to them. They were vicious destroyers, plain and simple.

Now I haven't said anything about it yet, but I guess you've kind of assumed the Casons owned some slaves, and we did. There wasn't any way we could've kept up with all the land we had without them. We weren't, at least in my years, slave breeders and traders. I don't know about before. I guess at some time, we were all traders. All of the slaves I knew during my lifetime were ones that were born here and grew up here just like I did, and over the years it just seemed like they were supposed to be here. It seemed normal, the way anything does you're around day after day, year after year. Now I know there were vicious, horrible slave owners, traders mostly, but most everyday people that needed the slaves for work understood that being tolerable to them was the best way to get good work out of them. I'm not defending it; the slavery I mean. Enough men died over it to prove it was wrong. I'm just saying that's the way it was.

We had an old couple that lived on the farm, and they had mostly outlived their usefulness as far as working in the fields, but the woman, Old Sis, was a good herb doctor and a mid-wife too. She helped deliver me. Her man, Tog, could read the signs about anything, from when to plant to when it was the right time to breed a mare. He was a good man at hog-killing time, and generally rendered the lard, and made the souse and the head cheese. He tended the smoke house and we never had to worry if it was right. I spent a lot of time around them when I was growing up, and I liked them. I believe they liked me too, just because they did, not because they had to because they were our slaves, but since the War I've wondered if what I thought was right or not. I hope they did honestly like me, but I'll never know because they're gone now, lying together up in the Negro cemetery.

When I got home from Durham, it didn't surprise me that everything around here was lying in ruins except the church and the mill. It was that way all down through the country from Durham to here. I didn't understand that way of waging War then, the trying to destroy a whole people, and I still don't understand it now. I remember thinking that to survive, we could get out of the weather and find a way to build things back by living in some of the old slave cabins until we could do better. It just didn't cross my mind that the Yankees would burn everything the slaves had too, but I was wrong. The morning after I got home, I went down to where the slave cabins were, and saw that Sherman's horde burned them too, and took everything the slaves had just like they did the white people. Old Sis and Tog had gone out in the woods and cut pine laps to make a lean-to with, and had set up living in there. All of us were lucky it was spring and getting on to warm weather.

Old Sis, being an herb doctor and Tog just being Tog, seemed to know a lot about finding a way to live. Old Sis knew all the wild plants a person could use to help stay alive and Tog was a good outdoorsman and trapper. They helped us stay alive, better than a lot of folks around, and just did it, not because they had to, but because it was the way they lived their lives, and always had. Even free, they were a part of us and we were a part of them. There weren't any hard feelings between Tog and Sis, and the Casons, even after they were free. We were all in it together, trying not to starve, trying to start up our lives again, and it stayed that way for a long time, until they died.

After Tog and Sis were gone, Mama told me a story about her and Sis going through the Yankee camps looking for scraps to eat after they'd moved on. They picked up kernels of corn from where the Yankee horses dropped them on the ground while they were eating. The horses trampled some of it into the soft ground, and they even found some of it embedded in the horse droppings. It didn't matter. Everyone was starving, and Mama and Sis worked together washing the corn, parching it, grinding it, and turning it into meal of thin bread and grits that went a long way to keeping everyone alive until we could get started up again with regular living. Every time I think about that story, I remember Keats' line from "Ode to a Nightingale" about Ruth standing in tears among the alien corn, and I can see Mama and Sis in tears too, in shock at all the devastation Sherman wrought, wondering if home would ever be home again, but still doing what they had to do to live. None of it was easy.

If the god damn politicians up in Washington had honored what General Grant, General Sherman, and the others signed off on during the surrenders, things would've gone a lot easier for us, and in the long run, a lot better for them too. In the end, it was the same radicals who talked like they took their directions straight from God and pushed the War so hard who seemed hell bent on retribution. They wanted to make us pay, and they did. They wanted revenge. After Lincoln died, and the radicals pushed through the Reconstruction Acts, another Yankee general, Daniel Sickles, ended up being in charge of both Carolinas. Sickles and the rest of the Yankees and carpetbaggers came down here to make sure we did what they wanted. Daniel Sickles was crazy. He proved it before the War when he used insanity to get out of killing Francis Scott Key's son, and he was just plain mean. It didn't sit well with any of us.

We started rifle clubs, some people called them hunting clubs, because the laws allowed it, and we needed the protection. In the end, it was the rifle clubs that opened a way for us to do what we needed to do to get the god damn Yankees out of here, and to get things back to as normal as they could be, what with all the wealth they stripped out of the land and the people down here during the War and Reconstruction. Even before the Red Shirts and Hampton in 1876, we used the rifle club to come up with a strategy to take control of our lives and land back from the Yankees. I went on the inside to do what I did.

What I mean by that is I did enough to be close enough with the Yankees up here around Scots Bend to where they asked me to help them keep the law around here. From our side, we needed to know what was coming from the Yankees and the best way to do that was to have someone on the inside. It turned out to be me, and it gave me some power, and some protection to do some things that needed doing. I was the one who went out and checked on lawbreakers and such. I went out to check on the first one of the Greer's bummers shot between the eyes on the road between the mill and the tavern.

The bummers who stayed around with the Greers were a nasty lot. By the time I got home about the middle of June, they had already been around here for a couple of months, well, since the end of March or first of April. They had helped the Greers keep the mill and all of their other things from burning. They had to be good horse traders to work the deal with Kilpatrick and Sherman, but whatever it took, they got it done and stayed with Henry, and Margaret and Julia. Most people say it was those girls that kept them here, and it's probably true. They both had babies that most people say was from the bummers.

The problem was those bummers were out in my area, and they seemed to have taken a special interest in what the Casons had. I guess we should've expected it since they lined up with the Greers and our two families had been at each other's throats for a long time. I couldn't let that go on. You can understand that, I know. I watched them real close, and it pissed me off the way they tormented the people out my way, trying to drive them off their land. We talked about it a lot in the rifle club and we knew that it was up to us to rid the country of those bummers out my way and some other Yankees and carpetbaggers that just liked what they were doing a little too much. It took a while. We had to be patient. I had to be patient to get rid of those sons of bitches, but that's what I did, what I had to do.

# Stash

L ate yesterday it rained; it was one of those easy rains, the vapor rising, the ground releasing its heat. It was a peaceful rain, one that comforts, one that the ground can take, one that adds to without washing away, a rain without worries. It eased me. A row of elms stands along the plank fence behind the jail, and at twilight a dozen pearl guineas assembled under them, their cacophonous calls rising to a day-ending crescendo; they flew up to the roost, then quiet. The light faded. I closed my eyes and thought about home. There is a warming fire in the kitchen. It's the first hint of real cold and the children want to be close, to sit in your lap, to squirm and giggle and hug while Ella puts supper on the table.

There's easy talk about nothing in particular filling the minutes, a little teasing with the children, them laughing, running out and then back into my arms, to warmth and comfort again and again and again. Ella comes over for her share of the closeness and sits in my lap with her arm around the back of my neck, and kisses me on the cheek. I close my eyes and breathe her in, feel her warmth. Then there's supper on the table, something to warm me inside, like fresh biscuits with butter mashed up in cane syrup to dip them into, a pot of this season's grits, creamy and warm, tasting like the sun, the water, and the soil, ours, maybe some coffee. Then, I see them without me, and the rain became melancholy. If they hang me, when I am dead, I will miss all of it.

I heard the front door of the jail open about an hour

after dark, and Tally called out, "Mister Stash, you down here?" I saw a light come on in the gathering room.

I've always known Tally, but you know how it is between white people and Negroes; even though you know them, maybe known them your whole life, you don't really know them and they don't know you either. I knew Tally was partly white. A lot of them are. It was kind of obvious from his color, and it was pretty clear to me that he had more schooling in him than most of the Negroes his age, so I asked him where he came from, how it was that he was with Big Lee, was he born around here, or just what. He said he was born sometime close to 1855 on the Bishop plantation up in Randolph County just outside Asheboro.

I was glad for the company. "Yeah Talley, I'm here."

"I got you some supper here. I'll bring it back."

"I'll come up there if that's all right."

"Yes sir, come on up."

There's a small fire in a pot-bellied stove that serves to heat the front rooms, and in a pinch, to cook. On a table with four ladder-back chairs set against the wall opposite the stove, Talley set a pot of black-eyed peas with onions on top, and a little basket with four squares of cornbread. We began a little conversation of sorts. I said, "Looks good. Did you cook, Talley?"

"No sir, I went begging for you at the Carolina Hotel again, Mr. Stash, Miss Lo says she hopes you like it."

"It's good enough Tally. Tell her I appreciate it."

"Not home though is it?"

"Not even close, but the food is fine, it's just the being here."

"I guess I know what you mean, Mr. Stash, missing home is hard, but home is so long gone for me, I just don't even think about it much. Mostly I try not to think about it. This isn't that bad though, the Sheriff and all you people have made this a good home, and there's a nice girl or two that I visit. I know it could've ended up a lot worse for me."

We talked a little bit more just passing the time and after Tally went up to his quarters, I went back to the cell and lay listening to the rain outside thinking about how fate moves around in the world, how sometimes it seems like God moves things, and how sometimes it seems like God doesn't have anything to do with anything. It just seems like it's all just things happening, just plain dumb luck, good or bad. I know all about the Bible saying "Trust in the Lord," and all, but it seems when you just lay back and "Trust," those people who don't lay back just chew you up and spit you out. It seems to me the Lord should look after you when you do "Trust," but in my way of thinking, it doesn't work out that way. It seems like you get caught out there standing alone most of the time.

The rain continued through the night. This morning a fine mist is falling, one of those times when the day tries to hang on to the darkness. Big Lee came in a while ago and said Judge McIver is in town and we had to walk over to the courthouse for my sentencing. Big Lee said if the Judge sentences me to hang, he and some of the other men will be contacting the General and the Governor to see what they can do. I got myself ready to go. Tally came in and said that Ella was over in the courthouse already and that I might get a minute with her before the sentencing. That would be nice, just to be close to her, and to try to let her know how much I miss her and the children too, and that if I had it to do over again, I wouldn't kill those sons of bitches, and she will know it's not true, but she'll act like it is, and I'll know it too.

This is how it went. We walked across Main Street to the courthouse. Big Lee and Tally walked on either side of me. Aiken White, the bailiff, walked behind. Big Lee and Aiken both carried side by sides. If Tally had a weapon, I didn't see it. Quite a crowd gathered between the jail and the courthouse waiting for the spectacle of it I guess. Ella was the first person I saw. I told her not to come, but I knew that she would. She fell in walking beside me. I wish she did not have to see all of this, but my not wanting her to have to go through this did not keep me from doing what got me here. I am sorry for putting her through this, and I am sorry that maybe I won't be here for her and the children, but I've already said that I would probably do the same thing again, and I probably would. Those sons of bitches deserved what they got and more.

Then I saw Tadlock and Julia Greer and their people. I knew they would be there too, them being at the root of what put me here, and Tadlock being one of the main ones who testified against me. Tadlock's white boy and a couple of other mulatto boys that people say are his too were with them. I guess they wanted to get them started early. Now I've already said his mama has undergone quite a change. By all accounts, when she was young, her sister was the only one around who could rival her looks. They were both pretty enough to stand out in front of that mill and entice those bummers to stay around and protect them from the rest of that horde that came through. Now she has turned herself into a man, mannish, to say the least. A person who didn't know her before would never guess that a woman is under all that garb and filth. She wears man's pants and boots, a man's shirt, and always has snuff in her mouth, the juice spilling down from the corners of her mouth. She makes no attempt to wipe it away, and as the day goes on, the juice begins to stain her shirt in the front. She wears a nasty old hat pulled down low over her brow. She doesn't care. It would take a stronger man that any I know including me to go anywhere around her with manly intent. I shrink to think about it.

Big Lee took my arm in a firm grip when Tadlock started spouting off, "Hey, Stash, I guess that Judge is going to put your ass on the end of that rope pretty soon," and Big

Lee just rumbling low, "Just keep walking son," and again, "just keep walking." I felt the fire rising in me, but not so hot that I could not control it; it was a test. The crowd parted in front of us, and we entered the front of the courthouse. Naturally, Sherman's crowd burned the one here during the War and the county put this one back up in 1884 on the foundation, and using some of the same bricks from the one Sherman burned. The courtroom is upstairs and we went up there with the crowd following behind. When the room filled, the bailiff opened the door to the judge's chambers and let him know we were ready. I should mention my lawyer by saying that Big Lee, Tally, and Ella sat behind me while I sat beside my lawyer, a fat alcoholic named Joe Swofford. I chose poorly.

We all stood up and Judge Harrison McIver came in. I should say here that he also rode with the 4th for a while. He lost his horse at Haw's Shop. The Yankee artillery shot it out from under him and it broke the Judge's leg when it fell. He had to come home, and never came back up to the fight. The bailiff is a good friend. Aiken White marched with the 8th Infantry and was one of the fifty-two men left when they surrendered in March of 1865 with the Army of Tennessee. As much as I have ranted about the bad people out there, I want to make sure I say good people are out there too, and Big Lee, Aiken, and Tally are some of them. Judge McIver too I guess, but good or not, friend or not, Big Lee says he's a stickler for the law. I guess a judge should be.

I think men who go off to War, men who face the random nature of death in war every day, who watch their friends die, who kill other men to keep from being killed, men who leave the violence behind, and then come home to rebuild normal lives by building back communities, by raising children, by loving wives, and a thousand other things day by day are rare men. I like to think I am a good man too, in my own place, in my own time, that I did and do what I need to do. At the same time, I know I can never get close to them, to what they did and do, and I just don't know how I measure up. You can decide about me for yourself as this story unfolds.

Anyway, Judge McIver came in, and the sentencing went pretty fast from there. First the lawyers talked, then some people, Tadlock Greer one of them, talked about the men that I killed, how good those bastards were. You would have thought they were monks. Then Tadlock gave a pretty good description of how it was that I killed them. Then Judge McIver asked me if I had anything to say. Big Lee told me the night before that the Judge would give me a chance to talk, but he said that unless I was going to get up there and apologize and say that I was out of my head or any little excuse like that, I just needed to keep my mouth shut. I told him that "I am a lot more likely to say that I wish those sons of bitches were still alive so that I could do it all over again," and he said, "Yeah, I thought so, and that's why you need to keep your mouth shut," so I intended to keep my mouth shut. I sat there for just a minute and the Judge asked me if I had any remorse for killing those men. I told him, "Remorse? Remorse for killing two sons of bitches that had a hand in my own Mama and Daddy burning up in a fire? Remorse, the only thing I'm sorry for is that Julia and Tadlock aren't lying in the ground with them, and if I get out of this shit, that's where they'll be real soon!" The crowd in the courtroom got pretty rowdy and I could tell Judge McIver didn't much like it.

After I told him what I had to say and the crowd settled back down, he passed sentence on me, and said, "John Brooks Harris, you are hereby sentenced to be hung by the neck until you are dead, said sentence to be carried out on March 21, 1898." It was just that simple. I guess somewhere in my head, I never thought I would be sentenced to death, not that I didn't know it was a possibility, but I just never faced up to the reality of it. Now it is right in front of my face.

Ella had an odd reaction. I expected her to be real upset, just like you did, but she was real quiet. It made me wonder if she hadn't been steeling herself for the hanging sentence for a while. Well, it's either that or she is just simply one tough woman. It might be a little bit of both. The Judge said he needed to see Big Lee in his chambers to get straight on how this hanging thing needed to work. The last hanging before this one was way back in 1855, so naturally, the Judge, Big Lee, or anybody else for that matter, knew all the ins and outs of getting one done. Judge McIver told Aiken White to escort me back to jail, and then told him, "You better walk with that side by side over there. There are some fools out there."

We all, me, Aiken, Ella, and Tally went down the stairs and through the doors to cross Main Street to the jail. A big crowd milled about, again just clamoring for the spectacle of it. I saw Tadlock and his crowd again, and I knew some of them would have something to say, and they did. Julia Greer sneered, "I will be right here when they hang your ass, boy," and Tadlock's little white boy along with his two mulattoes started circling us with a sing-song, "Stash, Stash, dancing a jig! Stash, Stash, dancing till he's dead! Stash, Stash, dancing a jig!" over and over again, "Stash, Stash, dancing a jig! Stash, Stash, dancing till he's dead! Stash, Stash, dancing a jig!" I felt the anger quickening in me, past the place where I can hold it, and when I saw my opening, I took a quick step and swooped Tadlock's boy up by the throat with one hand, squeezing him hard enough to turn him purple, and holding him off the ground, said, "You dance that jig, you little piece of shit! Dance!" shaking him, and him squealing like a pig that just had his nuts cut, dancing that jig.

Tadlock, pulling a pistol, got his hand on my arm, but in the next second, Tally slammed him to the ground, throttled him with one hand, laid an open razor against Tadlock's jugular with his other hand, saying, "Don't make me, don't make me!," with Aiken spun around, that side by side tucked right under Julia Greer's nose, her spitting, and sputtering, "My boys, my boys! No! No!" and in my ear, Ella, softly over and over, whispering, "Let him go, Stash, let him go," and the anger in me fading as quickly as it flashed up. I dropped the little pissant to the ground. He ran off crying and hollering.

In the same moment, Big Lee was there, firing a lever action rifle twice into the air, standing in the middle of the crowd with us, along with Judge McIver, him facing a crowd surging and pushing to break forward, the Judge brandishing his own side by side, hollering, "Back down, back down! This is not happening on my watch! Back down!" The crowd did back down, buzzing with excitement, wanting to get into the action, but backing down anyway, with Tally and Aiken releasing Tadlock and Julia, and we, all of us, walking to the jail, the crowd between us and the jail separating to let us pass, Tally and Big Lee in the vanguard, then me with Ella, the Judge and Aiken the rearguard, the crowd closing again behind us, surging to the steps of the jail, some of them ready to protect us, others fawning over Tadlock and his boy and still others adding to Julia's threats, "We aren't going to wait boy, we'll hang your ass and save the government the trouble."

Tally came into the jail with Ella and me, and took us back to the secure cell, locking us in, for protection I guess. Big Lee stayed out front with Aiken and the Judge. I heard some discussion, but couldn't make out any words. In about fifteen minutes, I heard the four men, Tally, the Judge, Aiken, and Big Lee talking in one of the front rooms, but again, being in the secure cell, I couldn't make out the words. In a little bit, Big Lee opened the cell door and came in scolding me hard for what I did on the street. He told me

I was lucky that the Greer's people didn't prepare for the chance I gave them, or I would be hanging from some tree by now. He said, "You're bold, but you're stupid too. Those things don't mix and that's why you are where you are. Don't you see it?"

I said, "I guess I do, but it doesn't make a particle of difference now does it?"

"None, except that you put Ella at risk; you don't care about that?" and shaking his head, "It might have made a difference if you had kept your damn mouth shut."

I just shook my head. He was right. Ella just sat quietly, and put her hand on my arm. "It's fine, it's fine," and me looking at her saying, "I'm sorry," knowing what I said is not enough, and Big Lee, shaking his head, taking her out, locking the door behind him.

# Tally

My mama was one of the house servants for Colonel Bishop and his wife Miss Bette. They had a big place, and owned somewhere around a hundred slaves. I was one of them. The Colonel was good to me and taught me how to read and write and how to keep his horses. Some of the other slaves said it was against the law for him to teach me to read and write, but he did anyway. Mama knew how to read and write too. Mama said I was his pet. I guess I was because he was real good to me and never did much without taking me around with him. Miss Bette was mean as a rattlesnake to me. She was the one that made Colonel Bishop sell my mama out to some of their kin people in Louisiana a year or two before the War started. The saddest day of my life was the day mama left without me because the Colonel wouldn't sell me too. I wanted to go with her bad. I just couldn't understand. I was too little to figure it out. Then the War came and everything changed.

Late in the War when the first of the bummers came, Colonel Bishop went out talking to them, trying to protect what was his. He was a prideful man, and he believed that civil talk could mend anything, but those bummers were so hardened against civil behavior by that time, if they had ever been any other way before, they just up and shot him in the gut and after he suffered for a few days, he died. I'll have some more to say about that later on. I was in shock from standing right there with him when it happened and kind of at loose ends, just living around the stables and sleeping where I could. After the Colonel died, I really didn't have a place.

When the fighting was finished, we heard rumors that the armies were standing together around their camp fires up near Greensboro waiting for the generals to work out the surrender papers. I went up to the house looking for something to eat. When Miss Bette saw me, she just ran me off, said I wasn't to come back, that if she caught me anywhere on the place again, she'd have me killed. She put her dogs on me and I just ran. I went down to the stables where me and the Colonel spent a lot of time, and one of the older stable hands told me the story again about the Colonel being my daddy, but I didn't believe much of what he said. He was one of those tall tale kinds of people, one of those that like to stretch things especially to a boy like I was, and the Colonel already told me that the older stable hands were wishing they were like me. I didn't pay much attention to what he meant when he said it, but now I think I understand it all. I guess he was telling the truth.

I didn't know what to do, so I went down to the main road. There were soldiers passing by every once in a while, headed home I guess, and a lot of other people on the road just wandering. I didn't have a way to go, or a place, so for some reason I just tagged along with all the movement, headed south, not with anyone yet, just kind of along. There were a bunch of people on the road wandering, trying to find a place. I guess I was smart enough or scared enough, or lucky enough, to stay away from most of them. There was a lot of killing right after the War for no reason, not saying that the War was a good reason, but just a lot of random killing like people didn't have feelings at all about it. I saw some of it.

After a few days of just drifting down the road, I was hungry, so I scrounged around for whatever I could find, and later that night when I was trying to stay warm down among the roots in the hollow of a blown over pine, I saw a little fire flickering off in the woods a little bit, and I slipped over to it. It turned out it was Big Lee, and when I eased inside the firelight and he saw I was just a scared colored boy, he gave me a little crumb of the food he had and a piece of a blanket to lie on. I know he felt sorry for me, but I think he needed the company too, and he let me stay.

I guess he was real tired because he slept hard, but I was still scared and unsure of what would happen to me, and I was up before daylight the next morning. By the time he woke up I had his mare worked through the way Colonel Bishop taught me, fed with what little I could scrounge, cleaned up and brushed as best I could. I led the mare - I found out later that her name was Maddie - out closer to the road, and found a little patch of grass for her to graze for a few minutes. When it started getting light, I heard some horses coming down the road, so I led her back to the camp. I built the fire up with dry wood so it wouldn't smoke too much and draw others in.

When Big Lee woke, he must have liked what I'd done, because after we ate a little scrap of food, and talked a little more, he figured out that I didn't have any place to go, so he let me tag along with him and I ended up with him here. If it wasn't for him there's no telling where I would be, or what might have happened to me. There was some rough people out and about back then, going from one place to another causing a lot of trouble, and I was just lucky to wander up on Big Lee, either that or the good Lord was looking over me. That was over thirty years ago, and I have been off on a little ramble every once and a while, looking for my mama and just seeing what was out there. One time I stayed gone for about three years, but every time I end up back here, and in all that rambling, I still haven't met a better man than Big Lee. There's not much I wouldn't do to pay him back for him looking out for me.

Generally speaking, white people - now I'm not talking about Big Lee - are a lot of trouble, not that I don't have white blood in me. Most colored people do, since we all come off the slave trade one way or another, but I've got half or more of white in me, especially if the Colonel really was my daddy. Mama wasn't black-black; she was one pretty caramel woman and had to be part white herself. The Colonel was a good man, but he and all that he had and is gone now since the War.

Before the War, I never thought much about being white or colored; it was just the way it was. I was just busy living, and the Colonel never treated me any way but good. The other hands around the stable said I was his pet like my Mama did and now I'm older and understand the ways of the world. I see that I was a lot more than just a pet to him. He didn't have any sons. If what everybody tried to say was true, and I was the one carrying on his blood, me being colored or not didn't matter. Carrying his blood on past him mattered to him like it would any man.

Like I said before, I was with Colonel Bishop when the Yankees came through, and I was standing right beside him when that one son of a bitch shot him right in the stomach. The one that shot him said to me, "Come on with us, boy. You're free now. He ain't got no rights to you."

I just blurted it out, "Free from what, you son of a bitch? You just shot my daddy," and I tried to pull him off that horse, but he just kicked me off him and rode off down the road laughing.

The Colonel was a proud man, and he expected that even though the Yankees were our enemies, some kind of manners still ought to be a part of what went on between men, but the Yankees didn't have any ideas about the right way to act with another person even if you were about to kill him. The ideas of dueling and honor, ideas that a man from the South knew and admired and lived by, especially if you were a man of the Colonel's standing, were wiped off the face of the earth by the War. So when the Colonel went out to talk to the first Yankees that rode up, he carried those ideas about how men ought to act with him, but the Yankees didn't know anything about how men ought to act, and when they got tired of talking, one of them shot him in the stomach.

Those bastards knew what they were doing. They could've shot him in the head or the heart or a lot of places and finished him off quick, but they shot him in the stomach and rode off laughing at the funny look the Colonel had on his face, and me lying in that road, while the Colonel staggered back against the fence in front of the house. He looked at me with a resigned look on his face and said, "I hate dealing with people who don't know how to act," and then he told me that he'd heard what I said to that Yankee about him being my daddy. He said, "I heard what you said back there."

I said to him, "Yeah. One of the hands told me a while back, but I was scared to say anything."

The Colonel held tight to me and said, "You're the only blood I'll be leaving. It won't make it easy for you. Nobody will give you anything because of it, but there's something inside you that nobody can take away from you. It's what will make you do what you need to do, just like I always have. Don't forget that."

I helped him inside and some of the house servants put him in the bed, and Miss Bette came in and looked at him, and then she looked at me and said, "Well, well, little Mr. Tally. Your easy days are over. Get your nigger ass out of my house," and I did. The Colonel lay up in that bed for four days suffering until the end came and all I could do was sit outside his window and listen to him moan. That just isn't a decent way to kill a man, to gut shoot him and make him suffer like that, but that's the way a lot of those Yankees were, kind of low class.

I've been down here in Scot's Bend since the end of the

War except for some rambling, kind of looking for my mama out in Louisiana, but there was always the draw of this place and the people I know here like the Sheriff and his family. I've kind of adopted them, and they've kind of adopted me, and even though I've sowed some seed around, they're my family, or the closest thing I'll ever have to one.

Once, about ten years after the War ended, I went back up to Asheboro looking around the old place, and found some of the same slaves living in the same little houses they were in before Mr. Lincoln freed them. They hadn't ever even thought about going anywhere but there, and they were still working for Miss Bette. The big house was just a shadow of what it had been, but I got to give her some credit. She was running that plantation, or as much of it as she could manage with the people that stayed there with her. I got to say, they were all doing about as good as anybody else.

I walked up to the house. I hoped she might be nicer to me after all that time, but I should have known better. She looked at me and said, "Well, little Mr. Tally, all grown up; I was hoping you were dead. You look just like the Colonel with nigger skin stretched out over him. It serves him right that his only blood left on this earth is running in niggers. Now get off my place; there isn't anything here for you," so I left again and I've never gone back. Now that I'm older, when I think about it, I like believe the Colonel would be proud of what he left behind. I've stood in my place and done what I needed to do, just like I did today, and that's what the Colonel always did and that's what he taught me. Well, he started and Big Lee finished teaching it to me.

Just like it was today. I was at Stash's sentencing and when we came out trying to cross the street back to the jail, some of the Greer men tried to get something stirred up. Tadlock's boys ran around singing some stupid song about Stash's hanging and Stash grabbed the white one by the neck and explained some things to him while he was dangling in the air. For some reason, a man or a boy listens better with their wind cut off, even when they're squealing like a little boy pig losing his nuts. Things just work better that way it seems.

Tadlock got his hands on Stash too and almost got his pistol on Stash, but then I got him down with a razor laid up beside his neck, and I was wishing that he would do something to go on and make me cut him, but at the same time I was hoping not. It would've made a mess of things, and Big Lee is always talking about being patient and doing things without other people really knowing what it is that you're doing. It's a hard lesson and not learning that lesson is what got Stash in the mess he's in.

Not being patient is what I'm talking about. He went out and took his revenge and killed those two Greer men without being careful about it. There was just two too many witnesses, with Tadlock and Julia both getting away. Stash should've let things lay for a while, and let a sniper do his work, either that or just waited on time to do to them what it does to everybody.

Not too many people can wait for time to take care of things. Stash is one that isn't. He's got a hair trigger, and he's never really been any good at all in controlling it. Big Lee says he's got some of that Indian blood in him, and that blood makes for some hard people to figure. Sometimes they'll be as soft as any people you might ever see, like Stash is with Ella and the children. I've seen him be that way with other people too, but then there's that other side, I reckon that Indian side. God Almighty! When something triggers that side, it's not a pretty thing to see. All of Papa Cason and Big Lee's teaching can't touch whatever it is inside him when that blood gets to burning inside him. It's a sight, and it's what's got him in this killing and hanging mess. It's about to worry Big Lee to death.

# Big Lee

I was awake all night fretting about what happened after the sentencing. It's got the Greers and their ilk stirred up again. Stash is under a lot of pressure facing what he's facing and I don't expect him to be any smarter or any more patient than he's always been, and that isn't too much. We've talked a few times about all of this drama. He's obsessed with God and religion right now the way a lot of people get when they're facing their own death. He's always been one to argue with God. Hell, he won't even keep his mouth shut with Him. I understand it though. I've had my own times like that, times when everything that was happening around me made me question whether there was a God, and if there was one, if it was one that I would even care anything about knowing. Hard times make you think like that, and I've had them, still have them.

When I did sleep, I dreamed about my first hardest time, and knew somehow that I dreamed it for a reason, so when I went to the jail this morning it was in my mind to talk to Stash a little bit, to tell him the story about that time, to tell him about the time living got so hard that my whole set of beliefs about life and living broke, about the time when I believed that God didn't have any part of what was going on. I needed to tell him that there is a life past those times, or if there's not a life past it, there's a restful place in your own head to lie down and die in. It's a man's duty to find it. A man just has to, or he's not really a man. This is the story I told him of what happened when I turned away from God and my faith the first time.

123

We hadn't been too long gone north, and joined up with General Hampton. Things in the cavalry were up in the air, with the General new to be in command of everything since Jeb Stuart died at Yellow Tavern about two weeks before, but you know the General, and once he was in charge, he took ahold of things pretty strong. The armies faced each other for a few days at North Anna, and then Grant tried to slip around us again, just to keep us moving I think, like he intended just to wear us down and in the end he did just that, the son of a bitch. We went down past Haw's Shop and set a line up in the woods to stop the Yankees from swinging around our flank. If they got around us, it wasn't but about ten or twelve miles to Richmond, and you know how hell bent the Yankees were to get Richmond, and how hell bent our damn politicians were to keep it.

Most of us carried Enfields and didn't know it at the time, but those Yankees had Spencer repeaters that shot faster, seven shots, but didn't have the range our Enfields did. When the Yankees showed up, we started firing first, and we killed a bunch of them quick. I read after the War that over two hundred and fifty Yankees died right there. Two hundred and fifty men died, and we celebrated like we won the horse race at a July 4th picnic. Some other Yankees pulled up some pieces of horse artillery near a farm house and had a clear view of where we were, but we were so enamored with killing those Yankees in front of us that we never saw them setting up. Those Yankees knew what they were doing with that artillery. We had them beat down good and we were all standing up shooting like it was a week-end sharpshooter contest when that artillery's first shot ripped right into the section where I stood. The sound of that metal buzzing and whistling into us is a thing I hope to never hear again, but at least I heard it.

Our one little section held six men, me with friends of mine, and when I looked around, all of them were tore up, bleeding out, moaning and dying, that is all except me. I never got a scratch on me, but five good men that rode with me, ate with me, talked about home with me, lay there on the ground, dead and dying. The hand of God was on me I guess, but I didn't know why then, and I don't know why now. I don't know why all those men died, and I lived, or even now that the years have passed, I don't know why those Yankees died either except all of us, Yankees and Confederates both, jumped up into something that we thought was important but didn't amount to a hill of beans, especially to all those dead men.

I know we hate those Yankees for what they did here, and for some things they did, we should hate them, and they should hate us too, but when those wounded men at Haw's Shop from both sides, laid up there in the sanctuary at Enon Church and died, it didn't matter whether it was a grey uniform or a blue one. Was God's hand on them in there? How could any mortal man tell which ones God's hand protected or didn't, because all those dying men prayed to the same God the night before, all of them, on both sides prayed, to be spared, to see their Mama and Daddy again, or to see their wife or their children again? So, tell me, what was the plan, and how did God choose who lived and who died out of all of those men who prayed to Him the night before? How did He choose?

It haunts me, and I just can't see it. It's all just too random. None of it makes any sense to me. It's too random that five men standing there with me, got all tore up from that one volley, laid there crying and praying and bleeding out on the ground, and died, and I didn't get a scratch, so that here I am, thirty four years later, living and breathing, watching the sun come up in the morning and set in the evening, all because I didn't die like those brave men. This is how life goes, and there's no way to see any sense of any of it.

Late the same afternoon, what we thought was infantry came in to reinforce the Yankees. I was numb from those men dying around me, and from all the killing I had done myself, but I had a cold fire burning in me that made me want to kill one more Yankee after another. In front of what turned out to be cavalry dismounted, a Union officer galloped back and forth rallying his men, acting like nothing could hurt him. It just pissed me off that after watching my friends die, that he could be so bold like that and not die too. We all tried to bring him down, and it seemed that no one could. I wanted that arrogant son of a bitch to die, to lie down on that ground and suffer like my friends had done before, and you know I can shoot. I followed him one last time with my Enfield down the line and back, waiting for him to pause; just a second was all I needed to kill the bastard, and finally he did pause.

He spun right in front of me and stopped to shout orders, about 200 yards away. I had him cold; in my head, he was already a dead man, but just when I squeezed off the shot, his horse reared and spun around shielding him, and took the bullet right in the neck. That horse dropped like a stone, and that damn officer walked back into the line as calm as if he was on a Sunday stroll, and do you know who it was? That son of a bitch was Custer. As hard as that might be to believe, I'm sure of it, because after the War I read that seven horses died under him and the last one was at Haw's Shop. Seven times that pompous, insane son of a bitch walked off a horse shot out from under him, and lived to lead a lot more men to their deaths before he was done.

I knew right then that if God does have a plan it's a plan so far past what I can understand that none of it will ever make any sense to me. Here's another thing I've never told anyone, not even Mae. I never prayed. I never asked God for one little thing. I never prayed at all, to live or to die, to see home or not to see it, because by the time we went north, something inside me had already broken, I'd endured too much of His silence, and I was so angry with Him I didn't want to talk to Him at all. Listen close to this, Stash. In my whole life, I never heard God; I never got an answer to anything I prayed for, asked for, even begged for, but what I did hear over and over were those dying men praying their guts out, begging to live, to see home again, begging for a chance, but they died, Stash. In His silence they died; twenty-seven good men from right around here never had the chance to come home, and they're still lying in one big grave beside that church in Virginia.

It was me that didn't pray, don't you see; I didn't ask for or expect anything. I got to come home and they didn't. I don't think I ever will know the why of it, but to live, to keep living, I've had to make my peace with it, to listen to the world around me and try to do what I think is the right thing, and to take what comes, and remember all those men who can't, all those men who are lying in that strange dirt in Virginia. I do what I do for them, and for Mae, and for Mama and Daddy, and for Little Lee too, and that's what you have to do, Stash, that's what you have to do before you go. Even when God is silent, you have to make your peace with all that is around you. You have to do it to live, Stash, and you have to do it to die.

# Stash

**B**ig Lee came in this morning and told me a story about Haw's Shop. It's legendary here; so many men from here died there. He doesn't talk much about those times. No one who went through it does, except maybe some men who want to make a piece of money on what they did or some who aspire to high political office, but that's not Big Lee. He told me the story to help me. I knew that much. It was the only way he knew. He poured his heart out to me. He holds his truths so tightly inside. I know how hard it was for him to tell the story and how important he believed it was for me to hear it.

We sat at the small table in the hallway adjacent to the row of cells. Silence hung between us. I didn't know what to say, how to respond to him. His struggle seemed heroic to me, so much more than anything of mine. The minutes passed. Sunlight moved across the table between us until it covered my hands. I felt its warmth. I stood outside my life watching, an observer of a drama I couldn't understand or hope to control. I was helpless, depending on others, or God, to see me to the end of it. Big Lee stared through me, off in his memories, waiting for me to speak.

Outside the window a lone mockingbird urgently trilled, singing one seemingly random song after another, but over the minutes I recognized a pattern, a complex one, but clearly a pattern as if the bird was delivering a coded message. I looked past Big Lee and saw Tally quietly leaning in the doorway between the front rooms of the jail and the cell area, his arms crossed, intently watching me. When our eyes met, one side of his mouth turned up in a slight smile and he shook his head and quietly walked away.

Big Lee's story challenged me; I wanted to avoid it. I had an odd thought. I remembered a time when I sat with Daddy listening to a mockingbird singing. He told me to listen closely, and tell him how many other birds I heard in the mockingbird's song. It was hard, but eventually I separated the songs and heard the cardinal, the robin, the thrush, and others, but there was one I couldn't identify. I told him I didn't recognize one. When it came around again, I pointed out to him and said, "There it is! That's the one. What is it?"

He said, "That's the one I wanted you to hear. I've never heard that song here," he said, "but I know it. It's the Carolina parakeet. I heard one outside Columbia along the Congaree one time but they're gone from around here, forever I'm afraid. They were here one time though. Your Papaw says flocks of them used to fly along the Pee Dee, and up Steerpen Creek. Now they're gone, but they left their mark here, a tiny mark in the mockingbird's song that no one notices, but the world remembers them, and somehow, the world will remember us too."

I heard the Carolina parakeet in the mockingbird's song outside the jail. I looked across the table to Big Lee. I thought about all that had happened and that we would all be gone too soon. Life was just time passing, carrying us with it, but if the world remembers a bird, won't it remember us too? I hoped so. Big Lee looked at me quizzically. Then he said, "You have to try to find some peace, some place that's comfortable to live in, Stash, and even beyond that, you have to find some place that's comfortable to die in. You just have to."

I thought, peace, find some peace? With all that's happened? It stirred my anger, and I answered sharply. "I'm too angry still, too bitter about everything. I'm just too pissed off because it seems like everything I've ever done played out into this, that it was all just a bunch of scurrying around, thinking I was living my life, thinking it mattered what I did or didn't do to get here in this thing to end with me hanging."

"You can't think that way; it just makes you the victim, and you can't be just the victim in your own life. A victim is dead already."

"I feel like the victim. God dammit, I feel like the victim! I feel like all of this living, all these things happening, drove me to a place where all I could do was what I did. What if there is such a thing as God's plan for it all? What if there is? What if I never really had a choice? What then? If there is a plan, doesn't it tell us that everything we do that seems like we're making choices, struggling and straining with what to do is all part of some petty drama that's already written out from beginning to end, and we're the ones who don't know it, who don't know the beginning or the middle or the end of it?

Who is making this life? The best we can hope for is the benevolent God, the one that guides us, the one that protects us, but it could be the God who looked at Satan and said, 'Go ahead and take Job's wife and his ten children; go ahead and turn him into a pauper covered with boils? Test him. Go on ahead and see what he does,' and it could get even worse. It could be the silent God who didn't answer his own Son that night in Gethsemane. It could be worse for us, the God who says nothing!"

"We don't know those things, Stash. We can't know. It's beyond us; we're stuck in this life for whatever reason, and it's beyond us to know everything, even to know anything, but we have to keep living. We don't have a choice. That's a hard, true fact. The only way out of here is dying, so we have to do things; we have to act like we don't know where it all ends up. We have to act like it is us making the choices, the doing, or else we'd just give up and lay down."

"The best we can do? The best we can do! That's what we all do, don't we, well, most of us do, and it ends up like this too many times for it to make any sense at all."

About that time, Tally came to the door again and told Big Lee that Judge McIver wanted him over at the courthouse, so he left, and I went into my cell and lay down, kind of melancholy. In a minute, Tally came and said, "Mister Stash, I can't help but listen to all this talk you and the Sheriff are having, and it seems to me that you aren't too much like Job. You haven't really done that much suffering outside of the regular things, so it seems to me that you're more like Jacob wrestling with that man."

"Tally, I feel more like Job right now."

"You just feeling sorry for yourself, Mr. Stash, but I see you wrestling with that man, or maybe it's a demon you're wrestling with, but you surely wrestling with something."

"It's hard not to feel like Job, Tally, and to just feel like giving up when you're looking at what I'm looking at."

"Well, I can say that the Judge and Big Lee haven't given up yet; they're sending telegrams every day to the Governor trying to get him to call it off. A lot of others agree with what you did, but they don't think you were smart about how you did it, stirring up all this ruckus. There's other ways."

"Well I can't see how that can help me much now. I don't even agree with how I did it, but at the time, it seemed like the thing to do."

"I guess not, but people will do what they can to keep you from hanging. I know that."

About that time, Big Lee came back in and told Tally that they had an errand to run. Big Lee looked at me and handed me a Bible. He told me he would be back in a little while to talk some more. I dreaded another talk. I didn't want to talk or think. I was alone in the jail again, and like usual, everything was unlocked, and I thought about taking off, just running to get away from all this, but like usual, it didn't seem to be the right thing to do to Big Lee and Ella and the children, so I stayed and waited for the time to pass, and it was passing faster and faster.

I read about Jacob in the Bible. Reading the Bible is one of those things drilled into me when I was just getting to know God and the church. That preacher took a special interest in me and Little Lee when we made the mistake of saying we might be preachers one day. He made us read and memorize that Bible like little demons every chance he got and he taught us a game, a sword drill, since according to him, the Bible was God's sword fighting evil in the world. He would read out some little piece of scripture and holler out, "Go!" and me and Little Lee raced to find it in the Bible to read it back to him.

It was quite a competition, and we knew the Bible inside and out before we slid back down into normal boys again. The preacher was mightily disappointed in us, but I think our Mamas and Daddies were relieved when we turned back to normal. It wasn't that they didn't respect the preacher. They just said, like most people said, that he didn't know how to do much on his own and they thought he was a little bit lazy, and like most hard-working people, they respected those who worked hard and could do some things for themselves. Anyway, this is what the Bible said about Jacob in Genesis 32: 24-26.

*Jacob was alone; and there he wrestled a man until the break of the day. When the man saw that he prevailed not against him, he touched the hollow of Jacob's thigh, and the hollow of Jacob's thigh was out of joint as they wrestled. And the man said, let me go, for the day breaks, and Jacob said, I will not let thee go, except thou bless me.*

So, maybe I am like Jacob, but I haven't wrestled with a man or God or an angel or whoever Jacob wrestled with. I'd like to though. I'm pretty sure I'm as tough as Jacob, and if I ever got my hands on that man, God, or angel, I could wrestle a blessing out of him too. The preacher says it is a sin to question the wisdom of God, and if what he says turns out to be true, it's just another in a long list of things I have to deal with on the other side, because I question God constantly. I always have.

# Big Lee

In the end, the task of hanging my own nephew seems like it is going to fall to me. Something I never thought I would have to deal with is one of my own caught murdering somebody, and being dumb enough to have people see him doing it. I can't really blame him for what he did. I would've killed those men too; I might have gotten around to it myself if Stash was more patient. What I can blame him for is that he didn't have more patience in trying to take care of his business in a way that could've avoided all that he's facing. I always tried to show him and Little Lee that there are ways to do things that don't put you out in the light where everyone can see you, but Stash's hot temper took over time after time.

He is like most of his generation; they think everything they do has to be out in the full light of the day, like they have to prove to everyone how tough and brave they are, and that's not how it ever should be. There is a smarter way. Most of these young men don't know how to just lie back a little bit and do real quiet what you need to do. I guess it's just the way the times are nowadays. If any of them ever had to go through what we all went through with the War and the hard years after it, they would know better, but I just have to deal with what's in front and do what I have to do. It's too late to do anything different.

A few of us here that fought in the War were shocked at how different things were when we came home. It was a really rough time for a while, what with the Federal troops in here and them trying to run things, splitting up land, and giving it to some of the Negroes and they even shipped some educated Negroes in here and gave them a whole lot of authority and other things that they had no way to be ready for. Some who went off and fought had to stand up to take hold of things when we got back home, just to get things back to a place where people could live.

I mentioned the rifle clubs earlier, and that's how we started getting organized since our surrender papers allowed us to bear arms. The club was just a way a group of us could be together with our rifles. Then the KKK came along out of Texas and Mississippi and we rode with them for a while. At first it was a good thing, not what it is now; no doubt it was a tough group, but the times were tough and what we did reflected the times. Then, like most good things, the rabble started drifting in and the KKK turned into a mean, nasty group who just tried to stir up trouble and settle any little grudge of the members with somebody else. It was predictable. That's what happens when you rip out what holds people together. Things happened that no one ever believed could, like white trash parading around like they were something and the Yankees thinking they could put Negroes in charge of everything down here and thinking they could run the government. What did they think we would do?

At any rate, some of us who went off and fought knew we had to do some hard things to make life livable once we got home and saw how it was going to be. Just in our group, there's me, there's Judge McIver who rode in the cavalry with me for a while before he came home. Then, there's Aiken White, who fought in the infantry, and Daniel Calder, who did the same, and there's some others, but those are the main ones. Some things we just took care of as quiet as we could, like getting rid of one or two of the officers with the occupation units here that just seemed to be doing their work with too much enthusiasm, having too much fun at harassing some of the men who served on our side and their families. In the end, just taking care of things as they came up wasn't enough, and we all decided we needed to take control in a bigger way. General Hampton saw it too, and we all, me, Aiken, Daniel and the Judge, went down and met with the General a couple of times when he was working to take over the government and get the Federals out of the state about ten years after the War.

When he ran in the election for Governor, we mapped out a strategy at a secret meeting down in Charleston; honestly, it was at a place called the Big Red House run by a Jewish woman from down there, Grace Piexotto. The rifle clubs from all over the state joined up in a group called the Red Shirts, and we all worked hard for the General, did what we needed to do, and in 1876 when he won the election, everything started getting some better around here. I won't talk about the Big Red House or Miss Piexotto; that's enough for a whole story by itself, but somebody else probably needs to tell it.

The General told that all of us with the skill and the courage to fight had a duty to stand our ground and take our lives back from the Yankees. That's what we did and that's what we still do. I worry about what will happen when all of us are dead because this younger group just doesn't seem to have what it takes. Hopefully, we've left something behind that's strong enough to keep things on the right track. All the rifle clubs banded together into a one big group called The Farmer's Alliance, and not bragging, just saying, we control most of the elections and other things around here. I don't want to say too much, but we do.

What we did to take control and to help win the election in '76 was a long time ago, but good people never forget, so I wired General Hampton about this mess up here. I still call him General even though he served out his terms as the Governor; to us who served, he will always be the General.

Anyway, when I contacted Gen. Hampton and told him about the sentencing, the General said to just to keep him up on the news about it. I told him I wanted to come down and I asked him if he could get me in to meet with Governor Ellerbe. He said he would speak to the Governor. Unless it's an outright pardon, it might not be enough. What I want to do is find a way to get Stash free of this mess once and for all. I leave the jail open and unlocked, and hope he's got enough sense to take the hint and get the hell out from here, but I don't think he wants to make me look bad. I don't care. I sometimes wish he would just go.

I think about Little Lee every day, but since Stash has been up here, I've been thinking about him more and more. I pass by the cemetery and every time I have some little message for him and his Mama out there, and I talk to them for a while every time I go to the church. Still, he's on my mind more than usual, like he's trying to tell me something. I wish I knew what it is.

After Little Lee drowned, Mae went down to Greer's Mill most every day, looking into that water for hours, hoping for some answer that never came to her. She said every time she went down there, Drip Greer sat with her by the water. She believed he wanted to talk, to tell her something, but he couldn't. It was impossible to know what was in his head. I know Mae felt sorry for him. She had such a tender heart anyway, and Drip was easy to feel sorry for, even for me. His mama left him down here with Henry and Julia, and Henry took care of him some, but once Henry died, Drip was pretty much on his own. The only attention Drip ever got was the torment Julia and Tadlock put him through, but he was a good natured person, and just kept staying around and coming back for more and more torment.

Other people around here didn't treat him badly, but they didn't take him in or try to help him much either. He was still one of the Greers, and that was enough for most people, but for a few others, like my Mae, they just tried to stay away from him because of the rough treatment it brought down on him. Anytime Drip sat with Mae, either Julia or Tadlock came out and beat him with a stick until he ran away. It seemed they didn't want him around, but at the same time, they didn't want anyone else to have anything to do with him either. Since Mae died, he's moved those feeling over to me. It's something about seeing Little Lee drown, I guess.

Once I got down to the mill and saw that bamboo handle sticking out of the water and that sow carp circling the pool under the dam, I knew my boy was in that water dead, and I'm sure Drip knew it too. As soon as he saw me, he started jumping around, pulling me by the arm down to the pool, trying with all his might to tell me something, spraying his spit all over me. He had that awl pike pretending like he was stabbing at something, jumping around, as agitated as I ever saw him. I can't remember which Greer started whacking him with a stick, but one of them did, and Drip went running off, down the creek, squalling and howling like a birdshot dog.

Even now, after all these years, Drip tries tell me things. He follows me out from the church to the cemetery any time he can. I've had to pull him off the grave so many times I can't count them all. He gets down on his hands and knees and starts digging and scratching at the ground like a little boy in a sand pile. It frustrates me that he's probably the last person to see my boy alive, and he'll never be able to tell me what happened. I believe with all my heart that he saw something that day, and for a lot of years, I was obsessed like Mae was, trying to get some meaning out of his babbling. I'd sit as long as I could, listening, looking into his eyes, trying to make some sense out of his babbling.

People don't think I should let him go to the cemetery with me. They say it's disrespectful Little Lee to let him come out there and scratch around on his grave. They think I'm too patient with him or crazy too, but patience and crazy don't have anything to do with it. I just want to know. I wish I could crawl inside his head. I will admit that it's nearly driven me crazy. After a few years, I came to the hard place of accepting what was true. Forever locked deep inside Drip is what he saw, and there's no way for me to know what it is.

Some people think it's odd that I spend so much time at the cemetery talking to my people there, but they're not dead to me. They're as much a part of my life right now as they were when they were here. I go out there and talk to Little Lee and Mae too, mostly just telling them about how everything goes now. Sometimes I ask them to speak up for me on the other side with problems here, like the one with Stash and what he's facing. There isn't any easy way to get him out of this thing he's in; it will take something beyond what I can do, and God's got to be real good himself to pull this off. There's no doubt about that.

# Stash

The cell is a lonely place at times. Since the sentencing I've been behind a locked door that I couldn't open. The cell door is solid metal; a small pass through is the only access to the outside hall. It limits light and sound, and I guess it protects me if a horde of fools try to break in to lynch me. I would hate to end up like Prince Williams, but lynching is not beyond some people out there.

I went too far after the sentencing, but it felt good seeing Tadlock's little bastard squirm. I have to admit it. Later, I did feel guilty about putting Ella at risk; I thought about it for a while last night, and it came to me that if I loved her as much as I think I do, as much as I say I do, none of this would be happening, because the need, the need to stay with her, to take care of her and the children would be enough to wash away the anger I felt, well still feel, and override my need for revenge. It doesn't matter; it's too late now.

They say that dying men pray, and last night I prayed, not that I am any good at it. I think some people's prayers soar up over the trees like a big red-tailed hawk high above the earth, but I'm afraid my prayers probably just skitter along, like a baby sparrow just out of the nest learning to fly, trying hard to get up out of the grass, but I prayed anyway. I can't say that I've repented, and if I haven't, then I know I can't ask for forgiveness, and how do you ask for to be forgiven anyway if you think what you did needed to be done to rid the world of that piece of evil standing in front of you?

I struggle with questions all the time. I have too much

time to think here. Does killing another man to destroy evil also mean that you've taken up the mantle of evil and wrapped yourself in it? Are you then lost to evil forever? It is that kind of thinking that keeps me from being first, apologetic, second, asking for forgiveness, and third, wanting to repent. Where does atonement come into all of this? I guess my atonement is going to be at the end of that rope.

When the hanging comes, I guess I'll be as close to Jesus as any man ever is; I'll be hanging there like he did on the cross, but my atonement will be just for my sins and his was for all of ours. At least that's what the preacher says. Are the two things, forgiveness and repentance, the same, or is repentance inside a man and forgiveness something that can only come from the outside? Sometimes I can almost get to the repent stage, but right up front, I am more penitent for the trouble I brought on my family than I am for those men I killed. I'm know that kind of thinking won't get me to the second step of asking God for forgiveness, at least if God is like what the preachers say, and to be honest, the way you would want God to be. Does repentance come before asking forgiveness, or does it just all hit you at the same time in one big avalanche of "Oh sweet Jesus, did I really mess up this bad?" I'm not sure.

Now earlier I talked about those "just in case Christians." Remember? It's those that haven't gone the whole hog yet, but are just dipping their toes in the water just in case. Well, I think repentance is like that sometimes too, well maybe more than sometimes. I see a lot of people trying to use repentance kind of like it is insurance. They do a thing knowing ahead of time it is a bad sin, thinking if they can just get past it, there will be plenty of time to repent later, and they do it or something else over and over and over again.

Now if I see it for what it is and get just plain sick and tired of it, well, what do you think God is doing with all that is in front of him to tend to? I'm just a simple man, but even I can see through those people, and that's why I don't just fall out here on the floor wailing and crying saying "Oh Lord. I repent! I repent!" That kind of thing reminds me of a little child crying to get his way, and being real sincere about it too with the snubs and everything, and then cocking his head up to see if it has done any good, and then falling right back into the snubs. You've seen it too, I know. God is too smart for that.

Anyway, I prayed last night, not a big prayer, just a simple, honest prayer. I'm not a heathen, in spite of what you may be thinking about now; I know how to pray and I did. In the end, I just asked for mercy; it was about all I could get right in my head. This is close to what I said.

*"Oh Father in heaven, I say now that even bound by my sins,*
*I seek your counsel and ask for your mercy, especially for my family.*
*I hear the words, 'forgive us our sins, as we forgive those who sin*
*against us.'*
*They roll like unsettling thunder in my mind,*
*and I see clearly that your judgment of me should be harsh.*
*Still, I seek your mercy and your hand in protection over my family."*
*Amen.*

That line out of the Lord's Prayer is the one that stops me. Faith is a lot harder for me than most people seem to make it. I don't think people read the line the same way I do. People think forgiveness is coming, think if we ask it from God, it's going to come no matter what. Other places in the Bible make it seem that way, I know, but it is too simple a reading of the line I think. That word "as" stuck in the middle there is a big word the way I read it. It takes the surety of forgiveness of sins out because the little word "as" means "in like manner, the same way, to the same degree," all of those things, and if the way I read it is the right way, well then, I am in bigger trouble over there on that side than I am over here on this side, and you know I'm in big trouble here.

A person can't earn God's grace. It comes unbidden, if it comes at all, like it did for Paul on the road to Damascus. God chooses the when and where of it, even the who of it. That makes it all hard to understand, to get to some point where you do something, fast, pray, atone, to help yourself, but even writing this I see that mercy and grace, unbidden, are the only things I can hope for, but I'm not Paul, so I am not really expecting.

Tally came in with some food a little bit ago. We talked some, and he said that the Sheriff told him to keep me locked in the secure cell for a while. He said maybe I would simmer down a little bit, and if I was in the secure cell it would be hard to get to me to lynch me if some of the Greer crowd came in. I said I appreciated that. Tally said, "Mister Stash, I sort of hate I didn't slice Tadlock Greer's throat when I had the chance yesterday. I hate it. It would've been good though, wouldn't it, to slice that evil bastard's throat and watch him bleed out right there on the street?"

"Yeah, it would've," I said and knew right then that my prayer had not worked. I was no closer to repentance than one of those whores out at the brothel.

See what I mean about how hard it is to get things right in your head to ask God for some help, and on top of that, how fast religiosity goes away. For it to work, Faith has to be real. God would be less than what I think he is to fall for something false, although it sure looks like it works for some people like those sanctimonious fools I talked about earlier. Speaking of sanctimonious fools, it's Sunday again, but Big Lee won't take me to church because of all the hubbub after the sentencing, and him knowing the Greers will be sitting right up front. It's a little bit hard to sit in the same church with people like them without trouble breaking out, so I guess my church going days are over.

Mama and Daddy have been on my mind, and I'm thinking I need to get on with the story about what happened to get me here, so I'll start with them. Mama and Daddy both died in the fire that burned the main farm house a little over a year ago. Mama had cancer they said, and lay there dreaming and moaning, not eating, just sipping water and laudanum every hour or so while Daddy tried to work the farm during the day with Estelle Pegues sitting with her, wiping her face, trying to keep her easy. It was a hard thing to watch. Mama dying, and me praying at first that some miracle might save her, and then praying that it would all go faster, and then just praying, just praying for some mercy and relief, for her and everybody else too, with her reaching out, seeing a world past us, and her saying, "Mama, Mama, Mama," while she was reaching out past us into that world we couldn't see for her own Mama, dead all those years. Now that she's gone, when I do pray, I just pray that Grandma was standing there to take her hand.

This is how it happened. Mama was sick and close to dying anyway, but a fire is no way for a person to die, especially a sick person who's weak, who can't get away from it, hears the flames licking up, crackling and popping, the smoke rising, filling up the room, and her lying there in her death bed alone, not knowing if it's a horrible laudanum dream of Hell or a real thing because the woman who's supposed to be helping you ran out to save herself. That's what Mama knew and heard and felt when Daddy saw the smoke and rode up to the house from the lower field on Sockeye, unhooked from the harrow, to find the house wrapped up in fire, caught from a brush fire that ran out from the pines beside it. We all got to the house about the same time, me, Big Lee, and a couple of hands, heard Mama crying out, "Jacob! Jacob! Jacob! Help me Jacob!," and saw Daddy never stop, just run into the house, with it falling in around him, to Mama's side, and that's where we found him, beside her, and both of them gone, so fast, so very fast.

I was in shock I think. Something happens to me in those odd times, like when Little Lee drowned, my emotions just shut down; it's not unfeeling; it's that my emotions suspend for a time, enough to do what's called for, and so I took the Winchester lever action from the barn and followed the track of the brush fire through the pines, starting by taking wider and wider circles, to find the start of it. The ground was still warm, hot in some places. I felt it through the soles of my shoes and kept moving fast. Smoke was still rising, and in places, fire on the stumps of old heart pine licked up like an eruption from deep in the earth. My Mama and Daddy were dead, killed by the same fire, and the reality of it seemed dream-like in the smoke and fire and heat, and me alone moving through it, a vision of Hell on earth, and a feeling of disbelief and anger and an idea way back in my head that God's hand was nowhere close to what was happening, an idea that God was looking the other way, letting Satan do what he would do. The track of the fire began to narrow, and I followed it down the hill through the pines in the direction of South Prong Creek.

The path narrowed to just a few feet at the source, about ten feet on our side of the creek, and lying at the birth of the fire was a heart pine brand still flickering with the last, dying flame. The idea of someone starting the fire, of them calculating the best wind, of them waiting for dry weather, of the fire being no accident, flashed inside me. I kicked the brand into the creek, putting out the flame, cooling it, and picked it up. I crossed the creek and circled once, that's all it took, finding two sets of footprints, one set of two men coming and one set of two men going back, and I tracked them through the woods until they crossed the road, walking up to Greer's Mill where they mixed in with others and disappeared there a few feet from the entrance.

I walked in the front of the mill with the blackened

brand in my left hand, the Winchester in my right. Tadlock Greer was on his stool behind the secretary stand, and he looked up at me, saying, "I hear there's a fire up at your place, everyone good?"

I said, "The house is gone. Mama and Daddy died in the fire. There's a track up through the woods to where the fire started. This is what started it," and I held the spent brand up and laid it on the secretary in front of him. "The track started here and came back to here." I watched his face for any sign, any little tell giving him away, and saw a slight flicker in his eyes, a nearly imperceptible rise of his right eyebrow, a long, deep exhale, resigned, like he did not expect anyone to follow the track to him in the middle of everything happening around the fire, and then him looking over to a group of five turpentine sharecroppers, his sharecroppers, taking direction from Julia Greer, their curved bark girdling knives hanging loose at their sides, standing in the double opening that leads back to the mill works, and two of them walking over to stand on either side of him, and Julia stepping back out of sight.

Tadlock asked them, "Fellas, Stash says there is a track over there in the woods where the fire started, coming from here. Did you see anybody over there?"

One of the men stepped forward a little and said, "Yes sir, I seen this one, Theo, right here walking beside me," and looked over at the other with that little smiling sneer like a dog showing his teeth that every piece of white trash seems to have, and the other one saying, "Yes sir, and I seen Charlie right here," pointing at the first man with the tip of his girdling knife, with the same dog-like smiling sneer.

The other three men edged closer too, so I lifted the Winchester, and laid the barrel across the top of the secretary pointing into Greer's chest, and said, "This isn't going to go good for you, you son of a bitch," knowing that I had no more hesitation about pulling that trigger, sending Tadlock Greer to Hell, than I would to chop the head off a snake or kick a mean dog in the teeth.

"Come on now Stash, you don't think I had anything to do with the fire? I've been here all afternoon."

"No, it wasn't you. You never have enough balls to do your own work; you've always got some piece of trash like these to do it for you." The two men beside Tadlock started to crab around to either side of me, so I watched Tadlock's eyes, and said, "I can pull this trigger faster," nodding to my right at one of the turpentiners, "tell this trash you drag in here to back down. They take one more step and you're going to look down at a hole in your chest."

Tadlock put his hand on the man's arm standing to his right, "Take them out, and get back to the camp."

About then, I heard the door behind me open, and Big Lee's voice, "Stash, it's time to go. Don't mess this up," and he walked up and laid his hand on the Winchester taking it from me. He stepped around, putting his arm around me and took me outside.

When we were clear of the people around the mill, he said, "You have to be smarter. Ella and the children need you and we have to take care of your Daddy and Maggie."

"I know, I know, but you know that son of a bitch or his Mama sent those men up there to set the fire."

"Yeah I know, and we'll get to them. Just be smart. The whole point is to make him pay, not for you to pay too. Don't you see?"

"I guess so, but I would get a lot more satisfaction out of blowing a hole in his chest just to see the look on that bastard's face."

"Listen to this, and listen real close. You could put every evil son of a bitch alive in a line and shoot five or ten or a hundred every minute for the rest of your life and never get to the end of it because new ones chomping at the bit, just plain itching to be evil, would fill their end of the line faster than you could kill them at your end. That's just the way it is."

"I know, but you're the sheriff. You know they did it, and I'm not worrying about every evil son of a bitch, just those!"

"Jesus Christ, you are bull headed! You're exactly right. I am the sheriff, so stay out of my way and let me handle it the way I want to. You hear me?"

I remember the funeral, the mass of people crowding in the church, more standing outside. A sudden death always draws a crowd, especially a tragic one. Some people are sincere; some are there for the spectacle. It's odd to me. If a person just dies with no drama attached to their dying, people aren't so likely to come around to the funeral and all, but if a person dies with some drama, like Mama and Daddy burning up, people flock to the house and the funeral just to see and to say later, "Yeah, I remember them dying. I was there." That's the way it was with Mama and Daddy. People came from all over to see what was left of the house, and finally, when I had enough, I ran a crowd off.

Grandpa Harris and two of Daddy's brothers, my Uncles Stephen and Isaac, came over to the funeral from Saddletree. I have to say we haven't been close to that side of the family, not that I don't know them, we just haven't been close. I went up there a few times when I was younger, and it wasn't much different than it is around here, except Grandpa and his family live mostly in the Indian sections, and they have as much separation from white people up there as we have down here between the Negroes and us, maybe even more because not too many Indians will work for the white people, and the only time the white people up there want anything from the Indians is when they want something they don't have much of like moonshine or pretty women.

As soon as Grandpa got down here he wanted to know

everything that happened. My uncles listened too, and when I told them what I thought, and what I found, that faggot thrown across the creek and all and about those turpentiners, it seemed the dark cloud that hung over me, descended on them too. I took them down through the pines and crossed the creek following the same track I followed a day or two before, and showed them Greer's Mill.

Our land comes down to a bluff that overlooks the millpond, and we sat up there for a while, looking down at the Mill, watching the people coming and going, us talking about what we might do, about what we could do to get revenge, but the funeral and family business over the next day or two outweighed the idea of revenge. After the funeral, I was with Ella and when I looked out, I saw Big Lee, Grandpa Harris, and my uncles under a big live oak near the barn talking. They talked for a least an hour and when they were done, Grandpa and my uncles came in and said their goodbyes and left. I knew Big Lee stopped them.

That song, "On Jordan's Stormy Banks I Stand," and its haunting refrain are about all I remember from the funeral. It was all just a haze of sadness. I still can't believe they are gone.

*I am bound for the Promised Land,*
*I am bound for the Promised Land;*
*Oh who will come and go with me?*
*I am bound for the Promised Land.*

I hope Mama and Daddy went there, but why did it have to go the way it did? Was all their suffering theirs alone and something they did or was it for me, to test me? If this is a just world, what did they sow and what harvest did Mama and Daddy reap? I don't know. That song is especially haunting now that I am up here facing what I'm facing. What the preacher said was unimportant to me. I know how that sounds, but I have to be truthful, and say that I was not concerned with what he said.

Mama and Daddy died in a fire set by Tadlock Greer. That is all I know. Well, not by him personally, but by those white trash turpentine sharecroppers, and it is all just the same as him throwing the burning faggot across the creek and setting the fire himself. An odd stillness stayed with me through the funeral, and for a month or two after. I did a lot of thinking. If I've heard it one time, I've heard it a thousand times how God has a plan. Maybe he does, well probably he does, but if it is God's plan that Mama and Daddy died in a fire set by some of the most evil people I know, I can't see it, and more than that, I can't accept it. If that is blasphemy, then I guess it is just one more thing to deal with on the other side after they hang me.

I've read all about Job's suffering, losing his family, lying under that gourd vine scratching his boils with those shards of pottery, and about his patience and faith and all the rest, but remember it wasn't exactly God who was behind it; Satan caused all of Job's suffering, although I will admit it was God who let him. Now was it all a laid out plan, or was it just something that happened during the conflict? The book isn't too clear on which one it was.

If you break away from the brand of Christianity that reduces faith to some kind of salve to put on every wound, big or little, to keep just plodding along with your head down like a plow mule with a bad owner, taking everything that comes and trying to be the best at suffering like that's going to get you into Heaven and instead, you go ahead and get mad at evil things and evil people enough to see clear that God and Satan are still in battle and things like Mama and Daddy dying in fire is Satan's doing, now that's something I can accept because fighting evil, railing against it, is something I naturally think I should do, but I wonder if either side has a plan so specific. Even when you read Job, it seems like it was all something that just came up like Satan saying, "Hey, I bet I can make that fellow, Job, renounce his faith," and God saying, "No, it won't ever happen, but you can try if you want to."

This seems to make more sense in the battle between good and evil. One side does something, and the other responds, and then those unexpected consequences pop up, like everything boiling up around Job, but doesn't it pull God and Satan down to the level of people and thinking like that can't possibly be right can it? So what is right, and which way is the right way? Do you want to be like Job and just lay there scratching, or do you want to be like Joshua at Jericho, and do something? How does "leave room for the wrath of God" figure into all of this? The Bible is a confusing thing, and there is one way that I am like Job. Just like Job, I am not smart enough to figure it out, and I don't think anybody else is either.

So, why did Tadlock or Julia Greer send those men up there to start a fire on our side of South Prong Creek? Did they do it intending to kill Mama and Daddy, or were both of them dying just one of those unexpected consequences that I mentioned? Was it just one more thing in a long line of things the Greers did over the years to be a constant torment for Mama and Daddy, a thing that blew up into something more than they thought?

I know I can't figure anything about their motivations with any truth to it, and if you asked Tadlock Greer or Julia or either of those two men that actually started the fire, they probably couldn't tell you anything that would make much sense. Neither of those two sons of bitches that started the fire and sneered at me in that mill, smiling and pointing those bark girdling knives around like they were going to do something with them are still here to answer any questions; those bastards are attracting worms in the cold ground. If you could go over to the other side, or let them come here, and you asked might say, "We had to; we work for the

Greers" or "It sounded like fun at the time," or some other stupid reason. Sometimes nothing makes sense.

# Tadlock

Honestly, I thought for a minute or two I was a dead man. It was over the fire up at up at the Harris place that killed Jacob and Maggie Harris; that's Stash's mama and daddy. Mamaju sent some turpentiners up the creek past the head of the millpond to set a fire across on the Cason side just for some mischief I think, and to see if she couldn't damage enough trees to maybe make them sell some of their timber off to us. None of us had any idea it would kill those people, not that we mind too much. It's just more Casons out of the way and it keeps us from having to get our hands too dirty. The fire did it for us. Maggie was a Cason, the Sheriff's sister.

Me and Mamaju and two or three of our turpentiners was out in front of the mill watching the smoke from the woods fire, kind of tracking it moving up the ridge when black smoke started billowing up from one spot. I said to Mamaju it looked like the barn or something up at the Cason farm was on fire. She said, "We ain't that lucky," and went on back inside the mill to check on the work in there I guess. It wasn't but a minute or two when those two turpentiners she sent up to the head of the millpond to set the fire came out of the woods across the road and walked up to where we were. I pointed to the black smoke and told them the fire caught up something at the Cason place, and they puffed up, bragging about what a good job they done.

About then, we heard a farm bell ringing and ringing and ringing, sounding an alarm off in the distance up about where the Cason house was, and it wasn't long until somebody came down the road off the ridge and rode across to tell us the main Cason house was burning and Jacob and Maggie was still inside, probably dead. Maggie was about dead anyway from the cancer so it didn't matter too much about her. They was all just waiting for her to die from the cancer, or that's what we heard, but they said when the fire started on the house, she was hollering out for Jacob and he went running into the fire and didn't come back out. Why would he do something odd like that for, especially for somebody who's about to die anyway? It's stupid, but that's how they are. Mamaju says those kinds of things are why before it's all over there won't be nothing left but people like us because people like them are too stupid to last. Maybe so, it makes sense.

Later on that day, something happened that caught me off guard pretty bad. What I really didn't have an idea about happening was that Stash would leave his dead mama and daddy laying there in that burnt down house for somebody else to deal with and come tracking off down through the woods to see where the fire came from. We all figured to have some trouble about the fire over time, but none of us thought it would come so quick, like the same afternoon! It's that damn Indian blood in him I guess, that makes him do odd things. It is scary sometimes, how them people with mixed up Indian blood act. You just can't tell what they might do. It just ain't normal, but I've heard some tales about those Indians up in North Carolina and about them Marlboro Blues right across the Pee Dee. It's a rough crowd any time but when they get riled, god almighty.

It was about three hours after the fire burned out. Stash came walking in the front door of the mill. I was sitting behind the secretary shuffling some papers around, not really doing too much, just thinking about what might happen with Jacob and Maggie gone, what it might do to the Casons, and he come walking right in. He was carrying a lever action rifle that I'd seen him with before, and he laid it right up on the secretary pointing it at my chest. Hanging from his belt was a fierce looking cane knife that swung back and forth with every step he took.

Thick soot from what the fire left in the woods he walked through from the Cason house down to the mill office covered his britches all the way up past his knees. You could see more of that thick black soot all up around his eyes and more of it under his nose where he'd been breathing it in and out. I have to say he was fierce looking, maybe something thrown out of hell if there is such a thing and a place with all that black soot covering him and those sharp, angry eyes peering out. He scared me a little, that simmering anger, but I couldn't let on; I was worried about more than him knocking me out like he did the last time, with him carrying that rifle and cane knife, but I'd had enough of all those turpentiners and Mamaju ragging my ass about Stash getting the upper hand on me, so I bucked up to it and determined to stand my ground, and I did.

Mamaju was standing with the turpentiners what set the fire when Stash came walking in. I had a few words with him and let him know real quick that I wasn't gonna take any of his normal bullshit. I even sent those men off. He had the gall to put that gun over the secretary pointing right into my chest, but I didn't figure he'd pull the trigger with all the people around. If he ever wanted to kill me that would have been the time, because he won't ever get another chance. The sheriff came in and hauled him out, but it didn't matter; he wasn't gonna do anything anyway. That was it for him, his last and only chance, and it won't be long until he'll get what he deserves, hanging up there doing the hangman's jig for everybody to see, and he'll leave the door wide open for me to move on Ella and take over his place there.

When Ella Quick and her brothers and sister moved up here with the Therrells, I thought she was the one for me, you know, a kind of respectable person, pretty and nice, to have at home when I got there. I had two of my boys already, but they were out. What I mean by that is that their mamas were some pretty colored girls that work around the tavern for us and they wouldn't ever be part of my house, and coming from where Ella came from, a desperate kind of life, I didn't have any idea that having those boys would get in the way of us, but that has to be what it was that made her choose Stash and not me. It couldn't be anything else, but it still ain't too late.

Going back to what's gone on between me and Stash over the years, it's been nothing but trouble. Life works like that; some people just can't fit in around each other. Mamaju says it's in the blood, but I don't know if what she says is true and I don't worry about it now. Stash won't be here much longer and when he's hung and gone, it'll be my turn with her. It's just that simple. She'll forget him real quick. I'll wait just a little bit of time, enough for people to quit talking about it all, and then one day when I see the sheriff heading out, I'll ride up that ridge with some candy in my pocket for her two little ones, and by then she'll be wanting and needing what every woman wants and she'll be ready for me. I despise that son of bitch, Stash, and when Ella is mine, and he's up there in that cemetery with the worms and beetles feasting on him while I'm doing all the things with her that he used to do, it will be some sweet revenge.

# Stash

Old man Henry Greer died a few years ago, back about 1892 I think, just before the cotton market turned really bad again. Now for about my whole life, growing cotton had been a good thing, not for the land, but for the pocket book. It was the way most of us out this way made our living, but Daddy and the rest of the Casons were a little bit more careful than most people. The better the market was, the more cotton most people planted, and like everything else, they thought it would last forever. I've seen cotton planted right up to the doorsteps of some houses around here.

Greed got the better of people like that, and they planted cotton right over their flower beds, kitchen gardens and hog pens. Then they wondered why food was scarce, or why everything just seemed so drab. They had that jar full of money though, so they could take it out and look at it and run their fingers through it to see how it felt, like that little bit of green and silver was going to take the place of a bed of spring flowers bursting with color, or a row of camellia sasanqua blazing red at Christmas, or a garden full of rich vegetables, or a big cured ham hanging in the pantry. Some people are just plain stupid aren't they?

I'm glad to say, the Casons seemed to naturally have less greed than some of those people, and didn't jump in as quick to plant more and more. I can't make a judgment on whether they were smarter, although it looked like they were in the end, but they sure didn't have that greedy bone gnawing at them like a lot of people did, and not having it kept them from over extending when the market was strong. I think it came from Papaw Cason down to us, and it came to him from his daddy I guess, and his daddy before that. Maybe they just liked flowers and good food.

I don't know why it always works out this way, but it does; really greedy folks like the Greers just hate somebody who's not, like the Casons. There's a crowd of people like the Greers that just want to tear down any good thing that someone else has or does. You've seen it, I know, and if you're not careful, you'll jump in with that crowd too. The Casons cared about their land, and when they settled down here, it became home and they tried to take care of it like a person should take care of home, but for the Greers, and a lot of others too, the land was anything but home; it was something to be used until it couldn't be used up anymore, and then it was time to try to get ahold of somebody else's any way they could and use it up too, or leave and take up somewhere else. The two different sides of doing things set up a natural conflict between the Greers and the Casons, not that the Casons wanted it, but on the other hand, they weren't shy about standing up for what was theirs either.

As bad as we thought the old man was, after Henry died, Julia and Tadlock didn't have anyone to hold them back, and they didn't have old man Henry's sense of strategy or his patience either, so they went after everyone hard, kind of bold and wild like, scheming and trying to destroy anybody that had an ounce of good about them, and they had a special hunger for what the Casons had because we always stood real strong against them and because of it, the Greers never got any kind of hold on anything that was connected to us. The fire that killed Mama and Daddy was just one more thing in a long line of things the Greers did over the years to torment the Casons, well, us, trying to beat us down like they did other people. You wouldn't believe it all if I told you, and there's not enough time to tell it all anyway, but I'll tell what I have time for. We weren't the only ones Julia and Tadlock and their ilk had designs on.

George Cason, one of the cousins, not too close in, but a cousin still, ran a little general store that his grandfather on the other side built about four miles up Scotch Road from the tavern. Tadlock Greer hooked up with a girl named Nell from over in Lee County and brought her up here. I don't know if they ever married or not, but she was up here with him and they had a little boy together, the same little pissant of a boy I snatched up after the sentencing. He beat that poor girl unmercifully - I've seen it myself - and it wasn't long before she left her boy with Tadlock and took off. The next we saw of her, that girl was living with George in the back of his general store.

Now George's place was never much competition for the tavern, there wasn't a brothel attached to it, but any competition for the Greers was too much, and Tadlock wasn't one to sit around when someone got the better of him even if it was him that drove that girl off. The Greers never paid a lick of attention to George before, but with Nell's help, George made wine and moonshine that was a lot better than what men could buy over at the Greer's tavern. There's a difference between proofing moonshine and just plain out watering it down the way they did at the tavern and believe it or not, the Greer's brothel didn't draw every man in like blow flies to a dead fish, especially once Nell was around for the men to enjoy looking at.

Some men just weren't that interested in measuring themselves inside those whores alongside every other man that went in there, so George and Nell began to build a good business from the men who were more interested in good drink and looking at good woman flesh. Julia and Tadlock didn't like it. I'll get to that good woman flesh in a minute. Now don't get me wrong, quite a few men flocked to those whores, more than enough to keep the brothel going strong, especially when turpentining and timbering was teeming with all those men who move up and down the turpentine trail during the season, but the brothel wasn't enough to satisfy those Greers. Nothing was really. They wanted everything plus revenge, and they determined to put George out of business and make him pay for what they said was stealing Nell from Tadlock.

The Greers had the woods full of those sharecroppers pulling resin from the pines, setting it out in barrels beside the road for the gatherers to pick up and take in to the turpentine still they built near the mill. With the cotton market down most of the landowners contracted their pines to the Greers hoping to make enough money to pay off their season's debts and have enough to start over the next year. Some farmers just tried to hang on since they already owed the Greers for seed and other supplies from the year before. It seemed that once a farmer started with the Greers for what they needed, they never got away from them, and a lot of times, they lost their land to the Greers and either left this part of the country or became sharecroppers on what used to be their own land. It was like that old tale about tar baby; once in, they never could pull away and got more and more stuck until it was too late. The smart ones simply left and tried to start over again somewhere else.

Now if you don't know, a turpentine sharecropper stays out, roughing it in the woods, usually alone, but sometimes three or four team up to work out of one camp. Each one of those men might be working as many as four or five thousand trees, and it is hard work, and you probably know like I do that a bunch of men together doing hard, rough work draws in the roughest kind of men, and those who aren't that way to start with usually turn that way over time. It seems that without women and children and family around, the things that make men care about living, men just naturally tend to run close to Satan. It is not always true, but mostly it is.

The Greers put the word out among those turpentiners to shut George Cason down and they told that they would pay a bounty to anyone who could find and bust up his still site, and there would be more bounty for doing other things to him, a kind of guerilla war against him. With all those men in the woods, it didn't take long to know where George was doing his stilling work, and one night a few of those turpentiners went in there and hacked up his still and dumped his mash in the creek. They slipped into his barn a couple of days later and turned over and smashed all his wine barrels, doing away with a year's hard work, pouring out everything that could turn to money for him, stealing as much as they could carry, watching the rest soak into the sand.

George wasn't sure who busted up his still at first. It wasn't the first time it happened because the competition was fierce in the whiskey business and it wasn't past most moonshiners to bust up another shiner's operation to get an advantage, but some people saw those turpentiners hanging around the store, and saw them slip out to the barn the same day George discovered his trouble. It was pretty clear to George then who and why all the trouble was raining down on him and he was like anyone else, and decided it was time to do something about it.

Now I hesitate to talk about this part of the story, knowing all the trouble it will cause for the men out my way, but I see it figuring into what happened, so it's part of the truth, and in a little bit, I'll be gone anyway. Like I said before, Nell was a good looking girl from over in Lee County somewhere; I never really knew exactly where she came from since I tried to stay away from her as much as possible, and George wasn't much inclined to talk about her and how she came up here with Tadlock and all that happened. She had a hard edge to her, one she brought with her, but it served her well around the store when all those men were coming and going, buying their liquor and wine, and hanging around outside the store drinking it, and doing all their big talking.

Now you don't need to tell Ella this part. I have to admit that I'm not a stranger to the shade trees around that store, and I was as admiring of Nell's good looks as anyone, and there's just something about a good looking woman that's left one man for another one that makes every man think he can be the next one. Men that wouldn't ever think about another woman can get pretty bold with their talk. When Nell was out working barefoot in the garden, or doing some other work on the outside during warmer weather, she gathered that dress of hers up, wrapped the hem around each thigh, and tied it off high up around her hips; it was as bold a display of female flesh as you'll ever see. Those were some pretty, long legs, and that girl could wipe sweat off her neck and chest in a way that put you in mind of, well, you know what it puts you in mind of, and not being used to that kind of display from the women around here, I freely admit that more than one time, I cut a pretty hot trail home to find Ella after watching her sashay around outside.

Even the older fellows from around took to hanging out there, and George, thinking he was helping business, put a bench out under the shade trees since those older men spent money too, more really than the younger ones. Those old fellows did a lot of urgent talking and wishing, but mostly they were past any serious activity if you know what I mean, but the Lord knows, they could do a lot of serious talking about what they might do if, just if, and Nell loved the attention and teased those old men unmercifully. We named that bench the wishing bench, and that's what it was; there was a lot of wishing and dreaming going on out there.

Now it turned out that once in a while, well maybe more often than that, one of the younger men hanging around would go into the store to occupy George while another one took Nell out to the barn or back in the little vineyard doing what men and women always seem to find a way to do. That might not be quite right; maybe it was Nell that took them, although you know it's always the man that thinks he the one doing all the doing. Now don't get any ideas; I never did, and that's the truth. I have to say it was a temptation, but over time I just felt real sorry for George, him being real busy trying to squeeze every dime out of that store and her dishing out good cheer to one man after the other. It got to be quite a busy store, what with the good drink and the extra benefits, and now that I think about it, her doing for free what the Greers were charging for might have figured into them trying so hard to shut George down too. I never even thought about until now, but it might be true.

It was some of those old geezers that told who they saw going out to smash and dump the George's wine and when he found out, he went to that turpentiner camp while they were out working and burned everything. It was fair retribution I think considering what they did to him, but I've said before that crowd is rough and they came back at him hard. Some say that it was Nell herself who betrayed George even more than she already had and told that he was the one who burned the camp, and while that could be true, it's hard for me to believe she did that to him even though she cuckolded him on a regular basis. However those men found out, they did, and in the end it didn't matter how, just that they did, and everything ended up the way the Greers wanted.

Some of that turpentine crowd came to George and Nell's rooms in the back of the store one night to get their revenge. The next morning, some of the men found him tied to a ladder back chair at the foot of him and Nell's bed. He was beat up pretty bad, his head tied to the back of the chair like they made him watch whatever went on in that bed. George wouldn't tell any part of it, and a couple of days later, when the store caught on fire, we found George out back in the barn with a side by side shotgun in his hand and the back of his head splattered on the wall behind him. It was suicide. I guess all that happened was just too much for him.

I don't have to tell you how people are, and how they embellish the story enough to make it like poor old George watched those men having whatever part of Nell they wanted and him just not being willing to live with it, setting his store on fire, and going out back to blow his head off. It might be so. It's happened before, but I don't spread that kind of talk around, well, except for now. The Greers even put the story out that Nell was the one behind the whole thing, and they turned her into the most evil thing to have ever lived around here, but I don't think her being willing to spread her legs and dish out good cheer among the men around here while she was with George makes her evil enough to do all that they say she's done except in the eyes of some of those holier than thou people we've talked about before. Why it's even some of those holier than thou men who dipped into that honey pot that do the most talking about how evil Nell was; I guess they do it to put up that good front for their wives. I know that all the things those people are saying about Nell just aren't true, and I'll tell why I think that if I have time.

You and I both know that some of those properly sanctimonious people, men and women, have a hard time keeping their britches up too in the right situation, some of them in any situation, but the edge they have over us, well, at least over me, is that armor, that just in case brand of Christianity that kicks in and forgives them ahead of time for all of their sinning no matter how bad it is. That's some awfully good protection when you can get it. To know that no matter what you do, the blood of the Lamb is going to wash you clean and save you for eternity is a pretty good deal. I wish I had it, that protection I mean, but somehow, I just can't get down on that level, and I really don't think God is as simple minded as some others around here believe, if you follow me. It kind of insults the whole idea of God, doesn't it?

# Big Lee

Too many times things happen in a man's life that make him face the same problems over and over. It seems like every time you work yourself past some hard time of your life, and get your head up above water to start moving again, the world says, "Ok, that's about enough of that, here's some more shit to stick your nose in." That's what I was thinking yesterday, kind of pouting I guess, flailing away at everything going on, being hard on God too, blaming Him for all my problems, when I remembered that what is going on may not be coming from God's plan, but instead it could be Satan's trifling.

Growing up I heard so much about God having a plan that even in the middle of the War and all the killing, I kept trying to get it all straight in my head that somehow God was responsible for all the hate and killing, that somehow, He was in charge of it all on both sides. For a long time, I believed with all my heart that what we fought for was righteous, that everything we were was right and good, and I knew there were people on the other side who believed the same thing. I remember the first time the idea of Satan became real to me, that maybe all we were was not so good, not so righteous. We were starving, sometimes fighting two or three times a day, other times just fighting all day and all night, the killing and the struggle to stay alive all running together.

We were on our own, without any regular supplies like they had on the other side, and we took what we needed when we could find it even though the country up there in

Virginia was bare from the years of fighting and scavenging. Sometime about then, I realized that all the good I believed we stood for when the War started had vanished, and we were just another part of the evil with its hooks deep in all of us. I wanted to survive though, and I did, barely. I did some things that I'm not proud of now that time has passed, and those old memories come back if I'm not careful to keep them pushed down.

You might think that I'm talking about all the killing I saw or the killing I did or some other big things, but you'd be wrong. It's always the little things that matter the most. One time I took a feisty bantam rooster from a little girl about seven years old with her crying and saying, "Mister, don't take Toby, he's all I got left. Don't take my Toby." and then when I had him, "Please don't hurt Toby, mister, please." That bantam rooster fed about ten men once I made a thin stew out of him and some cattail tubers I dug, but every swallow I took was a hard one. That sweet little girl's crying and the way her eyes cut into my soul still haunt me sometimes, more than the men I've killed, because it was right then, in that moment, that I knew evil had taken me too. It's odd I know, but it's the truth.

We became just another animal, not what a human being with a heart and a soul and a mind to make choices ought to be. We were struggling to survive, killing or dying, facing it every day, death I mean, trying to scrounge enough of any and everything to keep going. What we did find to eat, we fed to our horses if they could eat it, to keep them up and going, and maybe give us a way out, or maybe even a way back home when enough good men died for one side to give up. More times than I can count me and Maddie shared the same food. It was just how it was.

A thing I'll never be smart enough to understand is how during war time, politicians and generals do a lot better job keeping a good supply coming of what it takes to kill other men than they do supplying what it takes to keep their own men alive. I guess that's the way it is; those politicians and generals who like War count us all dead anyway, so feeding us, taking care of us after the War tore us all up isn't high on their list of things to get done. There's not as much money in that part of a War for the bastards and not as much glory for them either.

There was a big, spirit revival going on among the soldiers, men just outright begging for salvation. You might have thought God himself was riding with us like he did with those Jews in the desert. Every night around the fires, some poor starving soldier would get in the spirit and jump up and dance around spouting scripture or speaking in some rapturous tongue, saying God was talking to him or that he was actually seeing Jesus or God or both. The more dying we did and the more killing too, the more fervent a lot of men were, calling on God, hoping He might save them, or at least take them into heaven after the enemy killed them. The War starved us clean and pure into a futile army of maniacally violent monks sitting on the banks of the Styx ready to storm the actual gates of Hell.

It was then that I looked past any idea about God's plan and looked around for Satan and right then, I knew it was Satan - I saw him everywhere - on the other side killing us, and on our side killing them. People can say whatever they want to say, but around a War, God isn't ever the one winning, and War just can't be any part of God's plan like people say, trying to make it all seem right, and holy, and just. I know all about the Crusades, and believe me, those poor bastards got sucked up in all of it too, especially those pitiful children who went marching off under God's banner. It was all Satan.

To think that God would take a side and be a part of it, the killing and the hating, just can't be right. It's Satan alone that's doing the winning and the losing, all of it on both sides, stealing every man's soul caught up with that much hate and it never stops, even now. If a man ever takes up the Word of God, and says it's a reason to go to war, just go on and shoot that son of a bitch right there, before he can get a bunch of people to go along with him. It will save everybody a lot of heartache, and just to be clear, there are a lot of other perfectly justifiable reasons to shoot a son of a bitch.

I got used to the idea of killing men during the War. There's no way around it if you want to live and if other men keep trying to kill you. You just have to, and sometime along while all of the killing is happening, enough of what kept you from killing before dies inside you and it, the killing I mean, just becomes something you do. My Enfield did a lot of killing; I kept track of it, and before the War ended, I counted thirty-one men dead, men that I laid the sights down on and pulled the trigger and watched them die. Now, since the War, well that's another story; I haven't done any more killing than was absolutely necessary.

I've said before that when we got home, a lot was going on that we had to straighten out. Our little group here, men that went off and fought, men that could be trusted saw to it. We just couldn't sit by and watch land that our people settled and worked given to carpetbaggers, bummers that stayed down here, and Negroes. It just wasn't right and over time, we set most things back to right. It didn't take but a few examples to convince the Negroes that there were people out there that wouldn't tolerate what was going on. Prince Williams was a stubborn one and some rabble rousers took care of it, and after that most of the Negroes got in line. I was already working for the sheriff some then, but I never went after those men that did it. Those rabble rousers did me a favor, keeping my hands out of it, so when Doll came and told about it, I sort of already knew what happened and where we might find him.

The bummers that stayed around here didn't last long. I

shot the ones myself that stayed around sniffing after Julia and Margaret Greer, not at the same time although I could have. I was being nice, hoping the ones left alive would just leave. I've regretted that I didn't shoot Julia too. She's caused so much trouble. The funny part is that by the time I decided to shoot those troublesome bastards, I was working for the sheriff. I was the one that went out to investigate the killings. During the War, I usually didn't get to see up close who I killed and how good my marksmanship was. It was good to be able to ride up on that bummer lying there with his eyes open staring up into the sky. Not bragging, but I made quite a shot on that one, right in the middle of his forehead. That Yankee bastard never knew what hit him.

All those people who tried to ram the Reconstruction laws down our throats thought that just because the Yankees beat us in the War, all the men down here would just go meek and mild into living by what the Yankee Congress and the President said, but that wasn't about to happen. It took some years, but it wasn't too awfully long before we took back control of the government, and began to run things the way we wanted. When the General took over as Governor and Chamberlain went back North with the Yankees, we made sure to put things back to normal, or as close as we could get it. Still, there's a heavy price to pay for losing the War, and no matter how hard we've tried, things never have been the same.

# Stash

All I'm doing these days is sitting up here in the jail, twiddling my thumbs, waiting on the hanging, well, my hanging. I've already said it's not a pretty image, and I try not to dwell on it, but it's hard not to. I look back and see how a bunch of little things weaved themselves together over time, and ended up in one big thing that put me in here waiting. From up here, it's pretty easy to see how the one big thing happened, but you and I both know it isn't so easy to see real clear to the end while it's happening. If it was easy to see, a lot of things that go on wouldn't, and a lot of things that don't go on would.

The flow of living, of moving around doing whatever is in front of you day by day just picks you up and carries you to places you wouldn't want to go if you were in control of it, sometimes even if you are. I see it clear from up here how things hooked up like the links in a chain and kept building and building, carrying me along to a day that ended with me killing those two sons of bitches that were out doing dirty work for the Greers.

It's just the way it happened, but don't think that me killing those two slimy bastards broke the chain. The killing let off some steam, but it didn't break the chain, not by a long shot. The chain was stringing itself together long before I was born and it'll still be going long after Big Lee hangs me, for as long as Casons and Greers are walking on the earth. In fact, the killing started some new chains that nobody is smart enough to see the end of. After Big Lee came down to the mill office and pulled me out of there and stopped me from blowing a hole in Tadlock's chest the afternoon of the fire, I listened to what he said about how much my family needed me, and I knew that he was right; they did need me.

Ella talked to me too, and I understand why she wants me to be around for as long as I can be, for her and for Brooks and Janie, and the truth is that I want to be around for a long time. I swear to God I do. Any man that's a real man would want to, don't you think, but none of it mattered once I went face to face with those two bastards again, especially given what they were up to. The part inside me that reasons, that wants to be a gentle family man, just disappeared, like it's bad to do in those situations. The reasoning part of me went to sleep, and another part inside me took over. Sometimes I feel like I'm standing outside myself watching. That's the way it was when I killed those two sons of bitches. People say - well people don't; Ella and Big Lee do - this native blood running through me is the cause of it. I don't really know; I guess so, but it really doesn't matter. Something causes it.

I've heard all the stories about the Lowery Gang up there in Robeson County where Grandpa and Daddy's brothers live, about all the revenge killings they did up there, and how they caused a big stink for a while after the War. Some of the gang were my kin according to Grandpa Harris, and when Henderson Oxendine hung over in Lumberton just a few years ago, over a thousand people turned out to watch it, but some of the others, like old Henry Berry Lowery himself, walked away and blended into the big old world. I bet he's a white man somewhere. It'd be better than dying I bet. Daddy did the same thing in a way, walking away from everything that was going on up there, all the harassment and the violence, blending in when he came down here to turn himself white. It's a temptation for me to do the same thing. I could just walk away and be done; I know I could. I could walk away; go back up there and disappear into being Indian again.

The part of me that just wants to settle in and be a quiet family man with no trouble lost out I guess. The other side won. I couldn't get it out of my head that the two Greers ordered two men to set a fire that ended up killing my Mama and Daddy. It just stayed back in there, way off in the back of my mind, simmering. Even when I was doing other things, even when I was smiling and happy, it was still in there how four people who had a hand in Mama and Daddy being dead, were still walking around living and breathing, doing whatever it was that living was to them, just enjoying it all, thinking there wasn't ever gonna be a price to pay for what they did. I was just simmering along, building up a fire, bent on revenge if it ever presented itself to me, but at the same time, I was willing for God to take care of it. I was willing to leave room for the wrath of God like the preacher said.

I was willing to stay out of the way for Him to send down His wrath on those bastards and that bitch. I must've asked God a thousand times, "What the hell, I'm waiting. I'm leaving room for your wrath, the wrath of God like the Bible says, but it sure looks like you're just gonna let them walk around like they didn't do anything wrong? They killed my people, God dammit!!" I didn't hear anything back from Him. It didn't surprise me. I kind of knew how it would go, and I tried hard to be still, but I couldn't let it go; I couldn't get it out of my head how those leering sons of bitches looked at me in the mill office the day of the fire, and after a while revenge presented itself to me. The temptation or the opportunity, whichever way you want to look at it, came.

In the late winter and early spring after the fire, I started going out into the woods as much as I could. I knew it was time for the sap to start rising and that meant it was time for the Greers and their ilk to be in the woods trying to squeeze every bit of life out of the trees they still had on their side of South Prong Creek. Just like in every other year, I had to be on patrol to make sure they didn't come over on our side to poach trees. They always tried. I never expected to find what I did, or for things to happen to end with me being in here waiting to hang.

Carrying my Winchester and sharp cane knife at my side just like normal, I worked my way up our ridge heading in the general direction of the Mothers, and all along the creek that runs between our land and the Greers, there were signs of them poaching for resin. So many trees stood with the bark stripped completely around the trunk that I lost count. All these trees would die, and I knew the Greers would be in here next winter trying to buy the timber. Killing our trees, trees that we all worked hard to plant and protect, infuriated me. To me, for the Greers to send people over to poach on our land, to kill trees, to lay waste to work that stretched back through all the generations of Casons who lived here trying to build something up that would endure past them was worse than if they had gone to the cemetery and pissed on all the Cason graves there. Even if I wasn't stuck up here in the jail waiting to die, even if none of this had happened, I would let our trees rot into the ground before I would sell anything of ours to a Greer.

I was relieved to see the Mothers still standing, towering above everything else around them. Then I saw a thin plume of smoke rising out of the Mothers' amphitheater, so I went into a silent stalking gait, eased through the understory to the edge of the amphitheater, and looked over. Down next to the creek a man stood dipping water into a shallow pan, washing himself. A discreet fire burned next to a crude lean-to made from saplings covered with pine boughs. The man wore a pair of overalls with no shirt, the galluses hanging loose front and back, and he struggled to hold them up and carry the pan filled with water back to the fire. As he turned to walk back to the lean-to, I recognized him as one of the turpentiners who started the fire that killed Mama and Daddy, one of those arrogant, leering sons of bitches who were in the mill office when I poked the Winchester's barrel into Tadlock's chest.

Then I noticed the Mothers stripped of their bark, starting about two feet above the ground, and going up as far as a man can reach, with eight or ten pails attached around their trunks gathering resin. My heart sank. The Mothers were dying, not dead yet, but irreversibly dying, hundreds of years of standing over the forest spilling out onto the ground and into pails for insignificant men to haul away and turn into money. I felt a white-hot, calming flame of certainty. I would kill the son of a bitch.

I looked down the sights of the Winchester, following him while he walked towards the lean-to. He held up his overalls with one hand and carried the pan of water in the other. I began to squeeze the trigger, and waited for him to stop. He called out, "Theo, bring that whore out here."

Another man came out from the lean-to dragging a completely naked woman by the arm. She struggled a little bit and fell, and the man dragged her across the ground. It was the other turpentiner from the mill office, the other one who lit the fire that killed Mama and Daddy. He wore an unbuttoned shirt, no pants and a pair of brogans. He dragged the woman close to the other man and rolled her over on her back. "Wash her off, Charlie, she needs it. I just got done with her again."

The woman said, "You ain't done much."

The first man dashed the pan of water on the woman's stomach, and she rose to sit, looking venomously at the two men. It was Nell.

"You pin-dicks ought to turn me loose. You've had your fun. I swear to God, I'll just leave. I won't talk. Nobody around this hell hole will ever see me again. I won't tell it was you who went back and killed George. I won't tell. I'll just leave."

The men started laughing and jerked her up; stretching her on her stomach across one of the resin barrels, and Charlie tied her hands to a sapling in front. Theo let his overalls fall around his ankles and started hunching against Nell's backside. I shot him right then and he fell to the ground. I scrambled down the bank and intercepted Charlie before he could reach the lean-to. I held the rifle on him, and pulled the cane knife.

He was a pitiful sight standing there in his brogans with his tattered shirt open and his privates hanging limp in display. I said, "You're a dead man, you bastard."

He dropped to his knees, pleading, "No mister, no, plea…," but in mid-sentence, I swung the cane knife parallel to the ground, slicing through his neck and spine as easy as if it was a noxious weed. His head rolled off in front at my feet. His body stayed upright at first like he didn't need his head, his hands twitching, clutching together in a futile prayer pose. Blood surged from his neck stump while his hands began to relax, dropping down to his waist, and he toppled forward at my feet, his blood pooling in the pine needles like the Mothers' sap.

I walked over to Nell, cut the cords tying her hands, and she stood, turning to Theo lying on the ground. When he moaned, still alive, she kicked him again and again. Theo raised himself and cried out when he saw the head of his partner lying close, the open eyes staring blankly at him. Nell ran, stumbling into the creek and reaching down, gathered handfuls of sand, and scrubbed violently up between her legs and over her stomach and breasts. She began sobbing violently, scrubbing herself over and over with handfuls of sand, pulling herself open and scrubbing, trying desperately to clean herself. I called to her, "Nell, Nell, stop Nell."

Theo rolled over on his back and lay moaning, reaching

up to me, pleadingly, "Help me. I'm shot." Suddenly I saw the image of Mama reaching out of her laudanum haze crying out to her own mother long dead, "Mama, Mama, help me. Come get me," and I remembered the man lying at my feet, pleading for help was one who set the fire that killed Mama. I swung the cane knife violently into his face from the top of his head downward, and it splayed open like a ripe melon, not human. I had my revenge, and it felt good.

A shot rang out, and I saw Nell pitch forward into the water and spin downstream in the current. I heard the buzz and the report of a second shot intended for me. Instinctively, I fell to the ground and rolled behind one of the Mothers. I saw Tadlock and Julia at the top of the bluff across the creek, Tadlock holding a rifle trying to get another shot off at me. I shot twice at them before they disappeared. So I had my revenge, and this is what I will hang for. I killed two men who deserved to die, and left two witnesses. I should've killed four.

# Ella

Attached to the sill outside the kitchen window in front of the sink is an old plank cut to the same width as the window that John Brooks put up for me to feed birds on. The birds give me something nice to watch while I'm fixing meals or washing the dishes afterwards. The cardinals, purple finches and other birds are wary, and will seldom come to the feeder if I'm there at the sink doing whatever. I have to stand back or sit at the kitchen table with a cup of coffee or something to see those birds up close, and sometimes I do, just to see them, just to get close to them, but the wrens are different, and they're my favorite anyway. They come up close and don't mind whether someone is at the window or not.

Miss Maggie said the wrens were the most innocent of all the birds, like trusting little children she said. Miss Maggie believed that the wrens sometimes need a little help with their nests, hanging free like they do on some little twig that you would think is too thin to hold up a mosquito much less a neatly woven little nest full of baby wrens and their mama. So in the late winter, Miss Maggie always put out little scraps of thread and squares of leftover cloth just so the wrens would have something strong to weave into their nests. She said it always made her feel like she was helping God out with some of His best work, and she liked to see the colors woven into the nest along with the plain brown blades of grass and twigs.

One day last week it was still blustery cold, the wind coming out of the northwest, but somehow there was a hint of the winter breaking in the air, some tiny indefinable change that a person needs to slow down to feel, and when I felt it, I remembered Miss Maggie and her leavings for the wrens. Later that day I gathered up a few scraps of cloth and bits of thread leftover from a little dress I made for Janie and put them out on the feeder with some crusts of leftover biscuits. That northwest wind kept blowing for another day or two, but this morning, the wind switched around to the southwest and the sun came out. I was at the kitchen sink peeling some of the last potatoes we had from last year's garden, thinking about what I wanted to put with them for dinner when a Carolina wren lit on the feeder, pulled a thread out of the cloth and took it. In just a minute, the wren was back taking another and another and then another.

The next time the wren came it pecked a little bit at the biscuit crusts and then hopped up to the window. It turned its head to one side and looked right into my eyes for a few seconds, chittered a little wren song, and then it was gone. I started crying; for no reason at all I started crying, thinking about that wren looking into my eyes, flying off and leaving, and then I remembered Mama and Daddy and Paul, and Miss Maggie and Papa Jacob, and John Brooks, and what might happen to me and the children when John Brooks is gone. All of it flooded in and a deep sadness took me, and I just started crying, and I couldn't stop for a long while.

The hanging isn't but three days off. Time is running out for us. The winter was long, with John Brooks up in the jail, and nobody out here but us, and Big Lee, when he could be out here, and Tally every once in a while, making a reason to be out this way, making an excuse to deliver some little message from John Brooks, and taking him back some little scrap of leftover food, or a little trinket Brooks made for him, "so daddy won't forget me" he says.

This place used to be alive, what with Papa Jacob and Miss Maggie up at the big house, and me and John Brooks and the children down here, and all the going back and forth between the houses, and all the talk, and the good meals together, with the men out, doing all the big work around the farm and us, the women, taking care of the kitchen garden, and the chickens, and the other small stock, and the children too. Sometimes we worked together, all of us including Big Lee and the close neighbors, like on a hog killing day after the frost was coming steady, or planting the big garden in the spring. Those were good days. This whole place was alive.

Now it's a barely living place; it's a lonely place. Nothing is left of the big house but a few timbers lying on the ground charred black by the fire, a chimney rising out of the ruin, all that's left of the house, a cold chimney standing there mutely reminding us, marking a place and a time when the days felt like hope. It will be there until it comes down on its own, and it will come down; everything does. It's a sad place too, maybe too much for a lonely widow with two little ones to raise, and I can't see a way that it can ever be anything but a sad, empty place especially after John Brooks hangs, and we bury him up there with his family. I won't need to visit his marker to remember him and all we have been and all we could've been. I won't need to see the name and the dates that I know so well. This farm, that old chimney standing there, mine and John Brooks' empty bed, little Brooks' eyes, and Janie's questions will be enough. I will remember it all, the way it was, the way it will never be again.

The burden of it all could become too much. It's happened before, where a tired woman, or a man too, just wears out from all that life brings and just plain breaks down. It could happen. The days are getting longer, the crocus blooms past, the redbuds beginning to swell, but the nights are brutally long, silent, and still. It will always be this way with John Brooks gone, no hand to calm me, no warm embrace to ease me, to hope, to believe, and sometimes to help me forget other hard times. It will be this way when Tad-lock's crude courting comes, thinking he can wear me down, thinking he can have what he wants, thinking he can take me.

No one leads an easy life it seems. I used to believe I could get to an easier life, but we all come down to hard times in the end. Some people seem to be charmed for a while, a season in the sun, where everything seems to work. I've seen people like that, but more people are like me, carrying some curse around all the time, not knowing the why of it, not knowing where it came from, or even if the curse is God's punishment or just some random piece of living. I've heard preachers say that the sins of the father visit on the son, so I wonder sometimes if this is something I brought on myself, or if it was something my Mama or my Daddy did to make this life so hard for me. I feel the weight of it bearing down on me. It eased some when me and John Brooks were together and I fooled myself into believing that we were building a life and a future, but the curse intervened like it always does. John Brooks took the bait and betrayed himself and us too when he killed those two men. I have to quit thinking this way. I have to quit for Brooks and for Janie; never mind me. I have to get my mind on something else, something alive and hopeful.

I saw the first daffodils this morning up against the south side of the brick well housing, their heads up out of the ground, their blooms just breaking open. The sun warms the bricks, and John Brooks says his Mama planted them there because the bricks soak up the heat and warms the ground around the bulbs. They're always the first ones in the neighborhood to bloom. Most years, there's someone close around who's sick, sometimes even close to dying, and Miss Maggie always made it a point to pick some of those flowers and take them to whoever it was. She always said that seeing the flowers might give them some hope, and even if they were past hope, the flowers might be a sweet goodbye reminder of the beauty that just being alive gives us. One more flower might be all they have time for and one more flower might be enough to make them smile and remember all the good they've had in their life. I decided to pick some and take them up to the jail and visit a little while with John Brooks.

There were only four daffodils open, but that was enough. All I needed was an excuse really, just a little nudge I guess to have a reason to go up to the jail to see John Brooks. I picked those four and held them blooms down, so their sap wouldn't run all out while I was carrying them, and went in the house and wrapped the stems in a damp dish cloth so they would survive the ride. I gathered up the children and told them we had to go somewhere. I didn't tell them where since I knew they would be so wild I wouldn't be able to hitch Sockeye up to the wagon and get everything I needed ready to go if I told them we were going to see their daddy.

I got Sockeye hitched and them into the wagon and holding those flowers as best as I could, headed out down the hill to get on Scotch Road. When we passed the mill, Tadlock saw us and it wasn't but a minute or two until he caught up with us and rode along for a while trying to make conversation, with me ignoring him as much as I could, but him being real persistent even in front of the children, trying to talk to me like John Brooks was already long gone.

I just kept my eyes looking straight ahead and tried not to talk to him except to tell him to leave us alone, but he dug in his coat pocket and got some stick candy out and handed it over to Brooks and Janie and they didn't know any better than to like it and say they liked him, that he was a nice man to give them that candy. After a couple of miles I gave him a real cold stare, and he finally gave up and told Brooks and Janie that he would see them again real soon. He winked at me telling me he would see me too, that things were going to get better for me real soon. Something must be broke in his head to think that.

I pulled up to the jail yard gate, and I had to go around to the front door to get somebody to let us in. Tally went out back and opened the gate, and when we drove in, the gallows were standing right there and seeing it caught me off guard. My heart jumped up in my throat and I thought I might faint. I knew it would be there, but it didn't even cross my mind when I thought about seeing John Brooks. Seeing it right in front of me and thinking that John Brooks would die right there hit me right in the pit of my stomach and almost made me sick. Before I realized what he was doing, Brooks jumped down from the wagon and went running up the steps to the platform like it was some new toy. He was having a big time on top until I snatched him off there like he'd done something wrong. I felt bad about it for a minute since he really doesn't know what the gallows are for and what all this means for us.

John Brooks was back in his cell. Tally hadn't told him we were there, and Brooks and Janie busted in there and jumped on him when he rose up off the bed. It isn't like John Brooks to be lying around during the day like that, and I thought he must be feeling down to be lying there like that. What else would he be with what he's facing, but still, it tickled him to see us and he perked up real quick. We stayed for a while just talking, him playing with Brooks and Janie.

I put the daffodils in a glass that was sitting on a little side table there, and John Brooks looked at me, and said, "Those are Mama's early ones from out by the well aren't they?" I nodded yes, and the way he looked at me, I knew he understood what those little flowers meant. Then Tally came to the door and asked Brooks and Janie if they wanted to go up the street to the Q & Q and get a piece of candy. They were out of there in a second, and Tally just smiled and said they wouldn't be back for at least twenty or thirty minutes, and I knew what that meant, and so did John Brooks.

I was by the cell door and John Brooks was sitting on the bed. I closed the door. In the half-light I walked across to the bed. John Brooks gathered me in and pulled me down with him across the bed. We kissed, and I felt the distance and the time apart fade. I pulled his shirt open and buried my face against his neck pushing down on him hard, opening my mouth to taste him. I can't really describe it; I don't guess anyone can, but it has always been the way John Brooks smells, the way his skin feels against mine, the way his hands make me feel like a simple woman, all those things and so much more that make him the one.

Laughing softly, he held me and pulled my dress up over my thighs and used it around my waist like a cord to pull me tight against him. I pulled away from him and stood, letting my dress fall to the floor, sliding out of my underclothes while he watched me, smiling. He slid out of his pants and lay back, waiting on me, and I climbed back in the bed on top of him, and then he rolled me off beside him, on my back, and he spread my legs apart and was the man I love to love.

When we were done, I lay quiet for a few minutes and we just touched, both of us realizing that we may have been together for the last time. The euphoria of being with him faded into a deep sadness that saw into the end of us. I said to him, "John Brooks, I love you. I will miss you forever," and he said, "I love you too. I'm sorry. I don't want to leave," and I said, "I know."

"I don't mean die. I don't mean hang. I mean leave, run away. I can't leave."

"John Brooks, if you can, you have to. I can live apart, knowing you're alive. I can't live with knowing you're dead."

"I can't leave you and the children. I would rather be dead than to be without you."

"There's always hope in staying alive."

All the way home, I hoped and prayed that John Brooks would leave, that he would stay alive, but at the same time I hoped and prayed that even if he died, he would be alive again inside me. I told God that he owed it to me. It was the first time I prayed in a long time if you can call it a prayer. It's selfish I know, to think that way, to want something just for myself, to be that bold to God to just say right out what you want, but it's what I did, and I don't care. I hope we made another life.

# Big Lee

I took the train out of Cheraw down to Columbia to see
the Governor, hoping to convince him to commute
Stash's sentence to a term in prison, even a life sentence.
Hugh Calder, Judge McIver, and Aiken White went with me.
Tally stayed to keep an eye on things around the jail. We
hoped to convince Governor Ellerbe that the men Stash
killed were just trash, the kind of men that drifted around
causing trouble and even though we couldn't use the law to
get rid of them, all the devilment they caused were reasons
enough for them to die. We hoped he would understand.

After the War, we had to do hard things like what Stash
did pretty often to get things settled down again, but the
Governor is one of these new generation politicians who
don't put much stock in what we did after the War to
straighten things out. He seems to be too good, too clean to
soil his hands with the kinds of things it takes sometimes to
get things right; he's too civilized, thinking that reasonable
talk is always enough. It's not, and there's over a half million
dead soldiers resting in the cold dirt that would testify to the
truth of it.

General Hampton met us at the train station and went
with us, or Ellerbe probably wouldn't have given us an audi-
ence at all. We presented our arguments to him; about the
evil mischief those two dead men did in our community, and
who they were working for. We told him how Stash just did
what the law couldn't do getting rid of that scum. After we
pleaded our case to him, the best he offered was to take
Stash into state custody and do the hanging over at the

penitentiary, like that was what we were after, to shirk our responsibility for the hanging. He doesn't know, and probably doesn't care, that every men standing in front of him stood up under responsibility that he can't even imagine.

All five of the men standing in front of Governor Ellerbe went off and did what was asked during the War, came back home and tried live the right way, making families, doing what responsible men do, and the Governor didn't give us any more consideration that he would've given to five drunks. What we all did to make it possible for him to be sitting where he was didn't make a particle of difference to Ellerbe. In the most condescending tone I've ever heard, he said, "You men have been around. You know how it is. It's an election year and I can't take a chance on starting some trouble for myself less than a year before the election."

The General might be getting older, but he hasn't lost his fiery ways. I think he took the Governor's condescension as a personal insult. He lit into the governor telling him, "You arrogant boy, these men have earned more consideration from you than you just wanting to protect yourself. These are men, by God, good men! You don't even have opposition this election because good men like these, on my word, and your promises by God, turned the vote out for you last time! Is this is how you repay men who stood up on your behalf, you opportunistic ass?"

Ellerbe's face turned red. He stood up and slammed his fist on the top of his desk and started to say something, but right then a coughing fit seized him like the exertion was too much, and a couple of aides ran in to him, and one, another arrogant young boy, told us the governor was done with the meeting, and they took him out to nurse him I guess. I wondered if the coughing fit was just a ruse to get us out, but after we left, the General said, "To hell with him. He will be dead inside three years. I've heard that death rattle before. He's got consumption eating away at him."

I said, "That won't do us much good General. Stash will be dead by then," and he said, "Sheriff, tell that nephew of yours to get the hell out and leave. If he's anything like you are, Leland, he'll be fine. Just tell him to leave."

I said, "I've tried to get him to leave," and the General just shook his head.

"Out west is a big place, Leland. Tell him that, and tell him that a lot of our people are down in Brazil now, doing pretty good I hear. Tell him that, and tell him that anywhere north of six feet under is a pretty good place."

We rode with the General over to Millwood, or what's left of it, after Kilpatrick and his crowd of bummers burned it and everything else the General and his family owned. We dismounted from the carriage and walked with the General past the massive columns, all that is left of the grand house that stood there. He moved past them reverently, pausing to touch each one, looking up the height of them, with all of us a bit in awe, quiet, respectful. We followed him under the deep shade of a live oak gnarled and scarred by the fire. He stopped and leaned against the trunk.

When he turned to us, he said, "When I was a boy, I climbed down this tree from my bedroom, just to ramble, just to see what was going on. There was so much here, so many people, always something interesting to see and do, and when I was away for schooling or travel, I missed it. I was welcome anywhere on this place, in any of the quarters, and I knew most of the people here by name, and they knew me. Now I'm an old man, but I remember the way it was. I couldn't have that much time, but almost everything that was here is all gone, and I still miss it.

I miss it every day. So many memories, so many things lost, so many good times, but there were hard times too. I've buried both of my wives. Five of my children are gone. Some never had a chance. My sisters over there," pointing to a small house near the columns, "had their lives ruined by our uncle. You wouldn't think a governor would do something so evil to young girls, his own nieces. I should've challenged him; I would've killed him, but with me killing the sitting governor, it would've come out what he did, and my sisters' truths would've been out in the open. They would've been marked, and soiled on the outside for everyone else like they have been on the inside to themselves."

Judge McIver said, "We know what, how much you've sacrificed General."

The General continued. "I'm not looking for sympathy. I'm not telling you all of this for me; I'm telling you this for all of you, especially you Leland. Things change. Time passes. People live and die, but if I had a chance to save one, any one of all those that I loved, I would turn over heaven and earth to do it. If I could help Preston up off that ground, and brush him off, and put my arm around him, and walk away, instead of leaving him dead on that field in Virginia, I would give up everything, everything that I had before and after the War. I'd do it for another day, another hour with him and any of the others. I would."

I said, "I know General. I've lost a lot too, a lot of people. I understand," and I put my hand on his shoulder.

The General looked at me and said, "Leland, you do whatever it is that you have to do to save that nephew of yours, and you men help him. Don't lose anything else. That's not advice, men; that's an order, the last one I'll ever give you."

He told his stableman to drive us to the station. He said he just wanted to stay for a while to sit and talk with his sisters, and he walked away after wishing us well, telling me to send him a wire to let him know how it all turns out. He said, "I'll do what I can on this end to help out but I'm afraid it won't be much. Time changed things too much. People forgot what we did."

We caught the train back to the Cheraw station not talking much at all on the way home, just thinking I guess. The others were waiting for some direction, some plan from me, and even though I would've liked to give one, I just couldn't see the way. I just couldn't see a way to show how it was that I, or we, might save Stash. I couldn't see a way that we could do anything other than to hang him, give him up to the governor to hang, or convince him to leave, but with my next thought, I knew I couldn't convince him to leave. He would never leave Ella or the children either. He will never leave, and god dammit, I can't let anyone else hang him.

# Julia

A few years ago Tadlock ran up on a woman named Nell in some tavern down the country a little ways, and brought her up here. He tried to tell me she won't no whore, but I've been around it long enough to know one when I see one. She must've had some real magic with what was between her legs - I've seen it happen before - because even though Tadlock had some experience with some real good whores right here, women that I'd seen do their work out at the brothel, Nell put something special on him and took him, hook, line, and sinker. I told him nothing good would come from it, that he ought to find some regular girl if he wanted something to come home to. I told him he could do that and still tomcat around on the outside with whatever was out at the brothel, that he was welcome to any of them out there, but he had to have Nell. I got to admit that she was a fine looking woman; she stirred something in me too when she was around.

Before long, Nell was carrying Tadlock's baby and she gave him a son, and me a grandson. I softened a little bit to her after that. You know how a baby does that, and when that little pissant got up to running around and getting into everything, I thought maybe Tadlock hadn't done so bad after all. Nell was a looker, but she had a wild side in her too. Hearing them two go at it was something, It really was, but something went bad between them and they started fighting like men every once in a while. One time Tadlock got the upper hand and beat her down pretty bad. She laid up for almost a week, billing and cooing with Tadlock, and him waiting on her hand and foot trying to make up to her, but when she got up, she took off, left Tadlock and her boy too. I was glad about that, glad that she left the little pissant with us.

It wasn't long until we heard that she took up with George Cason out at his little store, and at first I couldn't believe it. I figured she would use that magic between her legs to get ahold of someone better than George Cason, even though I did hear one time that George had a tally-whacker that ought to be hanging under one of them stud ponies that people use to get the mare ready for the real stud. Maybe that was all it took for her, but whatever it was, that's where she ended up. It about drove Tadlock crazy thinking about her out there with George, and then when he heard about her sharing some of that magic between her legs with some of the men that loitered there sniffing around like they was after a dog in heat, it really did drive him crazy. He swore that he'd get George and her both, and he did, well, we did.

We put some of the hired men out to get George and Nell. It was easy once we had them set out in the woods do-ing their turpentining work. They could slip around with no one paying them much attention. The two that set the fire that killed Maggie and Jacob wanted the job of getting George and Nell, and I told them to go ahead with it. I told them if they got the job done on George and Nell, I might let them go after Stash. They really liked the idea of it. They didn't cotton much to Stash coming down to the mill office and being so bold to stick that gun barrel in Tadlock's chest and them having to back down and all. When I told them I wanted to kill off them special trees the Casons treat like they was planted special by God's own hand, they jumped all over the chance to get at Stash. Those two were good, just exactly what we needed to do the real hard jobs.

They made a camp right at the base of those two big old

pine trees the Casons worship and did all their dirty work from there. I don't never want the details, so I don't really know all that went on, but George Cason ended up dead pretty quick, and I told Tadlock that we needed to go out there and check on them men and tell them what good work they was doing. When me and Tadlock rode out to check on them, we heard one shot and when we got to the bluff overlooking them trees, we saw Stash had beat us out there.

He was the calmest killer I ever seen; I got to give him credit for that. He ran down that bank, catching one of them before he could get to his gun, and rolled that one's head off like it won't nothing. I've seen killing, and I've killed, but Stash rolling that man's head off was something else, and I kind of hollered a little bit just from the surprise of it. Then he turned Nell loose and watched her kick on the other man a little bit before she run off into the creek. That other poor bastard was reaching up at Stash for some mercy I reckon, but there won't none to be found there. Stash sliced down through that man's head like you would split a hog open, just as calm as if he'd done it a thousand times.

Later, I told Tadlock, "You need to go up there and get Stash to show you how to sharpen a knife. That was one sharp knife he used. Did you see how it sliced through them men?"

He said, "Shut up Mamaju. Stash ain't anything."

Anyway, about that time, Tadlock shot. It scared me to death since I'd been watching Stash kill them men and didn't see Tadlock pulling his rifle out. I about jumped out of my skin, and I saw Nell spinning off down the creek with red spreading out around her. I said, "God damn Tad..." and about then another shot rang out and a bullet whizzed by us. That son of a bitch Stash wasn't wasting no time, and we didn't waste none neither getting out of there. That son of a bitch Stash had done gone crazy and was on a killing spree that I didn't want myself included in.

Naturally, we had to be good citizens and tell about what it was that Stash did out there, and even though Leland tried every trick in the book to get him off, ain't none of it worked. So, it's a good time, maybe one of the best times in my life. In just a few days, Stash will hang for killing them two men. We tried to lay it off on him that he killed George and Nell too, but nobody ever found Nell's body, and Judge McIver who's an asshole buddy with Leland threw it out of court.

I got to thinking a little while back, and it came to me that Stash might just take off, or Leland might try to slip him out of there and take him off somewhere. I sent one of my regular men up to Barentine's store right up beside the jail to get a job. He told Daniel Barentine that me and him had a falling out and that he needed work. He got a job there, but what he's really doing is watching that jail for some of Leland and Stash's shenanigans. He says Stash comes over to the store most days, just rambling around like he owns the jail or something. That pisses me off.

When my man gets off work at the store, some other of my men stand guard at the jail overnight to make sure Stash don't run. I want to see that son of a bitch hang. We ain't had one around here in too long. I want to see that son of a bitch twitching and jerking at the end of that rope, but it he tries to run, some of mine will just shoot him. It won't be as much fun, but at least he'll be dead and out of the way, and Leland will be just about the last one in the way of taking everything they got and ridding the country of the Casons forever.

# Stash

The idea of leaving started a couple of days ago when Big Lee came in after they went down to Columbia. The governor told them he wouldn't help me, well that he wouldn't help them. Big Lee said the governor was a sorry excuse for any kind of man much less a man trying to be the governor. He told me I should to leave, that leaving is what he would do. He told me what General Hampton said about going out west or down to Brazil where some of our people went after the War. Brazil is too far for me. I can't even think about going so far away that I couldn't get back if I needed to, but going west is something I can maybe do, but I can't go too far. I'll come back for Ella, and then I'll go far.

In the end, Ella and Big Lee convinced me to leave. They said maybe she and the children could come to me after people forget for a while. It's hard to think about leaving what's always been home, but it comes down to one simple thing. I'm not ready to die. It's even harder to think about leaving Ella, and Brooks and Janie. I hope they get along good without me, and I know they will as long as Big Lee is around, and Tally too. I will send for them when I settle, wherever that might be. I don't know yet, don't have any idea. I'm just going wherever it is.

I talked with Tally and Big Lee for a while to pass the time, waiting for dark. I packed a few things to carry, not much, just a change of clothes, a broken arrowhead that Brooks sent up here to me, some cold biscuits, and a little money that Big Lee gave me to buy some things on the road. I went out to the stable. Tally closed up the gate a couple of days ago to keep the sightseers from congregating to watch them building the gallows, so it wasn't a problem with anyone seeing me packing things up and getting one of the horses ready to go.

Tally helped me some and Big Lee just watched us, talking a little bit like nothing special was going on, and then when it was good dark, he told Tally to go out to make sure no one was outside. He said I shouldn't go until Tally checked. Big Lee said he would ride a ways with me just to get me out of town, so I saddled up another horse for him and waited. He said the Greers weren't stupid enough to think he wouldn't have some kind of plan in place for me to dodge the hanging, and that I might need his protection for a little ways. Tally walked over to what looked like a solid section of the fence and slid one of the planks out to one side and real quiet, slipped between the planks like he'd done the same thing a thousand times and was gone.

We waited for a long time, almost to ten o'clock and he didn't come back, so I went back in the jail and went up to the living quarters upstairs. I found one of Tally's coats and a weathered old stockman's hat that Tally wore around town sometimes. I hoped anyone that saw me leaving would think I was Tally riding with Big Lee on some little errand. When I went back out, I paused to look around the jail yard, just taking it in to remember it all. It would be the last time I would be there, the last time I would ever be in Scots Bend. Big Lee was nowhere around.

The gallows was nearly complete. I walked under it, and stood looking up through the trap door that would drop under me if I stayed. The stars were bright in the deep night sky. They were all so familiar; I had used them my whole life to find my way home. They would be different far away from home. There would be so much to learn, and so much to forget. I climbed the steps to the platform, and looked out over the top of the plank fence.

Across the road, under one of the big oaks there, I saw the figures of three men. I dropped to one knee and watched them approach the gate. I recognized the gait of Tally and of Big Lee, but not the third man. Tally opened the gate. Big Lee pushed the other man inside and said, "It's one of Julia's men. He says they sent him up here just to keep a lookout, but he's probably up here to do more than that."

The man said, "I ain't up here to shoot you," looking at me. "I could've done that a month ago, and every day since. Tadlock said I better not shoot you. They want to see you hang. I ain't ever seen anybody want somebody dead as bad as them wanting you to hang. They hate your damn guts, both of ya'll too," talking to Big Lee and Tally.

We took the man inside and put him in one of the cells. He said, "I ain't got no stake in this. I ain't from around here. I don't give a shit about you people. You give me more money than they did, and I'll be gone, and you won't have to worry about seeing me no more. In fact, you don't even have to give me money. You let me out of here, and I'll be gone. I ain't got no stake in this."

Big Lee just looked at him. "Just shut up. You're not really in a position to bargain. You're lucky Tally didn't just slit your throat and leave you laying there. You're not going anywhere for a few days."

The three of us went back out to the stable. Tally went back out between the planks to make sure the man he found was the only one out there while me and Big Lee readied the horses. When Tally came back in and gave the all clear, we rode out together, the way Big Lee and Tally had a thousand times, and anyone watching from the dark would've thought we were Big Lee and Tally. We rode west about a mile out of Scots Bend and Big Lee stopped. "This is it for me Stash. You should make some miles before daybreak. Travel by night for at least a week, just to make sure you get far enough away."

"I will Uncle Lee." It was the first time since I was a boy that I had called him Uncle. He was Big Lee to me just like he was to everyone else, but it just seemed like the right thing to say, the right way to say goodbye to family. "Take care of Ella and my babies, Uncle Lee."

"You know I will, son. Don't worry about them. Be safe. Wait a long time before you get in touch," and he turned back to Scots Bend at a full gallop.

The quarter moon turned up like a shallow saucer sliced through the black night sky. I looked into it and breathed deep. I thought the word "freedom." It felt good to think it. I said it out loud to get the feel of it, "freedom." There would be no hanging, no dying, no pain, no feeling like the Greers won. I was free to be alive, free to breathe, free to think about tomorrow and the next day and the next, and then suddenly, I thought about Ella, and then the children, and then Ella again and again, and I knew I couldn't leave without seeing her, without seeing all of them one last time. I couldn't let her wonder. I couldn't let Big Lee be the one to tell her I was gone. I had to see her, to tell her why, to reassure her that I would come back for her, that I would never leave her for good, so I rode back into Scots Bend, and took Scotch Road south towards Greer's Mill and the Cason farm.

It was a bit after midnight I guessed. I rode past the church and the cemetery. I thought about the people who lay there, people that I knew, my family, my friends, and my enemies too, that they all came down to the same thing. I wondered what it meant that all the struggle, all the living and breathing, all the work and the play, all the days good and bad, ended with loved ones standing powerless at the grave, waiting to cover someone with cold dirt. Nothing else mattered; it always ended there.

In the pale moonlight the stones stood witnessing their memory. The Cason obelisk stood tall over the others inside the iron fence. Then I noticed an odd thing, a pale light glowing just to the right of the obelisk where I knew Aunt Mae and Little Lee lay. Curious, I rode into the church yard, tied the horse just off the road and walked quietly with my rifle across the yard and into the cemetery. I moved between the stones, and began to hear the sound of digging, and as unbelievable as it seemed, I realized that someone was robbing one of the graves.

The digging sounds covered my footfalls, and I stepped over the iron fence into the Cason family plot. Dirt lay piled on both sides of Little Lee's grave, and as I approached, a shovel blade filled with dirt rose from the grave and emptied onto the pile. I pointed my rifle into the grave and looked over the edge. In the light of a kerosene railroad lantern, a man stood on the casket lid trying to break into it with the shovel. I reached down with the rifle and poked the man in the back. He wheeled around. It was Drip Greer.

When he recognized me, he started his idiot talk, jabbering, pointing, and jumping on the casket lid, hitting it with the shovel blade. I'll say right out that it stunned me for a minute and I just stood there. Then I hollered at him to stop, but he just kept up his idiot talk trying to tell me something, trying hard to talk. I screamed at him to get up, to come up out of that grave, to stop bothering Little Lee. Instead of coming out, he fell down on his knees and started digging with his hands, breaking through the decaying lid, and in a minute he stood up with the skull, threw it up to me, and without thinking, I caught it. Drip scrambled out of the hole, jabbering away at me.

I was in shock, standing there with my cousin and best friend's skull in my hands. When Drip picked up an awl pike that was lying in the dirt and started jabbing at the skull, I thought he was trying to stab me with the pike, so I dropped Little Lee's skull on the ground and pointed my rifle at Drip. He dropped the pike and scooped up the skull, turning it over to the back, pointing at something there. There wasn't much left of Little Lee but some of his scalp, nothing really recognizable to me but the color of the hair. Drip pulled a piece of the scalp off the back and pointed to a perfectly round hole about a quarter of an inch in diameter at the base of the skull.

I took it from him and held it down closer to the lantern. It was a small, round, bullet hole I thought. Drip picked up the awl pike and handed it to me. He pointed at the tip, and then to the hole. I didn't understand. None of it made any sense. He put his hand on the awl pike and when I let it go, he gently slid the sharp point of it into the hole. It went in about three inches and stopped. He pulled the awl pike out and slid it back and forth in the hole. I was trying hard to figure out what it meant, trying to make something so unreal make sense.

Why had Drip robbed a grave to show a thing that he knew, but could never tell? All the years Drip tried to talk had come down to this desperate act of his, this grave robbing. All the years of pain for Big Lee, of Aunt Mae's wasting away and dying, and of my pain too, wishing I had been with Little Lee, thinking that if I had been, he would still be here, and finally, right here now, it suddenly made sense. The realization emerged that Little Lee's death was no random accident, no act of God even, and no plan of His beyond human understanding. Instead, his death was simply the bitter fruit of someone's evil act, a murder.

Drip pointed south in the direction of Greer's Mill, and then to the awl pike with one hand and to the skull with the other, and back again towards the Mill. He looked at me quietly, calmly waiting, like he was finally content, patiently waiting for me to understand what he had always known. I thought, trying hard to get it all clear in my head, inserting the tip of the awl pike into Little Lee's skull several times sliding it back and forth, and finally I looked at him. "I understand. It was Julia that did this." He shook his head, no. I slid the awl pike back into Little Lee and said, "Tadlock?" He nodded, yes.

I thought about the hanging I faced. I realized that going back might mean the chance to leave might be gone, that I might die at the end of that rope, but I knew I had to go back, no matter what the cost. I could hang, probably would hang, but I had to go back. Big Lee needed to know what happened to Little Lee. Everyone needed to know. I couldn't leave it to Drip. I looked over at him, "I'm taking this to Big Lee," and he nodded, smiling.

I walked to my horse, and put the skull in one of my bags. Drip walked along with me and when I mounted, he handed the awl pike up to me and I started out north along Scotch Road back to Scots Bend. I heard a strange howling behind me. I looked back. In the middle of the road, under the pale moon, Drip Greer was dancing and howling like a mad man.

# Big Lee

The morning before the hanging Tally was with me in the stable tending the horses. It was just a bit before dawn. The sky was lightening in the east. I was thinking it would be a busy day, maybe even a wild day with all the people coming in for the hanging tomorrow. I was thinking how mad all those people would be when it turned out there wasn't going to be a hanging, but I had to keep it to myself as long as I could to give Stash a good head start. I wouldn't go after him, but Julia and Tadlock and her crowd would go for blood once they knew he was gone.

There's a little trash burner stove out there in the tack room and we had a little fire going with a pot of boiled coffee on top and we'd had one cup apiece, and were beginning to think about cooking some grits and eggs when we heard a horse coming hard up Scotch Road from the south and then someone banging on the gate. I knew it was trouble. You get a sense for that kind of thing when you've been in the middle of trouble as long as I have, but I didn't expect the trouble that came if you can call it trouble. I don't really know what to call it.

What it was, was a mix of good and bad, because it was Stash banging on that gate holding the reins to his horse all rode out like he'd been in a race. He busted in the jail yard like a wild man as soon as I cracked the gate and his horse got a little spooked and nearly bolted when Stash dropped the reins and grabbed a bag off the pommel, and started running into the jail, telling me, "Come on! Hurry up! Come on!"

I said to him, "Slow down you damn fool, what in the hell are you doing back here? God dammit, you're supposed to be 20 miles away from here by now."

He said, "Come on, come on, you won't believe this!"

So I asked him what he had and he ran back to the horse and grabbed an awl pike that was strapped to the saddle, and said, "Come on! Hurry up inside before somebody sees us!"

I said, "Where the hell did you pick that up?" and he said, "You'll see!" and grabbed me by the arm, dragging me inside.

Tally took the horse into the stable and I followed Stash into the jail so I could see what in the hell it was that was so damn important he came back to face a hanging for God's sake. When we got inside, Stash put his bag on the table just outside the jail cells, and propped the pike against the wall. He looked at me and said, "Uncle Leland, you won't believe this. You need to sit down."

When I sat, he stood across from me, and said, "I wish there was an easier way to do this but there isn't," and he reached into the bag, pulled out a skull and set it on the table. I looked at the skull, and then at him, and then looked at the skull again. He was quiet for a minute and just waited, for some response from me I guess. I looked at the skull. I could tell it had been in the ground for a few years; just a few tufts of hair still hung on.

I said, "You dug this up, Stash?"

He said "Not me. It was Drip Greer." He told me that after I left him last night, he decided he couldn't leave without seeing Ella and the children one last time, and when he passed the cemetery on the way, he saw a light and walked up on Drip robbing a grave.

I looked closer at the skull, and I saw the gap, a missing tooth, behind the eye tooth on the right side, and it hit me like a shotgun blast. It was Little Lee. "This is Little Lee," and Stash nodded, yes. Then he turned the skull around and pointed to a hole in the base of Little Lee's skull. My mind was reeling. He took the awl pike and stuck the point of it into the hole. It slid in about two or three inches.

"They killed him."

I understood. It took my breath away. Stash might as well have stuck that awl pike between my eyes. I put my head in my hands and tried to breathe. The idea that somebody stuck that pike into my boy's brain and killed him like he was some animal at slaughter was too much to bear.

Tally had come in while all this was going on, and he said to me, "Leland, you alright?" I couldn't speak. I thought I might die.

So then Stash told the story about how he'd ridden out Scotch Road and saw the glow beside the Cason obelisk and when he walked over there, he found Drip Greer breaking into my boy's casket, and how Drip threw my boy's skull up to him, and how Drip got it across to him that it was Tadlock who stuck that awl pike into my boy's brain and killed him. Stash said, "Drip Greer knows a lot." Tally stood there waiting.

I looked up at Tally and he said, "I'll go kill that son of bitch for you, Mister Leland. You won't have to do a thing. I'll bring you that son of a bitch's head."

Stash said, "I'm going too. I want that bastard."

I told Tally, "No. Bring him. Bring him right here, alive," and then I looked at Stash and said, "You can't go; we can't risk you being out there again. You gotta get up to the quarters upstairs and stay out of the way!" He didn't like it, but he went; for once that stubborn nephew of mine listened.

# Julia

People are in here from all over. The tavern was full last night, and the brothel was busier than I remember it ever being in my whole life. It will be busier tonight, but I ain't worrying about none of this tonight. Stash hangs tomorrow. That's what I'm thinking about. People always come for something like a hanging. I had a man watching the jail last night, just to make sure Leland didn't try to pull some trick to let Stash get away, but I ain't heard nothing from him this morning, and Tadlock didn't come in last night either, but that ain't nothing different than a lot of nights. It's a little worrisome though.

Tadlock tomcats some, and he stays at the brothel with them whores of ours when he's restless like young men get sometimes. He's been keeping a pretty sharp eye on Ella too up at the Cason farm. I told him just to keep an eye out, and don't do nothing stupid. Once Stash is dead and gone, it'll be time then. Ella's a woman just like any other and it won't be long before she gets to looking around, needing what every woman does, and there ain't nobody around here better than my Tadlock.

I'm going in to town today and take me a room at the Carolina Hotel. I don't want to miss nothing that's going on. It ought to be a lot of fun around town tonight. I've done put out the word to all my men that I want them up there to have our back and to watch the hanging. Tadlock's boys, my grands, will be up there too. They ain't never seen a real hanging like this, one that the law does, and I ain't ever seen one either, one that the law does, but it ought to be something worth seeing.

We can talk about it and remember it later on. We'll talk about how we finally pushed them Casons far enough for one of them to go crazy. It might be as good a thing as ever happened around here. The only way it could get better is if I was the one to get to pull the lever on that gallows they done built up there to snap Stash's neck. You might could hear that neck of his snap up that close, and smell that piss and shit running down his legs while he's dancing around on the end of that rope. If I could, I'd give that bastard a short drop that wouldn't snap his neck. That way he'd suffer. A long rope is what they'll use though, one that'll be quick for that bastard.

One time I seen the Klan hang some poor nigger man. Well he won't much more than a boy really, down below Brown Springs that got caught slipping into some man's house down there to get at the man's daughter. I told Daddy when we was riding down there that the man's daughter probably wanted that boy, and he said it didn't matter. That nigger boy ought to have had more sense. It didn't matter what that girl wanted; they was going to hang that nigger and they did. It was a short rope. That's why I'm telling it. Them Klan people used a short rope a lot since it always put on a better show with all the kicking and squirming around the person did. They call it the hangman's jig. It's the last dance a lot of poor sons of bitches ever do. Them Klan people thought it might keep them others cowed down if they saw one of their own dancing around on the end of a rope. Anyway, I hope they use that short rope on Stash, but I ain't that lucky. They won't.

One of the Shaw men that come in the mill a little while ago said the Sheriff caught some man slipping around outside the jail last night, and he heard the man was one of mine who was gonna try to kill Stash. They locked him up, the Shaw man said, to keep him from causing trouble, and he heard that they was looking for more trouble from me and my crowd. They're stupid. I don't need to cause no trouble. Leland's gonna do my dirty work for me. He's gonna hang Stash, one of his own flesh and blood, and it's gonna end up killing him too. What Shaw said explained why my man ain't come back. I'll check on him at the jail when I get up there, and maybe I'll be able to give Stash a sweet good-bye while I'm in there.

I was up early. I gotta say that this hanging thing's got me stirred up. It's that way, ain't it, when something you worked a long time for is about to happen. I hate those Cason sons of bitches and getting to this thing what's about to happen took a lot of tricky planning. I was sitting outside the mill office enjoying the day, drinking a cup of coffee, when Drip came in covered from head to toe with dirt. There ain't no telling what he'd been up to, and there ain't no way for him to say. There ain't no way to keep up with him and I don't even try. I always thought that imbecile woulda been dead by now. Maybe I was just wishing, and I've thought a lot about having some of these men around here have an accident with him, but I promised Daddy that I wouldn't never kill our own blood no matter how much I might want to.

So later on when I got uptown and went to take a room with Lo Welch at the Carolina she won't the nicest person in the world to me. Me and her used to be friends back when we was just girls and she stayed the sweet thing she was back then, and I changed to what I had to be. She told me she won't looking for no trouble and didn't want me bringing any of my crowd to her place. I told her that trouble might find me, but I won't bringing none with me. I got up there about the middle of the afternoon, and she scraped a little food together for me because that's what she does. I guess that's enough. I'm feeling so good about the way things is going, I'll pay her a little extra when I leave. That ought to make her feel good about me again.

I walked down the street to the jail. If you know about Scots Bend you know I had to walk right down through all the businesses. I stopped in the Q & Q Market and bought me a banana and a couple of apples, and ate that banana right off, and put them apples in my pocket. I was feeling so good, I stopped at a lot of them businesses just to talk and have some fun. I don't usually do that, but I was feeling so good, it just came to me to do it.

When I got to the jail, it was Tally Bishop that I talked to first. I told him I was there to get my man out, and he said he didn't have no rights to let him out or take none of the money I held out to him, thinking any nigger would take money. He's an arrogant nigger though, with all his talk about being the only son of some big plantation owner from North Carolina, and thinking he's better than a white person like me, and he wouldn't take my money, and he wouldn't get me my man neither.

Leland was in the back of the jail somewhere, and Tally hollered for him, and in a minute he come out and said I might as well go on ahead and leave, that he won't letting my man out until after the hanging. He was just a plain son of a bitch about it too, telling me I was lucky that it won't me getting ready to hang, and I told him, "Well I ain't the one. It's your boy Stash that's gonna dance in the morning," and he told me to get the hell away from him or he might forget hisself and use me to test that door instead of that bag of dirt that was sitting up there. I wanted to trifle with him some more so I told him again I wanted my man outta that jail and he said to "Get the hell out or I could sit in the cell with him if I wanted him that bad." I figured he might really lock me up and I wanted to see Stash on the end of that rope, so I told him, "Ain't no man ever meant that much to me," and got on outta there, and went back up the street.

When I was leaving, I seen the Judge and Aiken White crossing the street from the courthouse, so I stopped to be sociable with them, just trying to be nice, and told the Judge it was a real good job he done sentencing Stash to hang, and I told Aiken to make sure he put that noose around his neck real good. I said it since I know they work real close with Leland and they would probably go on in the jail and tell Leland what I said. The Judge told me he didn't want no trouble up out of me or any of my men and I told him that I didn't have no chains on any of mine to keep them outta here, and they could do whatever they had a mind to. He said he was holding me to account for what they did, and that if I wanted to go to jail for obstructing justice, just let them act up. I told him, we was the good people and the worst criminal I ever seen was in the jail waiting to hang and why was he trifling with a law abiding citizen like me for. About that time, Hugh Calder came up and all three of them went in the jail. I guess Leland needed someone to hold his hand of pat him on the back.

# Tally

I always knew there was something more to it than just Little Lee drowning. I just knew it. That boy was a piece of work, him and Stash both, and I never for one minute believed there was a forty pound carp made that could drag him off in that water and drown him. At least now we know the truth of it; now we know who did it, and once I get Tadlock up to the jail, we'll get the whole truth. I'll skin that bastard an inch at the time if that's what it takes to get the whole truth out of him.

When Stash showed Big Lee the skull and told what he'd found out, Big Lee said he wanted Tadlock up at the jail, so I took the wagon we had loaded up with the stable manure like I was on a regular errand, and I headed towards Greer's Mill to see if I could get on him there. Big Lee didn't have to tell me to be secret about bringing Tadlock in. I knew why he sent me. I don't have any official title to go out and arrest Tadlock or anything like that, so when he told me to go I knew exactly what he meant for me to do.

Anyway, when I got to the church and looked across at the cemetery, two piles of dirt were still lying beside Little Lee's grave. I stopped there and tied the wagon off, and went into the Cason plot and looked over into the grave. About half of the casket lid was uncovered and broke open. A shovel and a pick were still in the hole, and I reached down and got the shovel, and threw enough dirt back in to cover up enough so that nothing would get in there and bother the rest of Little Lee.

I rode on out to the mill and walked in the mill office. A man was in there that I'd seen around some, one of the Greer's regulars I think, but you never really know. Even those regulars come and go pretty often after Julia uses them up for one reason or another. I told him it was Tadlock I wanted, and he asked what for, and I told him that was between me and Tadlock, and he said he didn't like for a nigger to be coming in there being uppity like that, and I said I was probably as white as he was, and he said that I didn't look like it. I just shrugged my shoulders at him. I didn't have time for it, and he was white trash, that's all, and I already knew Tadlock or Julia wasn't there or they would've been out there by then trifling with me too.

I left there and went on out to the tavern. It was pretty quiet with it being mid-morning, but there were people scattered about all through the woods around campfires and some just laying around on the ground not caring about being clean or having a fire to warm them or anything else either. I guess a lot of them were coming in for the hanging, but there wasn't any sign of Tadlock and nobody in the tavern that would know was doing much talking.

When I walked out, a colored girl that lived uptown before she turned into one of the Greer whores followed me, and played like she was flirting, trying to get me interested, and whispered that Tadlock was back in the brothel with another girl. I remembered her being from a good family, and I said to her, "Doreen, you're better than this out here. Your mama's been sick uptown. You need to get up there and get straight with her before she goes."

"Tell her to wait for me. Tell her I'm coming." She went back inside. She won't ever get away from all this. It's too easy if she can get her head past it.

About half way back to the brothel, I slipped over into the woods so I could come up on it without anyone inside seeing me. It really wasn't much to the brothel, just a one room cabin divided up into four spaces separated by some curtains, just to give a hint of privacy, but it really wasn't much. I took my open razor in one hand and my pistol in the other. I went in and pulled back two curtains on empty spaces before I pulled back one and saw Tadlock. The girl lying with him looked at me kind of scared like and then looked over at Tadlock asleep like she might wake him. Two liquor bottles were sitting on the floor, one on his side and one on hers. His was empty. Hers was nearly full. I put the razor up to my lips to give her the sign to be quiet, and she slipped out of the bed.

I eased up beside Tadlock and watched him for a minute. I thought how peaceful he looked and how that was going to end for him real soon. I leaned down close enough to him that I could feel his stinking breath, and put the barrel of the pistol in his right nostril pushing it up in his nose a little ways. He opened his eyes and they widened in surprise. I told him to stay real quiet and I laid the razor against the side of his neck. "Remember how this felt that day outside the courthouse. I changed my mind. Make me. Give me a reason, you murdering son of a bitch."

I did a little bit more sweet talking to him and then I thought about the empty chamber I always kept under the hammer to keep me from killing somebody in quick temper, so I just pulled the trigger for fun, watched him flinch real hard and heard an odd little sound from down under the sheets and after I smelled what it was, I just stood up laughing at the pitiful bastard, and told him to get up and put some clothes on, that he had to see Big Lee uptown.

He rose up. "I ain't going anywhere with you nigger. You better get your black ass out of here," and he looked over at that girl and said, "Go up to the tavern and get some help!"

I told her, "You don't have to listen to this piece of garbage. He won't be back."

Tadlock softened a little and asked me if he could clean up a little bit and I said, "You're not going to need it." When he pulled his clothes on, I tied him and gagged him. When I walked him out, that colored girl went outside with us too and she walked up to Tadlock and spit in his face and said, "That's for all the nasty things you made me do. You ain't got no hold on me now to make me stay."

She walked with us back up through the woods leading Tadlock's horse, and watched me move some manure until I had a space big enough for Tadlock to lie in. When I got him up in the wagon and tied his feet together, she helped me cover him up with the manure. She took a double handful and looked down at his face, and said, "Bastard!" and dropped the handfuls on his face. She mounted the horse and rode off, headed towards Camden.

It was nearing dusk by the time I got back up to Scots Bend, and the town was full of people coming in for the hanging. A little crowd of about fifteen people were standing outside the plank fence around the jail yard trying to peer inside to get a look at the gallows. Paul Calder, Hugh Calder's boy, was up one of the elms just outside the fence telling the crowd outside that all kinds of things were going on inside, when I knew there wasn't any of it true. That was just like Paul though, always into some mischief. I made sure the manure still covered Tadlock from view and drove into the yard.

I called up to Paul up in that tree. "Paul, you better get your ass out of that tree before you fall. Your mama would be mighty upset and I might not get any more of those apple hand pies I like so much."

"I'm not moving anywhere. Those people paid me fifty cents to watch inside the fence and tell 'em what's happening."

About that time, the sheriff came out and told Paul to get down, and he didn't waste any time listening to him. He looked at me. "You got him?"

"Yeah, he's just one more piece of manure on that wagon. It worked out good."

"Good. We'll wait for good dark to bring him in."

# Stash

A little after dark, Grandpa Harris came in. I'd been waiting on him; he sent a wire saying he would come to be with me when I die. After we exchanged our greetings, he told me that my uncles, Stephen and Isaac, were here too, but they'd walked on up into town to see the crowd, and to see how many of our people were over here to watch. He said they would be back in to see me in a little bit. We talked for a while trying to be normal, like about how the shad were starting to run in the Pee Dee and how the Indians from all over Robeson and Marlboro counties had already set up camps along the river to catch the fish and smoke cure them. They sell some, roe too, but mostly it's just a thing they do for their own since they've been doing it for hundreds of years according to Grandpa.

Grandpa said a lot of their people were over here since I was one of their own. He said they came to make sure things got done right, just like they'd done when they hung Henderson Oxendine over in Lumberton back in 1871. There was a lot of threatening back then too, just like there has been here, that people wouldn't wait for the law, but would take it on theirselves to do the hanging. It wasn't long before Stephen and Isaac came in to see me too, and we were having a regular family reunion. They asked me why I didn't just take off, why I stayed to die, and I told them about leaving and about how I'd thought about Ella and couldn't go and what I'd run up on out at the cemetery, and they asked if that wasn't the same son of a bitch that I thought had a hand in Jacob and Mama dying in the fire and I said he was the same one.

About that time, Big Lee and Tally drug Tadlock through the door. He looked like hell with hay and manure clinging to him and he smelled worse. Now stable manure usually doesn't smell that bad, especially if a man is used to it like all of us were, and I made a comment about the smell, and after they put Tadlock in the cell next to mine, Tally came in and told the story about how he got Tadlock and what that smell was all about, and Grandpa and the others had a damn big laugh over it, but in the next second, we all thought about the things we knew Tadlock was guilty of, and the other things we suspected he'd done, and we all just wanted to cut his damn throat and be done.

He still had a gag in his mouth; otherwise he would've been hollering like a mad man, and that's exactly what he did when me and Big Lee and Tally went in that cell to talk to him, and Big Lee took the gag off. He started hollering for somebody to help him, for his "Mamaju," or anybody else that might be in hearing distance. Big Lee cuffed him hard across the face with his open hand, lifted him off the floor with one hand and pinned him up against the wall squeezing down on his neck, saying, "You killed my boy you worthless son of a bitch! You killed my boy!"

Tadlock started turning purple, and for a few seconds, I thought Big Lee might go on and finish him right there, but then he just dropped him and Tadlock fell to the floor gagging. Tally offered, "Lee, I'll kill the bastard. It won't hurt me one little bit to do it."

Tadlock rose up catching his breath, and rasped out, "You bastards ain't gonna do shit, and you can't prove shit. There ain't a damn thing ya'll can do but let me go."

Big Lee swung around and hit Tadlock with the back of his open hand and sent him sprawling back on the cell floor. Tadlock said, "You're gonna pay for this!" with blood running down his chin, "All you sons of bitches are gonna pay for this!" and Big Lee grabbed him up and told Tally to gag him again, and then he slammed him down in a chair putting the barrel of his pistol right between Tadlock's eyes and told him, "Move you line-bred bastard! Just move so I'll have a reason! Just move!" but Tadlock sat as still as a statue.

Big Lee left the cell and came back in a few seconds with a bag and the awl pike and waved it in front of Tadlock. "You know about this pike, you son of a bitch, how about this? You used this to kill my boy!!" and Tadlock shook his head, no, no, no. Big Lee took Little Lee's skull out of the bag and stuck it against Tadlock's face, screaming, "This is my boy, you murdering bastard, my boy, my boy that you stuck in the brain like he was some pig you wanted to butcher!" and he took the pike and jammed it into the hole in the back of Little Lee's skull. Tadlock's eyes widened. I could see the fear in them, and he shook his head, no, no, no, no, until Big Lee cuffed him again with his open hand like Tadlock wasn't any man at all.

The tears started streaming down Tadlock's face, and I was watching him close, when Big Lee suddenly turned on me, and said, "It was you that let him down! It was you that ought to been with him that day! It was you that weren't there for him, just like your stupid ass isn't gonna to be for us, for your own family, for your damn wife and children! It was you!" and I knew he was right, but all the emotion that he'd held inside all these years shocked me.

Then he turned to Tadlock again, "You spineless piece of shit, you're gonna die! You hear me, you son of a bitch? You're gonna die!" and then he turned to me again. "I ought to put him in the casket with you! I ought to make you lay beside him for eternity! It would serve you right! It would be plain justice for you to have to snuggle up with this for eternity!" and then I saw his eyes soften, his anger spent, and he said, "Get your ass upstairs, and don't let anybody outside see you. Stay away from the windows."

So I left the cell. Grandpa Harris, Stephen, and Isaac were out in the hall, kind of big eyed, but ready for whatever action came. Grandpa said, "We're ready to get you out of here when you're ready to go. We got a lot of men over here, and we just got to give them the word."

I said "No," and he just shook his head, and asked me, "Don't you want to live son?" and I told him that I had to see all this out to the end. He shook his head again and sent Stephen and Isaac out to tell the other men to wait, but to be ready. I realized they had come to take me out whether I wanted to go or not, and the last thing I wanted was a face-off between the two sides of my family. As we were walking down the hall, Tally came out in a hurry, and I heard Big Lee tell him to go get the Judge, Aiken White, and Hugh Calder, so me and Grandpa Harris went on upstairs to wait.

I lay down on the bed upstairs. The events of my last day suddenly weighed down hard on me. Grandpa Harris sat in a straight back chair over by the window watching the people coming and going outside. "It always seems like it's one of us that getting hung, or shot, or beaten to death, but I never thought it would be one of mine."

"I brought it on myself, Grandpa."

"You shoulda got a medal for what you did. Trash is just trash that ought to be got rid of, and that bastard in there is just more plain white trash."

I was thinking about what happened to get in the way of me leaving. It seemed like fate coerced me to ride past the cemetery to come up on Drip and find out all that I found out there. It was destiny for me to come back to tell Big Lee, and to be sitting here knowing the gallows and that rope are waiting for me to walk up there early in the morning. I guess it's true that when it's your time, it's your time and there's not much you can do about it. I don't know whether it's God's plan or not, or just some random happening that we call fate, or destiny, or whatever, in a pitiful attempt to make sense of it. I've spent my life in a one-sided conversation with God trying to find some answers, but finally, at the end of that rope in the morning, I will find my answers, or I won't, and if I don't, it won't matter.

I'm just plain worn out, beat down like they say about people like me sometimes. Grandpa Harris was sitting over by the window real quiet, just watching all the coming and going, the people crowding around outside the fence trying to see inside. He said it was a damn sight how a bad thing like a hanging drew people in like a bunch of blow flies to rotten meat. I said it was, and I reckon I was the meat, and he said that wasn't what he was talking about. He kept watching and in a little bit, he told me that the Judge, Aiken, and Hugh were leaving. I got up and peeked out and saw them standing outside for a minute clustered up talking and then they went their separate ways.

It wasn't but a few minutes when Tally came in and got a change of his clothes out and laid them on the bed. He told me to change into his clothes and give him mine, so I did, and I asked him where he was going with them, and he said Big Lee wanted them, and I said why, and he said Big Lee was coming up to talk to me in a little bit. Grandpa Harris was quiet again for a few minutes, and then he just started laughing and said, "Well I'll be damned. This ought to be good."

# Julia

I didn't sleep much last night. To see anybody hang would stir me up, but to get to see Stash Harris hang is something special. I hate those Cason bastards, all of them. I got up early, and just sat there trying to wait a while, but it got to be too much and I went on out. The street was already full of people milling about waiting for the hanging at eight. My grand-boys ended up with me and all three, the white one that was Tadlock and Nell's and the two mulattoes too, went out with me. It wasn't long before we ran up on some of my men and I asked them if they'd seen Tadlock. I needed to talk to him before the hanging just to make sure we were ready to take care of things if we needed to.

They said they hadn't seen neither hide nor hair of him and it worried me for a little bit, but there was so much going on, I forgot about it. If he'd rather lay-up with one of them whores than to see one of our bitter enemies dance on the end of a rope, I guess that's his choosing. One of the biggest things to happen around here and he ain't nowhere to be found. It just ain't like him to miss a good time, and hanging a Cason is a good time, a real good time. I was thinking about that day when they sentenced Stash to hang and all that went on after it, and I told them grand-boys of mine that I wanted them to be singing that little song they made up the whole time when they brought Stash out and walked him over to the gallows to hang him, and they said they would and then they ran on off to get into some other kind of mess that boys can find.

It was just starting to get light. I had plenty of time

before the hanging to walk around town a little bit and see who all was in here to watch. A lot of people was just standing around waiting. I seen several camps in people's back yards and down along the creek with people milling about fires and such. I went around to a few and I started noticing that a lot of them camps was full of what we call Blues. Its them people that's got nigger and Indian and god only know what else all mixed up in them from over around Scuffletown and across the river all over Marlboro County. I always heard that people like that cluster around when one of theirs is in trouble, and there's a bunch of them in here. That's one of the things that really get under my skin about Stash. He ain't even close to white and he goes around like he's something big and special when he ain't none of it. People just don't pay attention anymore, I guess. So much shit has gone on, and ain't none of it good.

I steered clear of all them Blues. They ain't nothing but trouble, and I kept ambling around till I found a crowd of mine, and they was all laying around getting over drunk and some still drunk, and it pissed me off. They wasn't gonna be much good to me if we had trouble, and with all these damn Blues in here, there's liable to be trouble. I raised hell and got them bastards moving a little bit, at least up enough that they could be standing around and watching that pissant hang when the time came. I stirred up a little mouthful to eat from another little camp of people from out my way, and started making my way on over to the jail so I could be standing up close when they opened up the gate to let people in for the hanging.

My grand-boys was already outside the gate when I got over there, and some other boy was up a tree just outside the fence looking over into the jail yard, and it won't long before he started hollering that the Sheriff and Tally had come out and took a big bag of sand up on the gallows and was getting ready to drop it through the hole, and we heard the door open and we could just see the top of the rope when it tightened up and quivered a little bit with that bag of sand. At least that's what that boy in the tree said. Then he hollered out that the Sheriff was coming over to open the gate and the crowd behind me started pushing and me and my grandboys got smushed up against the gate and when Leland opened it, us and some others that was right at the front just popped through it into the yard, and I almost ran into Leland, and I said to him, "Well Leland, the big day's done got here ain't it. That little prick of yours is done for," and I expected something back from him, and I was ready, but believe it or not, he just smiled at me and walked away, the son of a bitch. I deserved more.

We got up to the front, right up to the gallows. I was gonna be able to see Stash when they stood him up there, and then when he dropped through that hole, I was gonna be able to see him twitching and jerking at the end of that rope under the gallows. It couldn't of got any better, and that's how it was when they brought him out. It was Leland and Judge McIver leading Stash out by each arm. He wasn't really walking on his own, kind of being drug along, like he didn't want to go, and I don't guess he did, but it was kind of funny to watch him, and then the crowd got to hollering and cat-calling, saying things like "Look there! That poor bastard is chicken shit!" and a lot of other things like that.

I almost felt sorry for him for a second, and then I remembered all the shit that's gone on between us, and I got to hollering too, things like, "Hey Stash, it's me, sweet Julia, here to watch your sorry ass dangle!" I just hollered out sweet little nothings like that. I wanted him to know I was here, and I was gonna be here after he's dead and gone. They had a hood over his head, and that disappointed me, that I couldn't see his face, and I hollered out, "Come on Judge, pull that hood off. We ought to be able to see that son of a bitch's face! Snatch that hood off!" and a bunch of other people in the crowd started hollering the same thing, but they didn't pull the hood off, and it really bothered me. I wanted to see that bastard's eyes while he's waiting up there to die.

Behind the three of them, Stash, Leland, and the Judge, was Tally and Aiken. Both of them was carrying shotguns, to keep the crowd off them I guess, and behind them Stash's Grandpa and Hugh Calder. I recognized Stash's Grandpa from him being around after Jacob and Maggie burned up. Ella wasn't nowhere around. They had to lift Stash up when they got him to the steps. He just wouldn't go up and the crowd went wild over that. I got my grand-boys to start that little song of theirs, and they was singing, "Stash! Stash, dancing a jig! Stash! Stash, dancing till he's dead!" over and over again, and in just a minute a whole bunch of people in the crowd was singing along too. You shoulda heard it.

They hauled Stash on up those steps and held him up to put the noose around his neck. He still wanted to just let go, but when he did, and that noose tightened around his neck, he went on and stood up on his own. Me and a bunch of other people was hollering for them to take that hood off, and then I seen that Stash had done pissed hisself, and I started laughing and hollering that "he's so chicken shit that he's done pissed hisself," and a whole bunch of people started laughing and hollering it too. I hollered up to Leland, "Come on Mr. High Sheriff, take that hood off and let that mealy mouthed son of a bitch of yours talk a little bit. He might have some sweet goodbyes to say."

Along then, that boy in the tree started pointing up at the jail and hollering out, "It's Stash! It's Stash! I see him! I see him!" and right when he was saying it, they pulled that handle and Stash dropped through the trap door and started kicking and dancing on the end of the rope, and the crowd just went crazy hollering and pushing about. It must've scared that boy because he fell out of the tree and hit the top of the fence. He landed right on the gallows platform with his arm stuck out at a funny angle, and laid there still as Stash would be in a minute or two. He was knocked out I guess.

Nobody paid him any attention at all for a little bit, like he wasn't even laying there. I was watching Stash dance around too, and I thought that it must be a short rope they put on Stash the way he was kicking and twitching like he was trying to run away from it! It had to be a short rope, and I thought how stupid Leland was not to get it over quick for Stash, for him not to make sure the rope was long enough to snap his neck like a twig, but I liked what was happening. Stash had shit and piss running down his pants legs over his shoes, and it took a good three or four minutes for him to stop kicking and squirming, and the people went wild, some of them trying to run away, and some of them pushing forward trying to get right up next to what was going on. He tried hard to run, and he fought hard, but there won't no running away from that rope. It had him good.

About the time Stash quit dancing, I felt a real sharp, hard pain right in the middle of my back and my legs gave out on me, and I fell straight back. I felt something jabbing deep in my back when I hit the ground. I thought, "God damn Tadlock for not being here to watch out for me." I blacked out from the pain and the shock for a minute and then I looked up and seen that other one, that other brother of Jacob's, the one that come down here snooping around after the fire, standing over me with some other people, and he looked me right in the face and said, "Bitch!" and walked away. I was trying to get up to get after him and I couldn't and the more I tried, the more I knew I couldn't and I finally just started hollering "I can't move my legs! I can't move my legs god dammit! I can't move my legs! That son of a bitch did something to me! Something's in my god damn back!"

Someone rolled me over, and I heard somebody say, "Jesus Christ! She's been stuck! Somebody stabbed her! It's still in there!"

All those people standing around over me was trying to decide what to do, and all of a sudden I heard Leland in the middle of it and then I felt something like a red-hot poker rush through me when he pulled something out of my back, and they rolled me over on my back. I was looking up and I seen under the gallows that they was lifting Stash back up through that trap door and his pants and shoes was all wet and nasty where his body had let loose with all that was in him, and then I looked up at Leland and he showed me what stuck me and he said, "Somebody stabbed you right in the backbone with this cobbler's awl, Julia. Somebody don't like you much," and I said "It was you that done it, you bastard! It was you!" and he just shook his head, and told some people to haul me up to the Doc's.

I kept saying, "I can't feel my legs. I can't feel my legs. Don't move me. Bring the Doc here you idiots," but they didn't listen to me. When they lifted me up, I looked over to the gallows and they was already hammering the top on Stash's casket. That son of a bitch was gone, but it didn't feel as good as I thought it would. I was hurt bad, and my boy wasn't nowhere around to help me. Some bastard had done stabbed me, and my legs didn't work no more. I started hollering again, "Leland done this to me! It was Leland done this, that son of a bitch! I know it was him somehow!"

# Stash

I watched them hang me. I died just a little bit after eight o'clock in the morning. Grandpa Harris went downstairs just before dawn broke and stayed a little while. I sat upstairs here staying back a little bit from the window so nobody could see me but where I could still look outside to watch the sky beginning to lighten in the east. I thought it might be the last time I would get to see the sun rise, at least from this side of being alive. The sun came on real slow like it always does, and then all of a sudden, it was just another day, like it wasn't ever the dark night at all, and a little bit after the day came, Grandpa Harris and Big Lee came up and told me I would live, that I wouldn't hang, that it would be Tadlock hanging in my place.

Something let go inside me when they told me, something I didn't have any control of, and first I started laughing like any old fool, and then in the next minute, I was crying like a big old unhappy baby. I said, "How the hell are you gonna pull that off?" looking at Big Lee, knowing that somehow, he had it all figured out, and he said they had it worked out, for me not to worry about it. He said Judge McIver, and Aiken, and Hugh Calder too, was all in on it, and I said, "Jesus Christ," and started laughing and crying all over again at the same time.

I was happy to be staying alive, living and breathing for a while longer even though I didn't know what was in front of me. I didn't have any idea what I would be able to do and what I wouldn't. I couldn't see a way past all of this, a way that would just let me go home and pick up with Ella and the children. I knew that couldn't happen, and I thought it might be better to be dead than to be without them, and then in the next second, I thought, "No, that can't be right. It's always better to be alive, to have hope, even if you can't see it." I'd lost enough it seemed to me.

I thought about all the tiny things that linked up to end up on this odd day where I was the one supposed to do the dying, but where another man, one that maybe deserved it more than me for murdering Little Lee and having a hand in killing Mama and Daddy, and George, and who knows how many others, was going to die in my place. It seemed as if Little Lee reached out of that grave to save me even though I hadn't been there to save him that day he died. It seemed that Little Lee and Drip got together to save all of us, me and Ella, and the children, and Big Lee too. It was like Little Lee couldn't lay peaceful and sleeping in that grave and let it go on that the man who killed him could just walk around in his life like he never did anything wrong.

I tried hard to see God's hand being in it, to see whether God planned everything out a long time ago to test us, to see how we measured up. I knew right then that if this life up to now had been a test, I'd failed it. Then in the next second, I was thinking about how impossible it all seemed. I decided I was just looking for reasons that weren't there; it had to be a string of random events that added up to this day of one man hanging in place of another who's sitting in a straight back chair watching it all happen, trying to make some sense of it. My mind ran wild; it just ran away in a whole bunch of ideas, and I just sat there crying and laughing and shaking my head, wanting the flood of thoughts to stop for a while.

I heard a commotion downstairs, and somebody said, "He won't walk. He won't go!" and Big Lee barking out, "Drag the son of a bitch if you have to. Drag him out there, and let's get him hung!" Then I heard them all going out and in just a second I saw them dragging Tadlock across the yard and up the steps to the rope. I saw the crowd surging and heard a lot of people hollering and taunting, but what I heard mostly was those little bastards of Tadlock's singing that little ditty they sang on the street that day about me dancing a hangman's jig, and I thought about what Tadlock must be thinking under that hood hearing his own boys singing his death song.

I saw Julia right up front, real close to where Tadlock would drop through the trap door, and she was hooting and hollering like she was at some big celebration or something, and it gave me a real odd feeling right in the pit of my stomach that it was a man's mama having the most fun watching her boy die. I heard her taunting Big Lee about me, not knowing that he was standing there taking out his best revenge on both of them, and in that moment, I knew it was all too much for it to be a random accident I was watching. If it wasn't God, it had to be Satan. The only question was which one of those crafty rascals it was.

The spectacle of the hanging felt like it was pulling me in, like I could feel what Tadlock felt, like I was a part of it even though I was standing off watching. I got careless and stood too close to the window staring down at the bloodthirsty crowd, and I saw Paul Calder up in that tree too late and he started pointing and hollering, "It's Stash! It's Stash! I see him! I see him!" I looked straight at him and I knew he did see me, and I thought, "Jesus Christ! I've messed this up bad!" but right then, the trap door opened and Tadlock fell through. A big gasp rose from the crowd, and I saw Paul lose his grip and fall out of that tree. I looked back at the gallows and the crowd and I saw Uncle Isaac real close behind Julia. In the next second, she fell and started hollering, and all hell broke loose around them. I backed away from the window and hoped nobody else saw me.

I lay down on the bed listening to the bedlam outside. I

could barely breathe. I imagined Tadlock's neck with him kicking and struggling to get away from the rope choking him, and I couldn't breathe. After a while, it quietened down outside, and I could breathe again. Grandpa Harris, Stephen, Isaac, Big Lee, Tally, and the rest - well, everybody but Hugh Calder; he had to take Paul off for the doctor to look at his arm - came in downstairs, and I heard them talking and laughing like they'd just come in off a successful hunting trip or something like that. Big Lee came up to get me and when we went downstairs they all talked about the hanging and everything that had gone on around it.

Tadlock was in the coffin nailed shut. They brought it inside to keep people from trying to open it to steal the body. People would pay big money to see a hung man's body, and some greedy son of a bitch might try to steal it. Tally and my two uncles sat on the coffin like it wasn't anything but a park bench. It seemed funny to me, them sitting on my coffin with Tadlock in it. The whole thing was so unbelievable that I started laughing again, pointing at them, laughing harder and harder, and they looked at each other like they didn't understand and I don't guess they did because I didn't either. Grandpa Harris put his arm around me and we sat down together and I cried a little bit and laughed, and we just sat there with everyone talking, trying to make things seem real again.

They buried me late that afternoon in the Cason section of the cemetery. Big Lee said my stone would be out there too. He said it galled him that a god damn Greer would be out there soiling the ground in the Cason plot, but there was a good side to it too. He had his revenge, on Tadlock and on Julia too. Later we found out that the stabbing paralyzed her from her midsection down; she wouldn't ever walk again, and she'd sit in her own piss and shit for the rest of her life. That's what Big Lee told me, and he seemed a little bit sad, nothing like I expected.

He said Ella and the children went to the funeral - they had to go - and that a big crowd was out there, mostly people from the hanging who just couldn't let go of the spectacle of it. Ella knew it was Tadlock, and the children were too young to understand what it was that took place. Big Lee said I had to stay out of sight, upstairs in the jail, for a little while until a good dark night came so I could slip out. Grandpa Harris said they'd be over at the fishing camp on the east side of the Pee Dee just down from Sneedsborough for at least a month and that I should come there when I could and walk back over into my own people and be an Indian again until enough time passed for Ella and the children to come over there, or me to come get them.

So, after a few days passed, I saddled one of the horses about one o'clock in the morning on the new moon, and said my goodbyes to Big Lee and Tally. I should've headed directly east to the Pee Dee, but I rode south, out Scotch Road and stopped at the cemetery. The dirt on my grave was still fresh and there was a little wooden cross at my head. It said "John Brooks 'Stash' Harris." It was an odd feeling, reading my name on the cross, but I smiled thinking about Tadlock down there with people thinking I was dead, and him just run off and missing somewhere. I pissed on the grave. It seemed right.

Then I rode on out to the Cason farm, to home. I walked around the yard, and listened, trying to hear Ella and the children inside, but I knew they were sleeping. I looked into the window of our room, but it was too dark. I thought about going inside, but I didn't. I knew I would never leave if I went in. I walked over to the well and picked four of the daffodils from beside the brick housing and I put them on the bird feeder just outside the kitchen window. I knew Ella would see them first thing in the morning. It would say to her that I was fine, that I was out and safe.

I rode to the Pee Dee, and when I got there, I released

my horse. It would find its way home or someone would take it to Big Lee. It carried his mark. I stood on the bank close to the ancient Indian weirs that Grandpa Harris and the other natives still used to catch fish during the spring run. Across the river, I could see dark figures moving around their fires, some for cooking and heat, but others were longer, lower fires for smoking fish, and I knew there were racks of shad and other fish hanging above them. I went down the bank to the water's edge. It was about an hour before sunrise I guessed, an hour before the men would be out in the river working the baskets and the nets. I would wait for daylight to hail one to take me across.

Then I heard a hound strike a trail upriver. I knew men would be following. I waited, listening. Was it moving away upriver or was it coming downriver towards me? If they came here, would the men know me? The hound was coming fast, its bass-throated baying leading the men to me. I couldn't wait for morning. They might know me. I had to cross the river alone. The water was still cold and about four inches of it flowed over the top of the weir. I found my footing and waded out into the river. I was just in time. When I looked back at the bank, the hound was there, its nose to the ground where I stood minutes before. The hound followed my track to the water's edge. It raised its head and bayed an urgent treeing cry. The men following it emerged from the woods and came to the water's edge. They looked at the tracks closely, holding their lanterns to the ground and then lifted them up high, peering out into the river. I heard one of them say, "These footprints are fresh. Someone just went into the river right here. Who would do a damn fool thing like that? It's still mighty cold."

I walked deeper into the river and struggled to keep my footing on the weir rocks. The water over the top deepened. I felt it pushing hard against my legs. I reached down to steady myself and ended up crawling on all fours, holding on against the force of the water. I paused to rest, and settled deeper in the cold water. I began losing the feeling in my legs and arms. The water was too cold. I watched people moving around the fires and thought about the warmth that waited for me, but the current was strong and the water stole my strength. The weir baskets were down. I knew that in the morning, the men would come out to harvest the fish in them. Maybe they would find me.

I looked up to the eastern horizon. It was just beginning to turn from deep violet to gray. Another day was coming, and with it, the sun. I moved further across the weir rocks, deeper into the river, trying to make it to the other side. I felt my strength going away. I lost my balance. The current was about to sweep me downriver, so I pushed off into the pool upstream of the weir. I was so tired. I wanted to close my eyes, but shook my head, struggling to move, trying hard to swim, but the cold paralyzed me.

The water took me. I settled deeper in the cold river, and slid under the surface, but a living thing swam under me nudging me to the surface. I felt something pushing me higher in the water. A massive sturgeon rose out of the dark water beside me. I put my hand out and it touched me with its long whiskers, its head high enough in the water to look directly at me. I looked back into its dark eyes, and saw a reflection of myself. I put my arm across the fish trying hard to stay on the surface and it swam along beside me, towards the eastern bank, close to the weir, out of deeper water. I was alive.

On the far bank, I saw a boatman go down to the river and pole across the pool, coming closer and calling out, "Who is it out there? You better not be poaching?" and I called back weakly, "No! Please! I'm about to drown!" The boatman poled the square-fronted punt close enough for me to grasp it and hang on. It was my Uncle Stephen. He looked at me and said, "Damn! Your Grandpa said it would be you. He's been looking for you all night. I don't know how he knows things like this. He just does. Hang on for a minute. We'll get you out."

The sturgeon followed the punt across the river, keeping its head under me, lifting me high in the water. We came close to the bank. I felt the bottom and tried to stand, but could not. I trailed my hand in the water and the sturgeon touched me with its whiskers again, and when Uncle Stephen dragged me from the water, it swam slowly back out into the river. Grandpa Harris was waiting. He and Uncle Stephen helped me up the bank, I could hardly walk. The cold water had paralyzed me. Grandpa Harris said, "Let's get to the fires. You'll be fine. You're home now."

While my clothes dried, I lay close to the fires wrapped in blankets and slept. When I woke, I listened to the birds in the dawn chorus greeting a new day. The sun rose. A great blue heron flew lazily downriver landing in the shallows below the weir, waiting for discards from the weir baskets. Four crows lit in the pile of fish heads and innards, greedily eating, calling their friends. Sitting in the topmost limb of a holly, a mockingbird trilled. Inside its song, I heard the Carolina parakeet. The world remembers, and God.

I watched the men hauling baskets of fish up for the women, girls, and boys to clean and hang over the smoking fires. One who said she was my cousin brought me a steaming bowl of broth thick with roe and potatoes. It warmed me. The sun moved further into the day. A loquacious flock of cedar waxwings lit in the maples feeding on the emerging leaf buds. I began to think about tomorrow, and the day after, and the day after, and all the days after, until the day that I can be with Ella and the children again.

# Epilogue

## Scots Bend 1912

The night was long. At times, the walk seemed insurmountable. Big Lee stopped often, and Tally waited patiently for him, helping when he could, almost carrying his friend some of the way, then standing back, allowing Big Lee to walk on his own when he was able. Big Lee's determination always impressed Tally and others too. It was part of him, and it had carried him well through his life, but it was waning under the onslaught from the cancer. Tally sensed his weakness, but then Big Lee's strength seemed to come back to him a little as the two men approached the bluff overlooking the millpond, and he actually seemed happy when they finally walked onto the bluff about thirty minutes before sunrise.

While the men were setting up, seven wood ducks flew across the millpond to land among the cypress trees standing in the head of the pond. The men watched them, remembering the times they hunted them together, better days than today, days with futures and hope. A pair of mallards landed in the deeper water next to the dam, and walked up to the road bed for gravel. The men set up places to sit, not trying to hide, just places out in the open on the bluff for anyone to see. In fact, Big Lee wanted Julia to see him; he wanted her to come out to the front of the mill office, and look across the mill pond to see him sitting there, watching her, waiting to take a good clean shot across the water. Tally set up a solid prop in front of Big Lee's seat, loaded the Enfield and put the barrel across the prop, and the butt of the gun in Big Lee's lap. He sat beside him, and they waited.

A farm wagon crossed the road between the two sections of the pond, a horse and rider, and then an automobile puttering along, disturbing the quiet, flushing the mallards who circled the pond three times, gaining height with each circle, and then after the automobile passed, came gliding back in a steep approach that ended just under the bluff. Big Lee leaned out, trying to follow them in but could not see them land. The rain was ending as the sun rose, and when it was completely above the horizon, the day warmed quickly.

Big Lee breathed in the fresh air cleaned by the night's rain, and closed his eyes, soaking in the first full rays of the sun, and for a moment forgot that he was dying, forgot why he was on the bluff, forgot the hard times. He remembered better times, like when he first brought Little Lee and Stash to the bluff and showed them how to jump out to the deepest part of the water, the safest part. From deep in his memory, he heard them laughing and saw them jumping into the water.

He relaxed into the memory, smiling, but it faded as quickly as it came, the task at hand taking over, and he struggled over them both, trying to hold on to the memory, trying to forget the present, the now, but he could not, and he remembered why he was on the bluff, and thought about his own imminent death. He felt emotion rising in his throat, his eyes filling with tears. He wiped them away. He was not afraid of death. He had lived his life so close to death, had seen it right in front of him so many times, and had seen others take their last breaths, men, women, even children. His life had run out; it was over, and he knew it. Death seemed a long-awaited friend, or enemy. He couldn't decide which. He only knew he would welcome it when it came.

Tally nudged him and whispered, "There she is!" and

when he looked across the water he saw Drip Greer wheeling Julia onto the stoop in front of the mill office. She was in her normal pose, in the wheelchair that had been hers since Stash's hanging fourteen years before where Isaac Harris had stabbed her in the spine with a cobbler's awl and paralyzed her. Everyone thought she would die, being confined the way she was, but she had lived because of Drip caring for her, and she hated it, hated that Drip forced her to eat, hated that Drip cleaned the excrement off her every few hours, simply hated still being alive.

Big Lee raised the Enfield and watched her down through the sights. She would die before him, he thought, and he tried hard to focus. He tried hard to hold the rifle steady for the shot that would send her to Hell in front of him. He was going to Hell too, he believed, for all the things he'd done, and he didn't think one more sin would hurt, even another killing, and he still hated Julia with every cell in his body, and wanted her dead too, wanted her to pay more. He felt Tally's hand on his shoulder, and heard him saying, "It's a good shot Leland. Go on and take it." He watched Drip leave her and go inside the mill office. He watched her sitting there in front of him, unsuspecting and unaware.

He began to slowly tighten and squeeze the Enfield's trigger. He would squeeze tighter and tighter until the rifle erupted, hurling the bullet into Julia's chest. It would be over then. Finally, it would be over. Tally said again, "Go on Leland. Take her," and then just inside Big Lee's field of vision to his left, Julia's right, a movement distracted him. A big yellow dog came out of the woods and trotted across the yard to Julia. Across the pond, Big Lee heard Julia's high-pitched screaming for "Drip! Drip! It's that god damn dog again! Drip! Drip! Get your ass out here!"

Big Lee eased off the trigger and saw Drip come out of the door, but instead of coming to her aid, he just stood there watching. The yellow dog trotted up to Julia and cocking his leg high, pissed on hers. Julia was screaming uncontrollably now, and Drip just watched. Big Lee imagined a smile on Drip's face and he asked Tally if he saw it. Tally said, "Yep, he's smiling, laughing really. Maybe that old dog comes every day." The yellow dog walked around to Julia's other leg and cocking his, pissed on it too. Then he grabbed the cuff of Julia's pants leg and started tugging on it, and eventually drug her out of the chair onto the ground. Julia was screaming madly, and the sound of it drifted across the pond to Big Lee and Tally. The dog played with her for a few minutes, tugging at her legs and arms, tormenting her, and then he cocked his leg, pissed on her face, trotted over to Drip who gave the dog something from his hand, and then went back into the woods.

Finally, Drip walked over, picked Julia up, and put her back in the wheel chair. She tried desperately to strike him, but he was accustomed to her blows and dodged them. When she was back in the chair, he positioned her again where she could look out over the pond and left her there. In a few minutes, the dog came out of the woods again, trotting over to her and started pulling on the cuff of her pants again. Julia was screaming and screaming for Drip to come, but he did not. The dog had Julia on the ground again in a minute and started playing with her like a puppy plays with a balled up sock.

Tally started laughing, and in a minute Big Lee did too. Big Lee lowered the rifle and handed it to Tally who started to pack it up with their other gear and the men prepared to leave. Then Big Lee asked for the rifle again, and pointing it skyward, fired one shot. He looked across the water at Julia, and when she saw him and started screaming for Drip again and pointing across the water at him, Big Lee raised his hand with the middle finger extended and held it there for a full minute. Then with Tally's help, Big Lee turned to walk home.